COLIN
FARRINGTON

# MR CHURCHILL'S DRIVER

## A MURDERER'S STORY

Copyright © 2016 Colin Farrington

The moral right of the author has been asserted.

Matador
9 Priory Business Park,
Wistow Road, Kibworth Beauchamp,
Leicestershire. LE8 0RX
Tel: 0116 279 2299
Email: books@troubador.co.uk
Web: www.troubador.co.uk/matador
Twitter: @matadorbooks

ISBN 978 1785893 643

British Library Cataloguing in Publication Data.
A catalogue record for this book is available from the British Library.

Printed and bound by CPI Group (UK) Ltd, Croydon, CR0 4YY
Typeset in 12pt Bembo by Troubador Publishing Ltd, Leicester, UK

Matador is an imprint of Troubador Publishing Ltd

*For Paul,*

*and for Charlotte Maria Burton (1877 - 1975)*
*my maternal grandmother, a great storyteller.*

## Author's Preface

This is a work of fiction. But William Gilbey's story refers to real events and to events that may be real.

In 1964 the last executions took place in Great Britain. Capital punishment was suspended in October that year by the incoming Labour government, and abolished in 1965 by Act of Parliament, for all crimes other than treason.

There remain many untold stories and undisclosed documents in London and Dublin relating to the events and negotiations of June/July 1940.

The United Kingdom had no European allies. There remained a strong peace party in Winston Churchill's government, led by Foreign Secretary Lord Halifax.

The priority of the Irish and their leader Eamon de Valera was to restore the unity of their island, against the fierce opposition of Northern Unionists. Some southerners wanted an alliance with Nazi Germany to achieve this, although many brave Irishmen also volunteered for the British Army. Officially Eire remained neutral.

# PART ONE

PART ONE

# 1

## 1.1

*A mémoire.... this is the beginning of a mémoire posted to important persons at Euston Station, London.*

My name is William Harrison Gilbey. My father, Herbert, 'Bert', Gilbey, a great storyteller, was the last man to be executed in England, by hanging, at eight in the morning on the 18th of July, 1964. He is buried in the precincts of Pentonville Prison, London.

I started this mémoire two weeks ago, on my own release from prison after I had served twelve years of a life sentence for the same crime as my father – murder. I did not commit that particular offence. But I acknowledge that I have been a criminal for virtually all my adult life. The story about Winston Churchill, which my father told me several times, each time slightly varied, is the main reason that I decided to research and to write this mémoire, incomplete though it is. It is the one story of my father's that, until now, I had written down. I transcribed it twenty years ago from a recording my father made, taped shortly before he was hanged. He used a German Grundig recorder, loaned by a wartime friend in Burnley, Lancashire, where we then lived.

'Well, it was like this, William. I was a driver, a good driver. My father had been in service as a chauffeur in a big house in Flintshire, in north Wales. My father taught me to drive. So, when the second war came in 1939, I was put into the elite driving pool in London for the government, the top ministers, civil servants, those sort of people. Only men of standing went into that pool. Only the royal drivers or the top military drivers outranked us. Anyway, my best mate, a bit younger than me, Roy Harvey, he got me into it. Both of us had injuries you see, so we couldn't go to the fighting front. I had a bit of a gammy leg, but above the knee, so it didn't often affect my driving. Roy used to wheeze, you know cough, a lot. But he knew someone high up in the Air Ministry who looked after him. I think I know who he was, but the name doesn't matter.

'Anyway, son, I used to drive mainly the top civil servants and ministers like Eden, Anderson and Butler. One day in July 1940 Roy came to me in our little kitchen. He said that he had been asked to do a big job that night. But he was wheezing badly. He said that it was an overnighter. I would be driving with stops all night. There would be another driver for most of the return.

'So, at ten at night on a humid evening, we left London in a big Humber. I had sealed instructions to be opened only ten minutes before departure. These directed me to my first refuelling stop at a military base, where there would be the next set of directions, and so on. There were no garages open, and virtually no other cars. There was what we called a blackout in operation.

For the first part of the journey there was a military outrider on a motorbike and sidecar.

'Imagine, son, driving in that darkness, air raid sirens going, planes overhead. Of course it was a critically important drive. To do it at all shows how important it was.'

*(My father stopped at that point: to drink beer, I suppose.)*

'You see, son, there were two passengers. One was Mr Churchill, Mr Winston Churchill, who had been Prime Minister for just a few months. The other was a General Brooke. It was a long and careful journey. In each stage we had some clear main roads, no lights though – remember, son, although the Germans had their motorways by then, we hadn't. They're only just starting them properly, in the 1960s, now, thirty years later. Well, we've always been years behind the Germans.

'It was a tough journey. Anyway, there were four stops. At each stop Mr Churchill got out and spoke to a welcoming committee. He was given a field telephone, down which I could hear him barking to Downing Street or wherever. Meanwhile, I opened my fresh instructions for the next stage. We were given tea and coffee, separately of course. The high–ups, the nobs, they didn't mix with us. Actually, Mr Churchill didn't drink much hot liquid. He was swigging from a flask most of the way, brandy I think. He had cigars always lit. Anyway, even with his lit cigars and his drink, he must have dozed a few times.

'Both men had papers with them. They talked, but the car screen was closed, so, even though Mr Churchill was shouting, I couldn't pick up much of what they said. I had to concentrate on the road. But, when we got to our last stop, it was becoming light. I opened the windows; and then General Brooke opened the interior screen as Mr Churchill needed to refuel his lighter. I left the screen open. Neither gentleman objected. At that point I heard Mr Churchill talking about a 'momentous encounter'.

*(Another drink, and a longer pause, a cigarette or two, the tape stopped and restarted. I remember my mother Marjorie moving in the background, ironing or cleaning, coughing, when father told this story.)*

'The last stage of the journey, son, took us into Wales, and over the bridge into the Isle of Anglesey. Mr Churchill then announced that we were early, 'a good thing'. Mr Churchill had worked out that if we went up a particular road we could get to a hill, a 'pwomontory' *(at various points my father used a rasping voice in imitation of Mr Churchill)* where there was a viewing point. They could watch the great man's boat come in over the mighty sea.

'In fact, when we got where Mr Churchill directed, I remained in the car as the others strolled the last twenty yards or so, to get a view. But my gammy leg then began to play up, so I had to get out. I stood at a distance from my passengers, yet close enough to see what was happening. Mr Churchill was waving vigorously at a ferry approaching across a calm, and otherwise empty, sea. As it approached the harbour Mr Churchill abruptly turned and glared at me, as if I was intruding on his private thoughts and was trying to read his secret plan. But Mr Churchill said nothing. I then drove to the ferry terminal as instructed. It was closed: 'services suspended' a notice read. Anyway there were other bowler-hatted men waiting, who acknowledged Mr Churchill.

'Then, from the pier, having come off the ferry boat, strolled up two men, both dressed in an old-fashioned way, even for those days. One was very tall and slim, with a proud manner. The other struggled to keep up with the tall man's strides. The second man was fat and had a black moustache. Mr Churchill walked towards them, indicating to the other Englishmen to stay back. He then shook the hand of the first, tall man. The other man was introduced. Then Mr Churchill brought the two of them to my car. General Brooke joined me in the front seat.

'Mr Churchill directed me to drive back to the hill 'so that the Prime Minister and I can take a stroll'. Another car followed, that was to take the visitors back to the ferry. When we reached the hill, Mr Churchill and the tall man got out. The tall man carried a briefcase, from which he took out some papers. Mr Churchill carried just a cigar. Then for an hour, or maybe more, they strolled together, up and down along the headlands, passing several times a plinth on which was a sundial and, I suppose, an engraved panorama. Son, you can see those often at the seaside or in the country. They serve to identify mountains and so on.

'Mr Churchill was occasionally animated, but the tall man was unbending. That man conveyed an impression of great reserve, serenity and confidence. He was a proud man, I was sure. I shall never forget him silhouetted against the sundial, and beyond it the calm sea.

'General Brooke and the other Irishman made polite conversation. But all eyes were on the two leaders. Eventually they stopped. The tall man leaned over the plinth with his papers. He wrote a few sentences on two sheets of paper that he rested on others. Mr Churchill then took the pen from the tall man's hands, and wrote and, I suppose, signed, something quickly on each of the same papers.

'Mr Churchill returned to us. The tall man went to the other car, where he was joined by his colleague. 'So, Prime Minister,' said General Brooke. 'So, General, it progresses,' replied Mr Churchill. 'The Prime Minister, the 'Tee-shirk' as he insists on being called, 'the Spanish onion in the Irish stew' as Mr Eamon de Valera is called by others, is a difficult, proud man who leads a difficult, proud and impoverished people. He still has choices to make. But I believe that they will come in. It will take a few months. The important point is that, if we can go on a bit longer, their certain moral duty is to come in our side.'

"And, in return, we give them their union, their united Ireland?'

"Yes, yes, the inevitable price, the inevitable bargain.'

"And the rest, their ideas? The proposals we were expecting?'

"I will deal with those later. We shall see. Time will tell. Everything is possible. But we will not be humiliated. Britain will *not* be humiliated.'

'I then opened my new and last set of instructions, son, and drove Mr Churchill and General Brooke to Chester. They spoke only quietly after that, even Mr Churchill. There was muttering, a sense of disagreement I now think, looking back. At Chester, a relief driver was waiting. I left without a word being said to me. Not thanks, nor anything. I stayed overnight at a fancy hotel, as we got good rates for an overnight. In the morning I managed to find a driver who, for good money, took me twenty miles or so to look at a house in north Wales, where my father had worked, and where I was born. It cost me a lot to make that trip. But history is important, son. The house was abandoned, I am sad to say. A little while later it was bombed flat. That war did terrible damage. Then I took the train back to London in the evening.

'Now, son, think about it! What a journey that was! I saw something historic then. Even though, when you learn the history, you will find that their agreements were never put in place. You know, maybe you and I alone know, that they were made all right. I saw a piece of history, a piece of unknown history. I am passing it down to you.'

That was the story told to me by my father, when I was eight years old. I lost the tape in one of my prison moves, but not the transcript, which I still have.

I think I knew, even then, that this story might be more important than my father's other stories, only some of which were about historical events. Most were fairy tales and fantasies. Yet the real significance of this story, and the other historical ones, didn't register. I never had the chance to learn history from others, nor, of course, to quiz my father.

But, after the waste of much of my last forty-odd years since I left our adopted home in France at the age of fourteen, I decided that, when I was released from my own long sentence in England this year, I must find out the truth behind such stories; if indeed there was any truth. And, of course, I wanted to know the true history behind my mother and I leaving England for France, and my father's hanging in 1964 for the shooting, so I had been told, of two women, a Miss Maeve Harrison and Miss Dora Lee, outside a post office in Manchester during a failed robbery. I wanted to know my father's story; and, by finding the truth, if possible, to restore his honour. Those who receive and read this will find that, since my release, I have been aided, and I have been followed, when researching the story. My 'mémoire' (I use the French spelling, because of my education) describes the past ten days, in which I met two remarkable women, Eireann Canning and Gillian Bevington-Ward; and when I found some comfort and some love – yet also the confirmation of much bitterness, fear and evil, in my life, and in your society.

I have found out things that I should not have found out. I have been driven to extremes. But I hope that in the name of truth I have made my, and my father's, case.

*William H Gilbey, Chester, June 21 2014*

## 1.2

*The beginning of my mémoire, in Hammersmith, London: Tuesday June 10 2014.*

'Why now, William? Why this sudden interest in your past? Oh, but I see, William, fifty years isn't it? Fifty years since your father died.'

I said: 'Since my father was hanged.'

But Mr Piercey, 'Lloyd Piercey', as his name badge on the breast jacket pocket of his smart dark suit stated, continued to read the bulky set of files in front of him. He didn't react.

My probation officer was meeting me at his office for the first time since my release on licence. I had outlined my plans. I had also tried to tell my father's 'Churchill and de Valera' story. But I don't think that Mr Piercey had been listening.

'Yes, you want to know your father, to understand what happened. Why you and your mother were left to fend for yourselves; why you lost the masculine influence in your life. I understand. Although, I see that you had guardians, the Wards.'

'Mr and Mrs Andrew Bevington-Ward.'

'Yes… they looked after you and your mother when you were taken to France, also in 1964. But the need to know more of their background strikes a lot of older people, not only people with your unusual, let us say *extensive,* history. And your mother, remind me.'

I said that my mother, Marjorie, had died in 1974.

'Oh, well yes, that's also forty years ago, a significant date again, exactly. Yes, I see.' Mr Piercey flicked through the recent papers. But he had already found his one angle on which to focus, as all social and such care workers have to. I have seen it many times.

I said that I had no brothers, nor sisters, nor other living relatives. Mr Piercey seemed relieved.

Then Mr Piercey said: 'Listen, William, do you mind if we relax and talk over a cigarette, rather than a coffee? I need a cigarette. The files tell me that you are a civilised man, a well-read man, especially of modern poetry. You are even a writer yourself, a man changed through literature, it seems. You love music. Your mother introduced you to choral music. You are a pianist. If you are determined, William, as the thorough prison report from your social worker Miss Ingham says, just to focus on looking over your history, and not to get into any more trouble, my job will be so much easier. You must look on me as a friend you can talk to, someone to help you gear yourself to the routine of modern life.'

I nodded. At that moment, I wanted to be agreeable.

'But to smoke, we'll have to go outside, to the car park, William. I'm sure we can chat better out there, anyway. It's not a bad day. This won't take long. Not much more we can do today. But I think I am beginning to understand you, your aims, your interests, which in my job is half the battle.'

Well, I wanted to say that, whatever Mr Lloyd Piercey might presume, I did have things to do. The priority was my research. But there were social ties to make up and good food to be had. Spending time with a probation officer or other social worker and general gladhander talking about myself wasn't part of my plan. Nor, as far as I knew, was it in the plan of those who watched out for me, those in my group I called my Uncles. One of them, a bearded man, had followed me to this probation office in Hammersmith. At least I hoped that he was one of the Uncles, and that there was a friend following me, not a foe. It could have been another officer of the state, or someone else with an interest.

I was certainly being followed.

I reined in. I smiled. I stood up, taking in the only two photos on Mr Piercey's wall. One was a family group, the other a probation service team photo. Mr Lloyd Piercey's was the only black face.

We squeezed out of the office and along a corridor packed with furniture, passing a door marked Elizabeth Llewellyn, Chief Probation Officer. Then we went down a dirty metal staircase, through a security door and into a concrete buttressed carpark. In the past it could have belonged in a corner of any of my prisons, penitentiaries, reform schools, centres correctionnels or borstals which I had passed through in England, France, Russia or Germany over my fifty-eight years. But this concrete square was, in a way, worse. It was masquerading as part of a new 'free' world.

I shuddered. I felt trapped. I swallowed hard. I will never again be confined for any appreciable length of time, whatever else happens. I have promised myself that, over and over again.

I have always kept serious promises, the sort you make at dawn and tell only to yourself.

When we got outside, Mr Piercey pointed a metal object at the flashiest car, a TT convertible, parked in the sunniest area of the litter-strewn car park. It let out three welcoming beeps. He opened the door and took out a packet of cigarettes from the glove compartment. He offered me one. I said 'no, thanks'. Mr Piercey then closed the car door and leaned back against it. He looked up at the building.

'She's sure to be watching me from her window, my boss, Mrs Elizabeth Llewellyn, I mean. But don't you look! Her window is always open. She looks out when I come here. But she'll approve of my meeting you here. So, don't worry. I can sense her smiling at us. She likes us to relax with our clients. She's a good boss really.'

Mr Piercey then corrected himself. 'Mind you, they can be the worst sort, the nice bosses. One of my colleagues thinks that even our offices are bugged. So, he records things on his own machine. As a sort of back-up. There are certainly closed circuit cameras. You can see them. But they're everywhere in this country now.'

As I looked round and admired the security, Mr Piercey laughed, glancing up from time to time.

'So, what can I do to help you now, William? I have to do something you know. Sure you don't want a cigarette? I thought all you old boys were addicted.'

The words were offensive. But I said nothing.

'So, what about work and money; and somewhere to live, William?'

'I'm OK at present.' I was more than 'OK' of course. But I wasn't going to tell Mr Piercey that. Years of wise investment in hidden, tax-free accounts arranged while I was most recently out of society meant that, yes, I was certainly more than 'OK'. In the past I may have lived well, while I was free. But I had seen that there was good money accumulated and stored for me, the products of half a dozen really big jobs, where nobody dared to tell tales.

Then, there were my mother's jewels. I didn't know the exact current value of the contents of the simple wooden jewellery box, the one my father bought for my mother two weeks before they took him away in 1964, two months before they hanged him. But the diamonds and pearls alone were worth hundreds of thousands of pounds, I was confident of it.

I had been told through my contact with the Uncles that the box was now safely in Hatton Garden. With the cash investments as well, I was sure that my wealth would amount to more than Mr Piercey and Mrs Llewellyn together would earn in a lifetime.

As for accommodation, I had been found a well-equipped and quiet two-bedroom apartment in South Kensington, luxurious by any standards, for however long I needed it. It had everything, including an excellent new American Rossi revolver (hidden at the back of a wardrobe), a new mobile phone, a specially programmed computer and £5,000 in fifty pound notes. I regretted that I needed all those things, especially the gun, but I had made enemies. My release had been publicised. There would be people who had found out through gossip or innuendo that I had wealth. I would always be watched. I would always have to be ready.

'You see, William, I know a lot of people, through this place and other contacts. I could get you somewhere nice for a very small rent.'

Mr Piercey's tone had become shakier. He was sweating. He was not looking at me. 'I've just been told for example of a little place, a terraced house not far from here, in Twickenham, minutes from the station, available from what I might call a well-wisher.'

I shrugged my shoulders.

'I could get it for you especially cheap, even rent-free for a while, William. There would just be an occasional caller, to store and to collect stuff. You know what I mean. You wouldn't be inconvenienced, honestly.'

This was a tone that I understood. I should have guessed this turn of events when he had brought me into the yard, out of earshot and bugging equipment, if not out of his boss's sight. It would be my 'old boy' word against his if I came over offended about his plan.

'Well, sir, I will take a look.'

It is always good to have a lifetime's insight confirmed: that we are all potentially bent, should the need strike. Most people can't actually get fulfilment in life, or even enough money, if they ignore the reality of the world around them and stick to the straight; if they always take their spirits watered, and even the best food tepid and unseasoned.

So I would play along. Although it was at a tangent from my mission and the promises I had made to myself, which were to get to the bottom of my father's history and of my father's stories, finally to understand my life and his life, why shouldn't I indulge Mr Piercey for a while? Why not go along with a probation officer if he can get to keep his Audi car, and his nice wife and his two plump children (judging by the photo) in a certain style?

Mr Piercey smiled.

'Yes, sir, I will certainly take a look, if that is what you want.'

'Great, good man, look here.' Then Mr Piercey stopped himself from further detail. He had gone far enough, I suppose. He had established the critical contact, the words that meant that a deal was on, the equivalent of my encounters with married women in business hotel bars, the conversation; the brushing hand, the agreement to meet. Or the moment you knew, from a whispered response, that a prison guard was bent.

'So, could you meet me at Twickenham, outside the station, early on Friday? I'm in court tomorrow and Thursday. Would eight in the morning on Friday be possible?'

Mr Piercey had had it planned all along, I was sure. It was already in his diary.

'Early birds feed with bright and watchful eyes, don't they? Of course, Mr Piercey, of course, thank you.' I held out my hand.

Thus my assigned help, Mr Lloyd Piercey, bade his leave. He showed me out via a side gate, his hand shaking as he entered the security code to open the exit.

'Good luck, William. I must just go back for a word with Elizabeth.'

I left the building, via the car park exit. The bearded man looked up at me from his car, parked directly outside.

## 1.3

The next morning, as I stepped into a taxi, I turned on the mobile phone that had been left for me in the apartment. One of my first messages was to the man I saw as the closest of the Uncles, Swiss Joe.

Swiss was also known to me and to others special to him as The Milky One, because of his passion for the original, never the dark or the fruit versions, of the

Toblerone chocolate bar. He required his guards in the French prison wing we had shared for two years in the 1990s to bring him a large bar regularly. Every new guard would get a telling-off, if they brought the wrong type: 'No, boy. I said the *milky* one, *au lait, au lait!*'

I knew that Swiss was getting instructions from someone higher up in the Uncles, the bossman.

I had not met the new bossman. His identity had changed while I was in prison. The previous bossman had been murdered, on a drugs run, I had been told.

Although I had been equipped at the apartment with money, as well as a bank card, I was still impatient to go with Swiss Joe and the bossman to see my jewellery and my money. Only when they were released to me could my life fully resume.

I sent the message to Joe twice, by voice and then by text. It was good practice. A handwritten note, left with the mobile phone, told me that texts and calls to and from it couldn't be traced. I didn't know how this worked. I was also told in the same handwriting, capitals only, that the modern computer terminal installed in the apartment on a desk was SPECIAL. It was permanently on, and well lit.

There was a twenty-four hour number to call a helpmate called Colin, should I have any problems with either piece of kit.

I hated the thought of using any machinery in a public place, so this was also welcome.

I had received computer training in prison as part of my pre-release package. I was determined not to be a 'rambler' or 'surfer', to use the words I had picked up in those sessions. I knew that I had to control things rigorously, to define and to refine my interests, and to focus on the jobs in hand.

I had also decided to continue by hand the mémoire you are now reading. I wanted, while I was writing, only one record, to be added to and edited every two days or so. Copying could come later.

To work.

I had explained from prison my plans to the Uncles. They had left for me in the apartment the details of what, they claimed, was a 'first class' private investigator, as well as another important contact that had been found for me.

I was at the investigator's office in Bond Street in the West End of London by nine-thirty. All was quiet. I pressed a door intercom pad. A slim, young man in a pencil-shaped suit eyed me from behind the window of a closed fashion shop on the ground floor.

I hoped that the young man could see that I was well dressed: a double-breasted suit, a striped shirt and silk tie, and on my feet my best brown brogues. Most of such quality clothes and shoes had been bought when I had last been out of prison for a longish period, in the 1980s.

The Uncles had offered me clothes. But I wanted those I knew. They were part of me.

I turned from the man's stare. I noticed down the street a 'Hermes' sign – Hermes, the winged angel, also known as Mercury, the God (or Patron Saint) of thieves. I laughed at that. It was a good omen. I felt happy.

I was called up, without questions. The office was on the top floor.

I stepped out of an ancient lift. I walked in through the only open door. I could see that the offices were ten times more chaotic than Mr Piercey's probation office. No-one spoke or moved.

But, with my eye for an ambush, I lasered in on two small, rather fat young men in pinstripe suits. They were just visible behind computer terminals and piles of old newspapers, with several bins overflowing. Their talk was over-ridden by the sound of machinery. Shredders, I thought. I had heard such machines in prison admin offices. Then, beyond them, appeared an older but equally small man.

However, the most striking feature for me was a large framed poster in a cubbyhole behind the man. Directly facing me in black capitals almost as tall as him, it read:

NOTHING WRITTEN FOR PAY
IS WORTH PRINTING

The man came towards me. He put on glasses and squinted, saying: 'Oh, my boys must have thought you were the sandwich woman.' Then he said: 'Welcome, my friend, and you are?'

I told him. The man looked up at me, and smiled, saying: 'Yes, yes, come in, Mr William Gilbey.' He then took me into his sloping cubbyhole, saying nothing to his 'boys'. With difficulty, he closed the door behind us. It was stiflingly hot. But I didn't take off my jacket.

'I like your poster,' I said. 'It is a quotation from Ezra Pound.'

'Ezra who? It was left behind by the previous tenants, Mr Gilbey, some sort of fancy publishers. They left all manner of rubbish. But we kept that. Is it worth something?'

'Anything of Ezra Pound has its collectors.'

When I thought of the hours that I had spent on the Collected Works of Pound and the Selected Works of TS Eliot in the prison library in Lyons, the Pound more difficult with some of the pages missing, and if this man only knew how much I knew about literature, its value, and the value of art, and how much I could teach him and his boys, well! Not of course, actually, that a poster was worth much.

I said: 'Pound was the greatest poet of the twentieth century. But he stayed in Italy during the war and made fascist broadcasts, which earned him spells in prison and in a lunatic asylum in his home country of America.'

'Loony, eh? Dear, dear. But the poster's worth something?'

'Everything is worth something.'

The little man, whose chair was unfortunately at a lower level than mine, moved some papers. He looked over his glasses across his desk, up at me. 'Well, well, anyway, a good early start has been had by all. So, to work, Mr Gilbey. Please tell me your problem.'

'There are two problems. I think that they are linked. But I want you to focus on just one.'

I then told the investigator about my father and because it seemed so important to my father's history, I began to tell again the story of his being Mr Churchill's driver when he met the Irish leader Mr de Valera, word for word as I had tried to tell the probation officer Mr Piercey. But we were interrupted, just as I had come to the point where the car driven by my father had arrived at Holyhead, by one of the younger men.

'This, Mr Gilbey, is one of my sons, Frank. The other is Charlie.'

Frank carried in two polystyrene cups of heavily milked coffee, with sugar on a white paper plate, on which the white of the sugar was tinged with brown. I accepted, squeezing my left fist with irritation at such filth. That is a habit of mine.

The interruption hardly mattered anyway. I could see that the little investigator, who was in his mid-forties, neither knew nor cared anything about Mr Churchill or Mr de Valera ('de who? Spell that'), so I ran through the rest of the story and the other history quickly, without drama. The investigator made notes, including the names of my father's victims, and also that of Roy Harvey, my father's friend and boss, which the investigator asked me to repeat and to spell. A name like that, he said, might be traceable. I said that I thought Roy Harvey would be dead. After all, the events I was describing had taken place between fifty and seventy years before. The little man put a large question mark next to Harvey's name. He asked me for any other names.

Several names came to my mind. The only one I told him about was saggermore, which had featured in several of my father's stories and sayings. It was a complete mystery to me. He asked if saggermore was a person or a place. I said 'a place, I think,' but I didn't know where. I thought it might be a hill. The little man asked me to spell it. But I had never seen it written down. The little man looked blank.

I then said that I wanted him, my own private investigator *solely within my pay* – I repeated with a special stress those words *'solely within my pay'* – to find out as much as he could about my father Herbert: the circumstances of his crime, his trial in 1964, and so on.

'Why now, Mr Gilbey?' asked my investigator, echoing Mr Piercey exactly.

I used the 50th anniversary angle that Piercey had spotted. I also said that of course it was a specialist job, looking at crime reports, old newspapers and files. I said that I couldn't face all that at present, so soon after my release. So I had decided that, while he, the investigator, was looking at the 1964 events, I would focus on my father's earlier history, especially his war service, including the Churchill story that I had told and others.

I said that, on the advice of Miss Lucy Ingham, a prison social worker, I had already sent a letter to the Cabinet Office asking where I could get information about my father's wartime service. I wasn't of course expecting a quick reply, or any real help from the authorities.

The investigator said: 'Are you looking for a pardon for your dad?'

I had never called my father 'dad'. To me Herbert, or 'Bert', Gilbey was, and always would be, my father. So I said: 'I just want an honest fresh look at what happened to my father, and why. What will it lead to? Who knows? I was told very little at the time. I have found out very little since. That is on my mind, and on my conscience.'

I clenched my left fist. 'Why did my father kill two women, as you can read on the internet. I looked at it again yesterday. Why did he kill those strangers, Miss Maeve Harrison and Miss Dora Lee, simply because they challenged him when he was parked outside a post office, waiting for other men to come out?'

I paused while the investigator made notes. He was a slow writer.

The investigator nodded.

I continued. 'Maybe it wasn't him. Maybe he didn't kill those people. Maybe it was mistaken identity. What was the story behind those murders?'

The investigator nodded again.

I said: 'Maybe my father was framed. I have been framed myself, you know. Or, to be more exact, I took the blame for something I didn't do. The framing of the evidence followed later to save others. But I don't want to go into that now. Look what happened to me. It could have happened to my father in 1964. Only at that time the consequences were even more serious. He lost his life. He was hanged.'

I thought to myself at that point: how shameful it is, that I know so little. All those years lost. I should have inquired years ago, indeed decades ago. Suddenly, I felt guilty and truly disloyal.

The investigator held up his hands. Then he winked, and nodded, and laughed. He had heard such things before, I suppose. 'And what's your timing on this? You want everything by yesterday, like everyone else, I guess.' He gestured across his wobbly pile of papers. He tapped his computer screen.

I kept calm. I said: 'Look, sir, you have been recommended to me by people that I trust. Please understand. Money is no object. I do not expect all my inquiries to be finished quickly. It all depends. But I have waited a long time – as I have said much too long – to start this. I am anxious to get on.'

The investigator replied, in a more serious and respectful voice, that he would get 'my boys' onto the basics straightaway. He was sure that he could let me have a first report 'within a few days'.

The investigator's son Charlie then showed me to the lift. As I left the building I noticed that the smart young man in the pencil suit was still in the same place, behind the plate glass window. This seemed strange. His shop was still not open. This time he could not ignore me. He nodded.

## 1.4

At eleven (precisely, trying to be on time is automatic after a lifetime in prisons) I pressed another buzzer, this one at the front entrance of a 1930's block of flats in West Kensington. This was the other contact I had been found to get me started.

The meeting was to be with Francis Bevington-Ward. I had not seen Francis for forty years. He was nine, when, at fourteen, I had left his family home, Les Arcades in St Laurent du Var, Provence, to go to college in Toulon, as his father, my guardian Mr Andrew Bevington-Ward, had arranged. I had lasted two weeks at the college. I had never returned to St-Laurent. I had never seen anyone from there again.

I had been told that Francis was now known only as 'Francis Ward'. And 'Francis Ward' was how he introduced himself, as he pulled open the door to his flat, once again at the top of a building.

The lift had been out of order. I was thus momentarily out of breath, and sweating from the long walk up. All I could do was smile.

'Well, well: you are William Gilbey! The man who came told me about you, and to expect you. Of course, you wouldn't expect me to recognise you. I hope you are not offended.' I continued smiling. 'It is a long time, isn't it William? I was a child. You were several years older.'

I managed to say that I was pleased to see him again.

I was about to say other polite things, but Francis turned his back and hurried through the flat's hall, bare except for an old-fashioned stand with accompanying umbrellas and scruffy coats. He then turned and beckoned me into what I took to be the main living room. This was at the opposite end of the designer range from my expensive and spotless rented flat in South Kensington, which was all beige and apricot, leather and silk. This top floor room in West Kensington was ill-lit and dirty, with decaying curtains and stained antimacassars, faded cheap magazines in racks, and dusty books piled everywhere. No windows were open. An old two-bar electric fire stood in the centre of the room.

Francis was dressed down, even street-rough, like I had been the day before, at my meeting with Mr Piercey. He wore a cream open-necked shirt, that might once have been white, and a pair of creased suit trousers. He was wearing red cord slippers. He smelled.

Francis said: 'You look well, old boy, in a smart suit and all that. My Pa and Ma said you'd do well with all your reading and your, er, artistic nature. Anyway, take a pew. Amazing that your friend found me. Clever people you have working for you.' Francis picked up and threw into an already overflowing bin a plastic sandwich wrapper, which had been lying on one of the three easy chairs. Each chair was of a different shape. The upholstery clashed.

Francis waved me down on to the chair. He stood over me for a moment. He looked at me intently. I had seen that look before somewhere. Maybe from his father?

'Of course you know that Ma and Pa, Andrew and Gloria, are both dead.'

I nodded, although I hadn't known that.

'It was a terrible thing, an accident, a car accident, on the Grand Corniche mountain road, between Monaco and Menton. It could not have been more dramatic. What a place to go! My father lost control of the car. It swerved off. Instant death. Two years ago, now, almost to the day. Pa shouldn't have been driving at all. He was well over ninety you know, but poor Ma, Gloria, liked to get out now and then.'

Francis paused.

So I asked: 'Was it his Mercedes?' Mr Bevington-Ward had had a classic Mercedes, and Mrs Bevington-Ward had had her own Rover saloon (although I never saw it move) when I was at Les Arcades.

'Oh, no, just a little car, I think. Things were much reduced you know. In fact some say, well even my sister Gillian would say if she were here, which she is not, but she'd love to meet you by the way, of course she was only a baby when you left for college, that the whole show wasn't an accident, as the police found.' Francis rambled on. I couldn't stop him. 'I'm afraid I even heard at the funerals some of Pa's chums comparing it to that Maxwell thing. You know, that newspaper man who was said to have leaped off a boat, as he was about to be declared bankrupt. But I can't believe that. Yet Pa had also lost everything, as we found out later. So you could say that, from his point of view 'logically and therefore' as he used to say, I'm sure you remember that favourite phrase of Pa's, 'logically and therefore'.' I nodded. Francis nodded back. 'Why not ditch it all, leaving us to fend for ourselves. He never liked supporting me and Gillian. He always said that we should make our own way in the world. There wasn't life insurance. There were plenty of debts.'

Now what I had gone to West Kensington to find out was not about the deaths of my guardians, nor their history after I left them. Interesting though it was to hear about them and the circumstances, to find out that they were dead was not unexpected. In fact I was surprised that they had died so recently. I had never imagined either of the Bevington-Wards living long after my mother, who had died forty years ago. Their going then would have seemed right. Their stories belonged together.

What I had come for was information about the Bevington-Wards' relationship with my parents, my father especially. There must be some explanation, which

I had never been given, why we went to France and why we were given sanctuary, why I was looked after by the Bevington-Wards when my father was taken. Maybe Mr Andrew Bevington-Ward ('His Lordship', my mother used to call him) had also been involved in the driving that my father talked about so much. He might have left some clue on that.

Francis stood up. 'Now, look here William, old boy. I'm really sorry. But I can't offer you much sustenance here. I'm not the domestic type, nor is Gillian, although she at least is employed, as a secretary. I'm an actor you know, but no work at the moment. So I've no coffee and biscuits and so on to offer but...' Francis looked purposefully at his watch and then at a 1930's clock on the mantel, 'but there's a good pub, The Duke of Connaught, not five shakes from here, so if you can hang on a few minutes, Tony the landlord, miserable Irish sod but good about my slate, given my irregular money, opens up at the stroke of eleven thirty, not a minute before. So, if we can time it right, we'll be at the head of the queue with a few other mates, when the gates are opened to us Gadarene swine. We can then share the first pearly drops of the day. Maybe we can snatch a pie or something, if you've got the readies, as it were.'

I had the 'readies', many thousands of them. But I hate pubs. The thought of The Duke of Connaught made me want to retch. Why do Englishmen live in pubs? One of my memories of my life in Burnley was of my father going off to his Wednesday evening and pre-Sunday lunch drinks at The Nag's Head or The

Sportsman's Arms. Sometimes other days too. And always coming back late.

I tried not to seem wounded.

But, in truth, I was hurt by the fact that Francis Bevington-Ward had not asked about my own history, nor about the deaths of my father and mother. I would have guessed that that would have been most peoples' starting point, if meeting a lost friend, almost a relative, after so many years. I assumed that the Uncles had told him about the hanging, and so on, even if Francis had not been told by his own parents.

Yet Francis was also an intelligent man. I could sense that. He had, like me, a nervous impatience that is the mark of such people. Although I suspected, well I had seen it almost immediately, that he was an alcoholic.

'Actually, Francis, perhaps not, if you don't mind. It's good to meet you. Maybe I should come back when you have more time. Maybe when your sister is here.'

'Oh, yes. We all like to talk about the old times, don't we, William? You and your ma were in a thingy in our garden weren't you, and all that, my Pa with his business interests, and Ma lounging in the villa. I guess you had some times out there, and some fond memories. Yes, a good chinwag, over a pint or three, mulling over the old days is my idea of a good night out.'

I decided to ask just one more question. 'What was your father's business exactly?' All I could remember was Mr Bevington-Ward working away at what he called 'catalogues'.

Francis flushed and looked, with a nervous tick, at his watch. I knew that I had been given exactly the wrong time to come, so soon before pub opening. He must have just got up from his bed.

I could tell that Francis had the running time between his flat and his drink worked out to a second. He would simply race out at twenty-five past the hour, with or without me.

'Well, oh yes, it was like import and export, bringing things in and sending them out. Not that I ever saw the stuff. The family had started it in Ireland.'

'Ireland?'

'Yes, er, Southern Ireland: Dublin, I seem to think. But some of the family moved to Wales, way back. They set up factories there. You know that there was a big steel operation in north Wales? They were ambitious people, not much style though. You know, 'nouveau riche' they called it then. Pa told me that. Then Pa moved to London. I don't remember exactly when.'

Francis looked at his watch again.

I said, 'Does the word 'saggermore' mean anything to you?'

Francis looked shifty. The name did mean something to him. Then he muttered: 'Well, I have got a history degree.'

I didn't understand. But I decided to conclude, a decision I now regret. I should have stayed with him, even forced myself to go drinking in a pub, to question him and to find out more, there and then. At the time, though, I feared that Francis would meet his friends, and get drinking. He might take offence at my persistence about long ago events, and my quizzing him.

There seemed on that day to be time for such things.

Of course, it was also in the back of my mind that, if later I had to be persistent or violent with him, to wring out the truth, I would be. I had every weapon of persuasion in my armoury, my new Rossi revolver if needs must. Just not to be used until other methods had failed.

'You wouldn't mind, Francis, if I research your family history? It is your er... Pa, after all. But it might lead me to information about mine.'

'Of course not, William, do as you will, me and Gillian, my sis, will be thrilled. Tell you what! In that little spare bedroom over there,' Francis flicked his wrist, checking the time on his watch again, 'there's three or four heavy, stuffed boxes which, to our shame, Sis and I have never gone through since the lawyer gave them to us. We've carted them around, well Sis, Sis insisted' Francis laughed as his panting tongue stumbled over the words. 'God, I haven't even had my first vodka chaser yet!

'Look, tell you what, William, the cases seem to be full of old business books of Pa's and other stuff, I guess. We always said that we'd ransack them to discover our inheritance or our heritage or whatever. But we never have. Sis gets worried that I might throw them on the fire. Well, actually there isn't a fire here. This is a rented flat, you know. But, if I've been on the booze a bit, I often try to light one, as it can get cold if the meter's run out. So she put extra strong black tape around the boxes.'

I nodded.

'Tell you what!' The hands on the mantel clock were showing eleven twenty-four. Francis moved towards the door out of the flat, me following him. He was still wearing carpet slippers. He had not turned off the electric fire. 'Tell you what, William! Why don't you come round on Sunday morning? We like a lie-in on Saturday, so Sunday is best, a bit earlier than now, before The Duke is open. Then the three of us, the two happy kiddies who grew up in Les Arcades, the best years of our lives, you can guess that, and you, one of the other boys, we can spend a good couple of hours tearing those boxes open, reminiscing, finding something useful. I might even get a few cans and mixers in, before we adjourn to the boozer.'

We went rapidly down the stairs.

'About ten o'clock on Sunday, then,' I called, as Francis half marched, and half ran, up the road. I could see the pub sign, The Duke of Connaught, at the next crossroads.

Francis Ward, or Francis Bevington-Ward, as I still prefer to call him, did not turn to reply.

Thus I started my search. It looked as if the history of the Ward family might provide an Irish link. And Wales too, where Mr Churchill had met Mr de Valera. I kept telling myself not to be impatient. Any leads were welcome.

This note added on 21 June when finalising my mémoire:

*This was to be the last time that I saw Francis alive.*

# 1.5

The following morning I misjudged the taxi time. For the first time in many years I was travelling across London at a peak hour, in heavy traffic. As I got out of my taxi, my hands were shaking. I had wanted to be on time. Then, I saw with pleasure that my comrade and Uncle, Swiss Joe, had waited for me at the corner of High Holborn and Hatton Garden. He was standing outside what seemed to be a temporary Portakabin toilet used by builders, his left leg reflexively kicking a cardboard box.

I hadn't seen Swiss for fifteen years. He had changed. He was slimmer and better muscled. He was casually dressed, in tracksuit and plimsolls. Before, he had been a formal dresser – suit and tie – when out of prison uniform. We were all more formal in those days.

Swiss Joe's unshaved face was pale and angular. I had thought of bringing him a milky Toblerone, a gesture to a true and faithful Uncle, but I hadn't had the chance to buy it.

I walked towards The Milky One. He jerked his head. I followed his gaze to look into the double plate glass window of a jeweller. He didn't turn nor offer any welcome. But he said clearly: 'At last for God's sake! Our bossman is waiting. Follow me.' Then he set off at a pace.

I knew the routine, to follow about thirty yards behind, to make it easier to sense if anyone else was following. If I suspected someone was after us, then I must walk on when he turned off, the meet was cancelled, and we would rearrange later. Although I had been worrying about being followed (indeed I was sure that I was always followed) I was a little out of practice. Maybe I showed unnecessary suspicion about a bearded man in a hard hat, who came out of the Portakabin, and the way he looked at me. Maybe it was because I was the only well-dressed man around. Anyway, he went another way. It might have been the same man who had been outside the probation office. I wasn't sure. It worried me.

I almost lost Swiss Joe as he turned up an alleyway off Hatton Garden, then down another snicket, then across a yard. I saw him acknowledge, with a slight jerk of his head, a younger man in tight bleached jeans, who had a shaved head and tattooed neck. This younger man stayed motionless until I drew ahead of him. He then followed close behind me. He muttered instructions to me, telling me to turn right, then to go in and up three flights of stairs in a modern-looking, but apparently abandoned, office building, covered with To Let notices. A black man was sitting at a reception desk. He smiled cheerfully, nodding at me and my skinhead follower. We turned into a small, crowded room.

'Welcome, welcome. Whoever thought we'd see you again, William Gilbey?'

A fat man, casually dressed and red faced, evidently the current bossman, about ten years older than me, faced me from behind a desk piled with computer print-out sheets, files, boxes and coffee mugs. This man gestured to me to sit in front of him in an old armchair, covered with ripped cushions.

'You look really smart, William, my son, so what a

great day this is. Now you know two of my guys, Swiss Joe and Artie, your artistic friend.' I nodded to Artie. 'But you won't have met Colin.' The fat man waved at the skinhead standing behind me. 'Colin may look like your average skin, with his tats and all that but he's a technology maestro. It's Colin you can thank for your A1 top of the range equipment, William, your phone, your terminal, everything in your apartment geared up for you, William. He learns quick, does Colin. While you get settled in to your new life, Colin is available twenty-four hours a day, and I do mean twenty-four hours a day, don't I, Colin? That's what Colin's paid good money for, a thousand cash a week. So you may be at your ease, William. You will never need to use hoipolloi systems again. You both understand?'

I guessed that this silent, clever skinhead called Colin had nodded at his bossman's remarks, from behind me. So I nodded too. I was glad to be told not to use the 'hoipolloi's' facilities – their internet cafes, their buses and their drinking and eating places.

Then, the fat bossman continued: 'So, I hope, and expect, William, that you are happy with the flat in Kensington, with the arrangements, with everything?' I nodded. 'And we know you followed up on that lead with Mr Francis Ward we gave you. You deserve it. We know, William, how much you want to find answers to your questions, especially about Churchill, good old Winnie they used to call him in the East End, and that Irish feller *'de Val-aer-ee-yar'* and the war; and what happened to your mum and your dad. So, if you need anything, as I said on the tecky side you contact your new fascinating friend and mine, Colin, for everything else you email or speak to your old chums, The Milky One, or Artie. OK?'

I nodded.

'Of course, we never expected you to get out again. You know that.'

I nodded again.

'How long have you been inside, William, exactly?' asked the fat bossman. 'Artie and me were just chuntering on it, before you lot came.'

'Twenty eight years, on and off. Twelve years my recent stretch.'

'Fuck,' said Colin from behind me.

'His recent stretch twelve years, twelve long years,' said Swiss Joe reflectively.

'But I had some good times too when I've been out, and I never let anyone down,' I said.

'No, William, as far as we know, you never spoke. You took your punishments alone.'

'And when I worked it out I reckon I got away ninety percent of the time, well, ninety-five percent if you only include the big jobs like the robberies in Lyons and the two murders. I was set up for the last murders, of course.'

The Milky One nodded and then sat down to my right. 'Yes, Pete, we had to do that.' Obviously Swiss wanted to claim a share of the French and the other big episodes for himself, as I had worked with him on those. To have been an English criminal working in France was always something worth mentioning.

'First, in France,' repeated the bossman Pete, 'then in England. And they really didn't want you out, the government, did they? Your lawyers, the ones we paid for, by the way, didn't think much of your chances. They had to go to the High Court to get your parole. But it's good, because you deserve it. As you say, you didn't kill those folks they sent you down for. We know that. You know that. You know, like us, who did it and you didn't say. So, that's good for all of us, because you kept quiet.'

The bossman paused. He looked around.

'Anyway, we like to see a loyal comrade free, well provided for and happy.'

Pete paused again, just for a moment. Then he stood up and pulled me, and Swiss, up, his fat hands tugging at our shoulders. He said confidently, 'In fact, let me say this, son. You're a big man, William Harrison Gilbey. You're a legend, my son. We all know that, don't we, boys?'

Swiss and Artie muttered something. Colin said 'fuck', in a gentle way.

'So, let's give him a proper round of applause.'

And they all did.

Pete, me and Swiss sat down.

'But, to get back to business, William. First, we've landed you on your feet getting Mr Smart Arse Lloyd Piercey as your probation officer. We know a lot about Piercey. He won't cause you no trouble. If he does start playing up, let us know. What's his current game at the house he's got you in Twickenham, well, we are not sure; but we think it's small fry and to be let go. So, go along with him, OK?'

I nodded.

'He's maybe running cheap drugs, see-kayz or calvin kleins, I mean coke cut with ketamine and talcum or chalk, that is to say five percent coke, a dash of ket, and ninety-five percent muck.'

'Shocking,' said Swiss.

'Disgusting,' added Artie, 'cheating your punters.'

Pete ignored them. Colin said nothing.

'We probably won't even bother to find out. He is a small man, Mr Piercey, not good enough to get the benefit of dealing with the big boys like us, nor to get on in his day job. He's stupid enough also to get a wife who likes her bling. And you may like to know, William, in case it comes in useful for you, our friend Mr Piercey's got a bitch on the side. Anyway, as I say, just play along with Mr Smart-Arse Piercey, until he gets boring. But, keep us in the picture. Same with your private dick we have given you, looking into your dad's story.'

I nodded.

'Maybe your dad didn't do what they said he did, either? What a world, eh? So, let us know how that gets on, as we may have other help to offer. To be honest, we just want to do everything for you, William: everything and anything.'

A voice – was it my father's voice? – at that very moment warned me. It told me to say: 'this is not what I have come here for.' Not the sort of help which spelled complications. Nothing to do with dealing drugs, nor even seeing them dealt by others. Not again. I had simply come to thank the Uncles, who had looked after me, who had got me out, and then to get my money and jewellery.

I was going to go straight. I didn't want to hear about crime, or to get involved. I mustn't have any risk of being confined again. I only wanted temporary help, which had been provided. I wanted to focus on the history, not the new.

But, when you are asked by comrades to do something, I had always been taught that you do it. My father had said that about his comrades. 'Always work for your own people son, not the nobs.' That's the whole basis.

So I said nothing.

Pete must then have read my mind. 'The other thing is, William, you want to know how you are fixed. You want to reap the benefits of all your wise tax-free investments over the years, things we Uncles have looked after for you.'

I said: 'Yes.'

Pete leaned over the table. He picked up a document. It was full of rows of figures, vertically and horizontally. 'You are very well fixed, William Gilbey, very well fixed indeed. What this shows is that in banks a few hundred yards from here you have ready cash totalling over a million, real English pounds I mean not dollars, and in longer term, some in dollars and some in euros and Chinese money, maybe approaching five millions, translated into pounds I mean. You look.' Pete pushed the spreadsheet at me. 'Isn't that good? Isn't that marvellous? Is that truly what you expected, William? Do you see it?'

'Yes,' I said, although the columns meant nothing to me. I had been hoping to see. Well, what? Piles of notes? Actually, I had been expecting to go to the vaults of a real bank, to see Arab bankers in their smart suits or flowing robes telling me that my horde of notes or gold bullion was in Vault 101, or Vault 666, or somewhere. So I said: 'Can I go to the bank?' although I had learned to hate banks and their usurers after reading Ezra Pound's essays. I preferred robbing banks to visiting them.

'Of course you can, son. Of course you can, but not yet. We will need to make an appointment. We will need to get dressed up, all of us, just like you, smart. Let's see now, let's make an appointment for later this or next week or yes… let's see.'

Pete looked at something on his fancy phone. He then pulled a face.

'Oh it may need to be the week after, as I have all this business with my Dubai visitors I can't let go. They're staying in a hotel not far from your apartment, William, as it happens. Don't let on though, if we bump into each other. They're very conscious of security are *A-Rabs*. They do business all day and expect play all night. But we'll go soon. You have my word on that, William. And when we do go to the bank we can certainly meet Mr Imoglu, our Turkish contact. Look, William. There's his name on the spreadsheet. He can go over it with you.'

I looked at the name.

'He's a good man, Mr Imoglu, very careful. Of course he gets his share. I can tell you, whatever the markets are doing, with all this credit crunch and Euro nonsense, your money will have grown even more by the time we meet. His investments are copper-bottomed, guaranteed, no questions asked. They've been in Cyprus money, Northern Turkish Cyprus, not in Euroland, ok?'

41

I nodded, without understanding. 'And my jewellery?'

'The same, son: it's safer than houses, it's in deep vaults.'

Pete opened the drawer of the desk he was squatting at. He took out, and opened, a folder. He showed me some glossy photographs.

I recognised several of the items straightaway: jewels that my mother used to show me, the ones that my father had given her, a necklace among them. Where he had gotten them, I never knew. They were in the wooden jewellery box hidden under the bed. They were only taken out on occasional evenings in the place we stayed at Les Arcades, with all the lights off, and just a weak torch shining on them, which caught their sparkle. My mother never spoke about the jewels otherwise. She never even mentioned them to the Bevington-Wards, as far as I know. They would be mine one day, she said.

So, when I left home at fourteen, I took them, to save her the trouble. I didn't ask her, and she never asked for them back. Well, I was never in touch with her after my brief stay at the college in Toulon.

But I have not had the jewels in my hands since I put them into safe-keeping after my second arrest. I got a message out to people I could trust. They took them from where I had left them. It was the beginning of my association with the Uncles. The jewels, like me, have survived on trust in the Uncles ever since.

Pete looked at the photo, then at the forms and spreadsheets, turning them over in front of me. He asked me to countersign some forms. My signatures were needed, he said, to arrange access to the banks and the vaults. The ones they had were out of date, and had faded. Some of them could still be seen on the old forms they showed me (which I couldn't remember signing, but it was a long time before).

True enough, when I signed again my signatures seemed thinner and smaller.

'Great,' said Pete. 'Great,' said Swiss and Artie. 'Fucking hell,' said Colin.

Tired, I felt a rush of emotion in that crowded room near Hatton Garden, when I heard all this. Despite that inner voice still pleading caution, and wanting certainty, not waiting around for skinheads, Turkish Cypriot investors and Arab bankers, I was happy. I felt among friends.

## 1.6

I went back to my apartment in Kensington. I looked at the computer. No messages; no new information.

I had given up believing that there would be references somewhere to my father's stories. I knew from my prison work that the meeting between Mr Churchill and Mr de Valera was not in the history books, nor was it referenced on the limited part of the internet that I could access from prison.

However, I have kept an old cutting from a newspaper where, in a review, a famous historian stated:

*History is always written and re-written, historians constantly reassess official lines, and new first source material, such as files and diaries, lost buildings and artefacts, emerge which throw startling and fresh light on even well recounted events.*

Yet, my task was a specially challenging one, wasn't it? My father's story about Mr Churchill and Mr de Valera, which had seemed so interesting, almost romantic, when I had first heard it as an eight-year-old in 1964, and later when I wrote it down from the tape, was hugely controversial.

Yes, it was a discovery. But to release it, without proof, would be to risk the final destruction of my father's character, equivalent to a second, and this time public, hanging.

From my reading I knew that there would be many who would immediately want to deny that there had been the possibility of an agreement in 1940 between Britain and Ireland; or that Ireland might have entered the war on Britain's side; or that the Unionist and Imperialist Winston Churchill might have ceded the claims of the Northern Unionists to the Republicans.

Without giving away my story, I had talked to many Irishmen in prisons, from all parts of Ireland. A lot has happened since 1940. But attitudes to history, and the memories that stem from that, still seemed raw.

There would be ideal material for those who like to ridicule and to demonise others. First, to denounce my father, Herbert Gilbey, the convicted, hanged criminal, the 1960's murderer of old women, a fantasist storyteller. Then to denounce his mouthpiece William, his criminal son, who had run away from home at the age of fourteen, a gang member, a serial criminal and a convicted murderer. I had been spared from the state's murderous hands only by the accident of later birth. By the time I was tried for murder in 2002 civilised societies in Europe had stopped putting criminals in nooses or chopping their heads off in guillotines. But I was still considered a danger to society.

Who would believe such a father and son, given that we would be pitting this notorious Gilbey name against the great Churchill?

Then, looking out of a window on to the quiet road below, I saw someone standing behind an old-fashioned lamp post, a rather obvious place to watch my coming and going. I could not see if it was the bearded man again. Or might it be Colin, standing by to help? Or even Pete the bossman? But he was a director, not a player.

Yes, it could be Colin. Was it really worth his or others' time to watch me? I must know something worth knowing, or at least have the key to unlocking that knowledge. I must be worth following.

I turned back to the computer that Colin had fixed up. I decided to focus on the Irish connection, now that Francis had confirmed the Bevington-Ward business interests there. I entered de Valera's name. I wanted to know as much as possible about the Irish leader.

Up at the top of the results that stared at me from the computer was 'The de Valera Foundation'.

I clicked. The Foundation had a simple website, stating that it was an organisation in Dublin devoted to the study of the former Irish President's life and works. I had not come across it when I had made similar searches in prison. There, the computer systems had been restricted and censored.

The website read that The de Valera Foundation was non-political. Its main focuses were historical and editorial. Based in Dublin it had only two named staff. There was, however, a long list of apparently famous Irish men and women as trustees. It was run by a woman with the nice-sounding name of Miss Eireann Canning.

I drafted and redrafted. I was sorry that Miss Ingham was not on hand to help me. Eventually, I managed to send Miss Canning my first ever email, signed William H Gilbey.

I wrote that I was interested in the work of the foundation. I had come across a story with a de Valera connection in my family that I wanted to check. I wrote that I didn't want to put anything in writing; but that I hoped to visit Dublin very shortly, maybe as early as next week. Might she be able to spare me half an hour or so? I would be very grateful.

I tried to make the email as correct, and as courteous, as I could. I checked and re-checked the spelling.

That email began a relationship, and a sequence of events, which determined the course of the rest of this mémoire, and the course of my life.

# PART TWO

# 2

*the mémoire, posted to important persons, continued.*

The next day, I was early in Twickenham for my second meeting with Mr Piercey. I had again misjudged London's traffic. My taxi, driven fast along half-empty roads, had dropped me off almost an hour before I was due to meet him.

I walked along the main street. I looked in shops and found a cafe. I bought a mug of coffee and took it to a table in a corner, looking carefully for any followers. I didn't drink the coffee. I picked up a free paper. Fortunately, this was not a stakeout where I had to remain one hundred percent focussed on the business in hand. Here, I could let my mind roam free.

I must have looked ordinary, just an early morning worker in an old shirt, torn trousers and a windcheater, someone whose best period of life had come and gone. I could have passed for an office cleaner. I had dressed that way with a view to Mr Piercey, of course. I could not show my true self to him.

A hand touched my left shoulder. Mr Piercey said: 'Hello, William, a nice coincidence. You are even earlier than me.' I shook my thoughts away. I put my notepad into my bag.

As Mr Piercey sat down, I caught a glimpse of his Audi car, parked across the road in shade. It was facing in the opposite direction from the station. My acute criminal's eye saw a woman in the passenger seat. She was leaning back. No mention was made of her by Mr Piercey, then or later. But a woman had come with him.

'I often call in here, William. Anyway, I'll get a coffee. Do you want another one?'

I said: 'No thanks.'

We walked to the three-storied house Mr Piercey had chosen for me. It was in a terrace in a cutting just fifty yards or so from the railway line. I heard train announcements from Twickenham station.

I saw a curtain twitch on the second floor of the house next door to the one we were visiting. Otherwise the houses seemed boarded-up or empty. Some of the front doors were newly painted.

After Mr Piercey had unlocked the door, everything else followed quickly.

'It's smart and new isn't it, William? All these houses are, after they are renovated – they are what estate agents call sought after. Soon, the whole terrace will be like this.'

I looked down along the ground floor hall to what was evidently a new kitchen. Indeed, the whole house seemed new. But, unlike my Kensington apartment, I could see that it was cheap. Everything you could see from the hall was dull. There were a few prints on the walls, and a few patterned cushions. But otherwise it was pine, chrome, anonymous and unlived-in. Everything had been bought from a catalogue or a cheap department store, I guessed.

The patio at the back beyond the kitchen was well-scrubbed with minimal greenery, no maintenance expected. That was OK by me.

Nothing has ever matched, nor could ever match, the vibrant colours of the south of France. Since then, I have never wanted any sort of garden. I hate the greens and browns of parks, prison gardens and countryside estates. They make me want to retreat behind one of their low brick walls, and piss.

We went up to the first floor, which consisted of a bathroom and two bedrooms. Mr Piercey said that his friend's 'business' was on the upper floor. So the doors to that were locked. 'You have no need to see anything. You will be introduced after you move in. You won't need to see much of him or anyone else at all.'

Mr Piercey clearly didn't expect any reaction from me. Everything was taken as read. 'There will be no rent or bills to pay at the moment. All you have to do, William, is to live here, for the next three months, say. I only ask you to look after the place and to let me know of any trouble. Well, you can guess who with. Keep me informed. Be my associate, William. It will be great to get your feet back on the ground in a place as comfortable as this, won't it?'

I began to explain again about the apartment my friends had already found for me. But Mr Piercey said that I had no need to move in for a week or two. Again, I heard the voice within me telling me not to get involved. But it was too late. Mr Piercey said: 'No doubt your friends would be glad to have their apartment back sooner than they expect.' He added that if his boss, Mrs Llewellyn, knew that I was living under supervision, he maybe would not need to see me so often. 'Or even not at all at the probation office itself.' Then he corrected himself. 'Although, on second thoughts, maybe you ought to come in once in a while, to keep the record keepers happy. We do have to observe guidelines.'

Mr Piercey did not seem to want any comment from me. He ran his fingers over some of the furniture and held them up to me to show how clean everything was. He then said that he might 'drop in occasionally for a coffee', and that he might 'even bring Mrs Llewellyn. I would let you know in advance, of course, so that everything is prepared. Mrs Llewellyn would like to meet you, I am sure. She is a nice lady, William. You will like her. I know that you will speak to her carefully, and in a kindly way.'

Well, yes, I thought. I could spend nights here to keep Mr Piercey and his Mrs Llewellyn happy, while I sorted out my affairs. Then, with my money and the jewellery cashed in with my Uncles' help, and the private investigator's and my own researches also completed, for good or for bad, I would have done my duty to myself and to my father. Then I could disappear. I knew that this stage of my life, important though it was, could not go on forever. I had to do my best to find out the truth about my father and his story. But after that I would have a new life to lead. I had maybe twenty years to live a 'normal' life. More practically, it also occurred to me that, if I did need a sudden flit from Twickenham,

I need only tell Mr Piercey that I might call the police to the house, with its suspicious goings-on. Or I could even ring Mrs Llewellyn direct. That would surely finish Mr Piercey, if he was doing what the bossman Pete had alleged. Yes, I had been offered neat solutions to the problems of the authorities' last hold on the Gilbeys.

Anyway, as I had decided that for the time being I would go along with Mr Piercey, I felt that I must look more interested and grateful. So I went into the ground floor room, uninvited. I opened the double doors that led into the second room at the back. This then made for one large living area. Eureka! To my surprise and delight, concealed from our hallway view, there was a piano. It was only an old upright, not a 'baby' or a 'boudoir' grand; but it was something I didn't have at all in the Uncles' flat in Kensington. I pressed a few of the piano's keys at random. It was playable. 'That was left by a previous tenant. It doesn't fit in here, does it? I can get it taken away,' said Mr Piercey.

'No, no,' I said. 'Please, no, leave it.' Mr Piercey looked alarmed. It was my tone of voice, I suppose. 'Mr Piercey, can I tell you something?'

Mr Piercey looked at his watch. 'Of course, William, that is what I am here for.'

'Mr Piercey, I want to tell you a story, a story about me; about me and the death of my father.'

This is the story that I told Mr Piercey. I reminded him that I had gone to France in 1964, after my father was taken.

On 18 July, several weeks after our arrival at the villa Les Arcades, and, uniquely in my memory, my guardian Mr Andrew Bevington-Ward pushed open our outbuilding door without knocking. Mrs Bevington-Ward came in behind him. She put her arm around my mother, and led her up to the villa.

Mr Bevington-Ward sat down on our only chair. I stood in front of him. He sniffed the air and lit a cigar. I hoped he would offer it to me after he had inhaled it, just as my father had poured me a glass of sherry the previous Christmas, saying as he did so that 'the boy should have the odd glass, so that he gets used to the idea'. But on that occasion my mother had called out: 'He's only seven, for God's sake Bert.' So I had not tasted alcohol.

However, Mr Bevington-Ward did not offer me his cigar, or indeed anything. Instead, after a moment, he stood up. He took a final, long inward breath. He pushed his cigar butt in our sink, through the dirty dishes. He said as he sat down: 'Well, William, my boy, you have to face up to some bad news. You will soon be a young man and that is what, *logically and therefore*, young men have to do.' I did not reply. This seemed to please him.

'Good. The plain fact is that you will not see your father again. Earlier this morning, there is no easy way for me to tell you this, William, my boy, your father has died. He, well he, he was executed. He was executed by hanging in England, at a prison in London. Mrs Bevington-Ward took the telephone call.'

This reference to the telephone especially excited my interest. It proved the gravity and reality of the news. We did not have a telephone in Burnley, nor in France. I had never used one. My mother had told me that she had gone to use a telephone in Les Arcades a week earlier.

But I had been left behind in our building (the first time that had happened, I think). She gave me no account of the call, nor what news she had had, or what she had discussed. Mr Bevington-Ward looked at me, worrying perhaps that I had not understood. 'Hanged,' he said again. 'Hanged,' I said.

I do not know whether I understood the matter fully. But I knew about death. Many of my father's friends shown in his black photo album had died – he had said – in 'the war.' I had seen photos in magazines of burned-out buildings in Aden and Cyprus with men's bodies twisted and bloody, as well as the trapped and murdered rabbits and foxes in the grounds of Les Arcades. I think also that I had already assumed that maybe my father would not appear in France, and that his role in my life had come to an end. After all, cold and foggy Burnley was his place – not warm, thunderous St-Laurent du Var. Whether that theory was the same in my mind as death, I do not know. But, frankly, there was a point that was conclusive. I enjoyed being alone with my mother. My father now existed only in sweat stained shirts and trousers with turn-ups, his beery or whisky breath, and in his stories, the one about Mr Churchill and Mr de Valera being the most told. There were others about Anthony Eden and so forth, and folk and fairy tales from his and his family's past. But none seemed so dramatic, so unmissable, none was intended to remain in my memory or require my action, as that Churchill/de Valera story. Mr Bevington-Ward continued. 'Yes, my boy, your father has been hanged. The bastards.' Again, a word excited me. I knew 'bastards' to be a bad one, one of the three or four such words that I had heard my father use, and which greatly annoyed my mother. So 'bastards' and a telephone call on the same day! Mr Bevington-Ward then stood up and took me by the hand. We walked up to the villa together, not by the winding path we Gilbeys used, but across the lawns. Mrs Bevington-Ward, her gurgling baby son Francis in a basket at her side, and my mother were sitting on the terrace that looked towards the mountains, our building concealed from view by trees. It was the only time that I ever saw my mother there. Gloria Bevington-Ward was on a low settee (a 'chaise longue' is the correct word I now know) that had been set outside for her. The maid brought lemonade and tiny biscuits for all of us. I remember Mrs Bevington-Ward saying that 'soon' Francis would be 'old enough' to play with me, 'young William'. 'In a year or two they will be good for each other'; 'out here'. Then Mrs Bevington-Ward added: 'William, you should call us 'Uncle Andrew' and 'Aunty Gloria' from now on.' 'Uncle Andrew' looked up to the ceiling, and lit another cigar. My mother said nothing, and looked away.

A few moments later, my mother and I returned following our path, in silence. However, I remember her saying, as she laid me down in the bed that we shared: 'Remember this all your life, William: *Violence begets violence; evil begets evil; and good begets good."*

After I had told him this story, I remember that Mr Piercey looked again at his watch. He said: 'But how did you get there in the first place, why were you taken to, what was it called, St-Laurent du Var?'

That was a good question. Of course I had no answer to give him. I thought I had explained to him that I was ill-informed and that I was an innocent. Yet, like Parsifal in one of the books of old mythology I regularly read, I was resolute in my quest. But Mr Piercey hadn't understood me. Few people have. Maybe no-one has.

I said: 'Mr Piercey, I remember policemen coming to our house in Burnley and brief, muffled conversations with them. Then, on one of the trains to the south of France, my mother told me that we were to be met by a 'kind and nice' couple, who would look after us. But when, after changing trains many times, we reached our destination, there was no-one at the station. We had to use a taxi, an enormous fascination for me, Mr Piercey. I had only read about taxis, just as I had only read about other countries.

'The taxi took us about ten miles. We stepped out, and saw in the evening light, behind grand entrance gates, a large stuccoed house. I saw glimpses of a dark swimming pool and a tennis court. I smelled the perfumes of night-scented stocks and herbs. They clashed with the strong French tobacco smells of the taxi. I heard my first cicadas, and the moan of the outside generator that was to provide occasional electricity for our outhouse.

'A man came out and paid the driver. Then we were shown round the back, stumbling in the dark, with a uniformed maid's weak torch to guide us.

'My memories of the first few weeks include the walks up to Les Arcades, always staying on the path, and the first meetings with the Bevington-Wards – Mr Andrew in a straw hat and immaculate clothes (pressed linen suit and starched white shirt with spotted cravat), ignoring me, but polite to my mother and his wife Gloria, a bird-like lady, always smoking, silent, smiling and reclining, not moving even during the piano lessons I later had with her friend Mademoiselle Prevert.

'I remember the sense of luxury in their house, the sparkling chandeliers, the paintings on the walls, of every size and description, the wonderful smells of food. I remember the visit of two Frenchmen in double-breasted suits, and a woman dressed as if for a funeral (as my mother described her). They were from the local schools, I was told. But I was offered no formal primary education. It was said that the French schools could not cope. Or maybe there were other reasons. Anyway, it was accepted that education was to be my mother's (and the Bevington-Wards') responsibility, at least initially. Forms were signed. I was to be sent away to an English-speaking college when I was fourteen. My mother and Mrs Bevington-Ward talked about that regularly. Mr Bevington-Ward was often said to be 'making inquiries'.

'Thus, before being sent to college at Toulon at fourteen, Mr Piercey, I never had much formal education. I do not regret that. I hope that tells you something about me.'

Mr Piercey opened the front door. 'I guess you'll get a train back to town, William. This house is certainly convenient for that. I'll say goodbye for now, William. I'll ring you. I'll see you again next Friday, if not earlier. Good luck, William!'

I sat down. I looked again at the piano. I thought of all the things about me that Mr Piercey, my supposed helpmate, didn't know. I thought about the knowledge that burns inside me: the learning that life has given me, whatever other deprivations I have suffered.

It was to be my joy to be mainly self-taught in France and later, to experience the literature I love at first-hand, and to encounter difficult poets and impossible language in English and French, in magazines, in the village bibliotheque, the local bookshops and in the Bevington-Wards' own collection. I have always been able to confront literature, above all poetry, without interference, in my own choice of libraries, reading rooms, hotels and apartments, and in the limited and torn collections of borstals and prisons.

Of course, I realise how that freedom deprived me of a lot of what the average person learns and knows – the routine stuff, the politics, the shared assumptions, the cheap culture on television, the bus stop conversation. But let me be clear. From that time in the south of France – which was, according to my mother, in her happier moments, 'paradise' – I learnt many of life's true realities. I realised the place that the Gilbeys had been given in the world.

I remember long walks into the village with my mother. We would arrive just as the twice-weekly market was closing. My mother would beg for a few cents, or rescue from pallets over-ripe and squashy fruit and vegetables, or oatmeal for porridge. She would plead with stallholders for the last of their cheese and meat. The baker would give away for a few centimes the last of the morning's drying bread.

My mother would then walk back with her full pannier and with clothes, wool and silks for Mrs Bevington-Ward from the cleaner or the haberdasher.

I would skip ahead. If it had been raining I would jump on the fat white and brown slugs that lined the road. If it was dry I would pull flowers from the roadside, tossing them into the path of cars. I remember that my mother was often distracted, talking to herself to learn better the slang phrases in regional French, which she had just heard.

My mother sometimes seemed happy. She often sang. To me, in my age of innocence, people seemed generally kind. I remember a few raised voices, but generally a sense of distance and privacy, of the Gilbeys being ourselves in our own world. That was a demi-paradise of mother and son, never to be regained.

## 2.2

The taxi driver at the Twickenham rank smiled when I gave her my South Kensington address. 'Don't mind if I try this out do you?' she said, waving at one of two machines on the dashboard, a satnav. 'I never had one before. My mum got it for my birthday. I always thought they were the work of the Devil, satnavs!' I had learned about such things in prison lessons. Miss Ingham had briefed us on iPads, iPhones, digital television and satnavs, to prepare us for the Brave New World, she said. But, yes, I can see that the satnav is the work of the Devil, the Devil that spies on us through satnavs and closed circuit cameras, the controlling Devil, the Great Satan leading you on His dance through London, the most corrupt city on earth, as Ezra Pound described it.

I almost said such words out loud as my irritation with the chattering taxi woman rose, but I stopped myself. I clenched both fists at my sides instead. Anyway the woman rambled on with her trivial nonsense, until her second device, her fixed mobile phone, rang. She then shouted at her husband, mostly about the satnav's idiocies. It was a long, slow, noisy and dirty journey. I closed my eyes and tried to think not of noisy people, nor of Pete and Colin, Swiss and Artie; nor of the bearded man who was surely still following me, nor of Mr Piercey and the person in his car and his doings in Twickenham. I thought of good things, mainly my plans to discover truths, and then to build a new life. I thought of jewellery and money, fine meals and great cooking. Above all, my thoughts kept coming back to the piano in Twickenham and the pianos at Les Arcades. I have always loved the piano, the resounding music it can produce through its elaborate construction of fine wood and taut wires. And, to give her credit, my talent as a pianist was recognised early by 'Aunty' Gloria Bevington-Ward, who remained otherwise a remote figure in my life, never what I imagined a real aunty would be like.

One day, my mother and I had come back from one of our shopping trips. My mother was especially quiet. There had been a scene in the town cobblers, when it seemed that the shoes my mother had taken in were too far gone with holes and scuffs to be mended. I remember my mother saying to the man that they were 'Madame's', and that perhaps she had sent the wrong pair. But I doubt that the fat little cobbler, who spoke French too fast for my mother, believed her. I knew that the shoes were my mother's, but I didn't say.

I always remember contemptuous looks. I have suffered many in my life, from 'good honest working people' especially when they are sitting on juries, or when they form booing crowds to watch people like me being led, handcuffed, from court or police station, to a van. The look on the face of that smelly French cobbler, when reinforced in my mind by my mother's distress, her breakdown in tears, when she called on Mrs Bevington-Ward to give her the cleaning and the new balls of wool, has never left me. On that occasion, Mrs Bevington-Ward gently asked us to stay and to have some coffee. Without being asked, or being given permission, I crossed to the upright piano, similar to the one we had in Burnley. I played two early, easy, Bach preludes. Even then, I knew how to make them 'sing'; but also to keep the line strong. 'Why, Mrs Gilbey,' said Mrs Bevington-Ward, 'William has a natural talent. He must have lessons from my friend Mademoiselle Prevert. Then he can play for us, all of us. I will have the piano tuned, of course.' My mother was proud. She loved music. She told me that as a teenager she had secretly joined a choir in Belfast and had sung in oratorios like 'Elijah' ('those Baal choruses William!') and 'The Creation' ('The Heavens are telling the Glory of God'!). They were, in her Catholic parents' view, Protestant music, sung by the enemy, and to be disapproved of. Anyway, my mother never seemed to disagree with Mrs Bevington-Ward's plans. So, at first it was once a week, then twice a week with the teacher. Then in a matter of a few months my studies escalated, so that I was going every day to play, and Mademoiselle Prevert was coming three times a week, or more, to teach me. Mademoiselle was a tiny woman, who talked to me only about music. She never asked me how I was; nor did she comment on my old clothes or untidy hair. I don't remember being able to wash much. There was limited hot water in our building. But Mademoiselle's teaching was remarkable. She had no qualms about forcing me along. She would often push me off the piano stool and demonstrate technique. She would take me from the pin-sharp accuracy required in Scarlatti and Mozart; through the romantic breaking of chords, and the different placings of the hands and wrists to achieve correct gradings of cantabile' ('singing tone') in Chopin and Liszt; to the arched hands of Rachmaninov, and the correct way to play his arpeggios and glissandi. Mademoiselle Prevert had the composer Maurice Ravel and the pianist Alfred Cortot as her heroes. Sometimes, without any introduction, Mademoiselle would put on old-fashioned 78 rpm discs to illustrate her points. She said that Cortot was not allowed to play or record much in France 'after the wretched war', which was 'a wretched pity'. A collaborator, he spent most of the post-war years recording in Japan. We always listened in silence to the records. Mademoiselle told me that technique was innate. It was style I needed to learn. From Mademoiselle and from Alfred Cortot.

Mrs Bevington-Ward often reclined in the opposite corner of the room during my playing. But she would never say anything. 'His Lordship', as my mother often called my 'Uncle Andrew', would nearly always be in the house too. He was a shadow, a distant presence. He was working on catalogues, it was said. On a few occasions Mademoiselle's son, Nicholas Prevert, dressed in a sailor suit, came with her. He would be put in a corner and told to sit quiet while I played, and to learn from me. Apparently he had no aptitude for the piano. I had a great 'aptitude' (Mademoiselle pronounced that English word very carefully). But, when I turned to the right when reaching for the upper piano registers, I could see Nicholas's reflection in a mirror. When he had realised this he used to wait for my movements. Then he would time scowls, pulling horrible faces. I would stumble in my playing as a result, and Mademoiselle would scold me. Nicholas used to catch my glance again, and laugh. How I hated that boy, how I wished that I could strangle, or drown him, or crush him like a slug, or have him hanged like my father had been hanged, whichever would have been the cruellest and most painful death.

One day, about six months into my lessons, I had come into Les Arcades when I found that the upright piano, a Challen, had been replaced by a boudoir grand. It was a magnificent, shiny Bosendorfer. I have been asked, during numerous assessments, to state the greatest moments of pleasure in my life. Outranking my first taste of pan-fried fresh foie gras, or my first sip of armagnac, or even my first fully unleashed sex with a virgin in Toulon, I always identify the first experience of that Bosendorfer piano. I had only ever seen 'grand' pianos on the sleeves of records, or in books. Now there was a magnificent instrument, devoted only to me. Of course the upright in Twickenham could not compare. But it was mine, and mine alone. It was a new, and welcome, link to my past.

When the chattering woman's taxi had finally dropped me back in South Kensington, I looked at the computer. I found that there were two new emails. One was a simple and welcoming message from Miss Canning of The de Valera Foundation. After several attempts, I managed a reply. I said that I would travel to Dublin the next Monday, 16 June, and that I would call her on my arrival. After I did this, I remembered to turn on my mobile phone. It bleeped.

The first email was a request to arrange a meeting, following the letter drafted by Miss Ingham. The message was in the name of 'Harry Ross'.

The second email was from Swiss Joe. I had wanted to eat out in London regularly, alone, and in style, after my release. When I had confided this from prison to the contact man, he had come back to say that The Milky One and the new bossman were worried. They thought it an unwise idea after I had been in prison for twelve years. I would take time, they said, to get into the routine of a free man. But, when I said how important it was to me, and how I had dreamed during my twelve years in prison of eating good food, just as I had dreamed of playing a proper piano again, he said that the Uncles would make arrangements.

I used the prison training computer during my last weeks of confinement to locate the best restaurants in London. Now, in his mail, Swiss told me that I would be a 'special guest' in all of them; that I would have my own table set well away from others; and that I could order anything I wished – but that no charges would be made. However, I should take cash, from my apartment, to reward good service, as well as to pay for taxis. I would have the best of the restaurant staff at my command. I could not vary the dates, nor any of the arrangements chosen for me. I saw no harm with that.

Swiss's message also told me that a table had been booked at Claude, a Michelin starred restaurant in Mayfair, one that I had been very much looking forward to, mentally right at the top of my list, for eight o'clock that evening. There was no need to confirm.

I will not record in this mémoire the evening, nor the meal of smoked salmon, kidneys and tarte tatin in detail. But I can say that I greatly enjoyed Claude, its style and its perfectly timed cooking. Yes, I was happy again for a while.

A famous chef I worked for used to say to staff and to customers, in his more sober moments, that his sole purpose was to give 'a few moments of pleasure. What better thing can a man do in this vale of tears?' For two hours, Guiseppe Carnarolo's maxim was proven.

But I was not as focussed as I should have been. I was thinking of travel and upcoming meetings.

The trip I planned to Dublin on the next Monday and Tuesday excited me. It was so new and offered so much, especially meeting a knowledgeable person who could help me, I hoped, with my story about Mr Churchill and Mr de Valera.

By contrast, the meeting with Mr Ross of the Cabinet Office (I had left an immediate message for him, to meet me early on Wednesday, after my return from Dublin) began to trouble me, mainly because he was an officer of the state. I also wondered whether he would be annoyed by the delay in taking up his offer, and that he might be condescending and obstructive. The more I dwelled on it, the more likely that seemed.

Before all that, on Sunday, would be my second encounter with Francis and my first meeting with Gillian, and an opportunity to know more about the Bevington-Wards' role in my life.

My inner voice was silent. Nobody told me to hesitate, or to change course. But, in the background, there were thoughts of my mother and father. My father, especially. He was the essential actor in all this. He was the only person who knew the truths that I wanted to discover, especially of his stories that were my inheritance, and which formed such a large part of my own history.

I would always retell the stories my father told me. I would defend him. That was my duty, as it is every son's duty. But did I really know any of the truth? The most important thing about Herbert Gilbey was the way that he had died, the fact that 'the bastards' of the state had executed him. Was he truly a cold murderer, like me? Why, why had he become like that?

I had heard nothing from my investigator. I decided to call the little man and his boys on Monday, from Dublin if necessary. I also thought that I might call on them unannounced, in Bond Street, within a few days, if I sensed no progress.

Saturday was for writing this mémoire, and choosing clothes for the Dublin trip; Sunday for the Bevington-Wards. No more extravagant eating and drinking. No more fantasies. No pleasures of any sort. But I reminded myself to remain on alert, for the followers who, I knew, were ever present in my life.

# PART THREE

# 3

*MI5 HQ, Vauxhall, London*

William Gilbey was right about being followed. His every movement had been noted.

The bearded man's reports – and the letter below, forwarded from the Cabinet Office – were the latest additions to files that went back seventy years. They now sat on Harry Ross's desk. The letter had been bookmarked for him by his senior colleague, Morgan Janvir. Harry shared an office with Morgan.

Long Lartin Prison, June 6 2014.
Prisoner number WHG 22/LL 84692

*Dear Sir,*

*My name is William Harrison Gilbey. I am being released next Monday. I have been advised to write to the Cabinet Office by Miss Ingham, my after-release assistant here.*

*My father, Herbert ('Bert') Gilbey, was the last man to be executed in England, by hanging, at 8 in the morning on 18th July 1964. He is buried in the precincts of Pentonville prison in London. My father worked at No 10 Downing Street during the Second World War, as a driver. He told me stories about his time there. The most important one was when he described taking Mr Winston Churchill, then Prime Minister, to meet Mr de Valera, then Prime Minister of Ireland. This must have been an important event. I want to find out my father's part in it. I want to discover his history generally. Please, would you kindly advise me of how I can trace my father in your records. Please help me in any other way that you can. Miss Ingham is writing below the name and contact details of my supervising probation officer, who will have my contact details.*

The name and contact details of Mr Lloyd Piercey of the Inner London Probation Service followed.

Harry read the letter quickly. His roommate, and senior, Morgan Janvir, who had been on the phone to his father when Harry had arrived, said 'Good morning Harry; or is it good afternoon? I've put a new agenda for the 10.30 on top of your files.'

Morgan and Harry were booked in to see Wilfred Robbins, the head of their division, A2, at the same time every Thursday.

Harry picked up the agenda. Virtually all A2 matters were put on paper. Most were shredded daily. Emails were not trusted. Scanning or copying of documents was not permitted.

'Any changes you can help me with?' Harry said.

'That letter in front of you from Gilbey is now there, in fact at item three.'

'Important?'

'Better read at least the top file now. In fact if I were you, better read all the files, back to 1940. Robbins's imprint has been on and off the case for at least twenty years. It seems to have followed him round. You've been on the speed-reading course, haven't you, Harry? Better make use of it!'

It was already ten o'clock, so Harry focussed hard for twenty-five minutes.

At 10.29 Amy Moynihan, Robbins's secretary, opened the door to her boss's room. This was larger than that of Janvir and Ross. It was dominated by a heavy bookcase, whose contents (dictionaries, biographies of English statesmen, twentieth century poetry – Eliot and the like) never seemed to Harry to be moved from one week to the next. In the middle of the room was a circular table and a small globe; at the side a heavy safe with several dials and, facing as visitors entered, an old and battered desk. There were no paintings, no photographs, no plants nor ornaments in the room. Just two phones, one black, one red, on a side table at the right of the desk.

But the centre of attraction to any eye was always Wilfred Robbins himself – a tiny, angular man of fifty seven, upright behind the desk, on a raised chair. Known to juniors as the monkey, Robbins's face was washed pink, 'like Germolene', his first secretary had said. His hair was always close cropped. He wore the same type of old-fashioned wire spectacles, one for everyday use and one for reading, prescribed by a National Health Service optician thirty years earlier. He dressed in creased pinstripe suits, starched white shirts and spotted ties. Today his tie was green.

Morgan Janvir, small, dark and intense, sat down, opposite Robbins, first; Harry Ross, tall, tousle-haired, breezy and tieless, after him. Robbins nodded, and then took up his reading glasses, clumsily peeling his other glasses from his face as he did so. To Harry, Robbins's movements never seemed fully co-ordinated.

'We'll go straight to agenda item three, Mr Gilbey, as I have been summoned to The Second Floor at eleven. I hope my time there will not be wasted.'

Harry smiled. Morgan did not. Harry knew that Morgan was an ambitious man. Wilfred Robbins was no role model for ambition. Wilfred, with his regular and indiscreet sallies against his superiors, was behind the ideal career path. Sir Rory Armitage, the Head of A Group, was ten years younger, yet on The Second Floor, and already a knight. As Harry Ross saw it, Robbins knew no caution. It seemed that he was prepared to challenge everything and everyone, often in exaggerated language. Harry Ross admired that. Ideally, he would do the same as he went up the ladder but, maybe, less noisily than Wilfred.

There was a class issue also. Unlike Sir Rory and Morgan (who had told Harry this on the first morning they met) Robbins was not an Oxford man. He had taken a degree in Anglo-Saxon in Aberystwyth. Harry had taken a degree in English at Lancaster.

Yes, Harry admired Wilfred Robbins. Morgan clearly did not.

'So, the letter from Mr Gilbey, gentlemen? What is to be done? Mr Janvir?'

Morgan said, 'Well, actually, Harry has most recently had the papers.'

'Well, Mr Ross?'

Harry said: 'It is a variant on an old story.'

'Yes, that is true, pray continue.'

'And it is clear that the decision to suppress it, or whatever, has been taken many times at the highest level, Mr Robbins.'

'Yes, you will have seen that the matter was put to Prime Minister Macmillan over fifty years ago, then to Heath; to Callaghan; to Thatcher; to Major, and even to Blair, in his case during the so-called Good Friday talks on Northern Ireland. Never to Harold Wilson, though. Wilson couldn't be trusted. Our predecessors showed as little as possible to Wilson. Nor did it go to the wretched Brown. The man never stopped talking long enough.' Robbins looked over his glasses, as ever waiting for a challenge to an outrageous statement. Harry Ross laughed. Morgan Janvir did not.

'The immediate problem, though, is that William Gilbey has come out of prison a roused man, keen to make up for lost time, and, from what we know so far, a determined man.' Robbins sipped his coffee. 'So Mr Ross, you are fairly new here. May I ask again: what is to be done?'

But Morgan Janvir interrupted before Harry could reply: 'I wonder why we are bothering with this. Why are we so concerned? It is history. As you, Mr Robbins, and indeed Sir Rory, have always said, A Group does not stand in the way of truth.'

Robbins smiled and coughed. Morgan continued: 'I repeat, Mr Robbins, A Group does not stand in the way of truth, save as authorised by ministers. And only then in the most extreme cases of national interest. Nor are we archivists. Unless there is something really dangerous that is bound to come out, why not steer clear? Safety first, surely? And, if Gilbey were to find something interesting – so be it. Let him get on with it. If we are determined to slow him down, then give him a pass to the government archives at Kew. He could be lost there for years.'

Robbins did not comment. He looked to Harry, who after a few moments' thought, said: 'Morgan is probably right. But from what I have seen and absorbed, surely we risk Gilbey opening a Pandora's Box if we stand aside and do nothing? And we have to reply to the letter.'

Morgan Janvir shook his head in that dogmatic and confident way which the easy-going Harry found superior and annoying, especially when he did it in front of more senior colleagues. 'Well, maybe so, maybe so Harry; I doubt it, as Gilbey wouldn't find anything at Kew and he will hopefully give up there and then. If he doesn't, we can review. Continue to watch him, by all means, if that is a sensible use of MI5 resources. But nothing is likely be gained by interference now.'

Wilfred Robbins nodded. 'Yes, yes, Mr Janvir, of course. I wish that you were right, but there are problems in staying aloof, in not getting involved aren't there?'

'I think, Mr Robbins,' said Harry Ross, who was warming to a theme, 'that you mean Ireland, the Republic, the de Valera history, reopening the wounds of that era. That is where you see a real problem. Even now, it might not be safe, given what has been achieved recently, to stand aside. We may be risking too much.'

'Quite, Mr Ross, yes, that allegedly beautiful place Ireland. I have never been there, Dublin nor Belfast, Armagh nor Cork, so I cannot definitely say. But I know, like all Englishmen, how it is steeped, maybe even obsessed with its history.' Robbins looked over his glasses. 'Do either of you know the works of Ezra Pound? They're in the bookcase somewhere. He wrote: 'there is no topic more soporific; nor more generally boring, than Ireland'. That caused an outrage at the time. Mind you he also wrote that he had 'never known anyone worth a damn who wasn't insane'. Pound himself was judged to be insane after the war.

'So, yes,' Robbins continued, 'Ireland is a problem, Mr Ross. But a bigger problem is money, money that, even as we speak, is being thrown at this conundrum. It is money from people who believe that there may not only be historical truth, and truth itself is dangerous, we know, especially in the Irish context, but also a pot of gold, maybe several pots, some now in Gilbey's own hands; but they believe that there is a great deal more unaccounted for.'

Robbins paused. Then he said, in a sarcastic tone: 'Perhaps neither of you gentlemen may yet have understood the importance of money. You were both born with silver spoons in your mouths, I suppose.'

Harry wanted to protest. But he said nothing. Robbins said provocative things. That was Robbins. What he had said was clearly true of Morgan, though.

His father had come to England as a political refugee from Iran. He had set up a business. Morgan's father was now a millionaire, several times over, so Morgan had said.

'And what is our biggest problem?' Robbins continued. 'I'll answer that for you. It is that there have always been big holes in our own understanding of what happened in 1940, and subsequently.' Robbins paused and lifted his hands to his chest. 'I fear gentlemen, whatever The Second Floor may tell us, that A Group is not all-knowing. We don't know the full truth. Even Sir Rory acknowledges that. The most important document is missing. We only have drafts. The Irish papers from the period are similarly incomplete. If Mr de Valera was indeed involved, which Gilbey's father's story states, then he probably took the relevant papers into his coffin in 1975. Whether that was from a sense of shame, or a sense of disappointment, we do not know.'

Robbins stared, first at Janvir, then at Ross. 'So what do we conclude, what am I to report to The Second Floor?'

But, before Morgan or Harry could speak, the door between Wilfred's and Amy Moynihan's office's opened suddenly. Amy came in, saying: 'I'm sorry, Mr Robbins, but Sir Rory has called me personally, on my own line. He has asked if you could go to The Second Floor now, as he has had a call from Sir Brian.' Robbins smiled and raised his eyes upwards again, his left arm reaching behind his head to scratch the opposite side of his neck. 'Thank you Amy.' Harry also smiled at Amy, a warmer smile, and said 'Thank you.'

Amy smiled back at Harry and left slowly, leaving the door open.

'So, no more hesitations. Really, we have to decide here and now what to do.'

'Gilbey continues to be followed,' said Harry, to break the silence.

'Yes, we should wait on that before doing anything rash,' said Morgan.

'Yes. He is indeed being followed,' said Robbins. 'He is being regularly reported on by A8. They sent Nicholson on the job. No-one else was available. He's one of those seconded people, a policeman from Glasgow. He's not that good. I suspect Gilbey has already spotted him. We will take Nicholson off the case soon. A8 agrees. I will get Sir Rory's agreement as well.'

Amy Moynihan had now come back to the doorway, looking more anxious as the seconds ticked by on the clock on her wall. She and Harry exchanged more smiles.

'We need to reply to Gilbey's letter, at least,' said Harry.

'We need to do more than that. We need to talk to him ourselves.' With these words, Robbins took a Top Secret': UK eyes only file from Amy Moynihan, whose personal phone was ringing and flashing up *Sir Rory Armitage – personal line.*

Robbins then went through the door, as Amy said on her phone: 'Yes, Sir Rory, Mr Robbins is on his way.'

But, only a pace on, even before he had stepped into the corridor, Robbins turned back, as Janvir and Ross stood up. Robbins spoke with unusual force: 'Yes, Mr Ross, we must talk to him. Or more accurately *you*, you,

Mr Ross, must talk to him. You must deal with him, this criminal fantasist, as we shall agree to call him, William Harrison Gilbey. You will devote yourself exclusively to this case, from next Monday. I will dictate instructions after lunch.'

## 3.2

It was only after they had lunched that Morgan Janvir and Harry Ross talked again properly. They had not spoken more than a few words since the morning meeting's premature end. Both had worked on until their usual eating time of one o'clock – writing, filing, telephoning, all routine.

Morgan said that really he ought to have been given the task of talking to William Gilbey. He was the senior. It was an important case (not what you said before! thought Harry). There was some truth in this. If Harry could have conceded, he would have done. Well, perhaps. But he said nothing.

Morgan went on. He had, by heart, Robbins's words at one of their meetings, prior to giving Morgan his best case (he had described it to Harry in detail twice), when Morgan had had to trail and interview an Arab spy. 'And if you say, Mr Janvir, that you want to remain rooted to your desk why did we waste all that training?' Morgan had not argued the point at all. But Robbins had continued: 'No, whatever your reservations, sometimes it is our duty in the national interest to show ourselves, to get out in the world, acting sensitively, solving difficult problems, those that are beyond the police or the other agencies. Only the most difficult, mind, for A2. Nothing easy for us. So what you have to do, Mr Janvir, is almost beyond duty. It takes courage and skill.'

'That is what Robbins said, Harry: 'only the most difficult'. You weren't here at the time, but I'm sure you would have been told much the same thing at induction. You would have been told that external visits by our division, dealing with political and national issues of the highest sensitivity, are rare, and to be handled with the utmost caution.'

Harry nodded.

However, Morgan admitted, as he picked his teeth, that neither of them could ignore directions on the Gilbey case. If Robbins had made up his mind to send Harry, it would be pointless to protest, even if 'a disaster for the service' was impending, said Morgan. Anyway, he, Morgan, was sure to get a transfer soon. He had endured Wilfred Robbins for three years. Robbins would soon not be able to 'block' and 'thwart' him. So Morgan said.

Harry kept quiet. He didn't want to add to Morgan's hurt. For Harry, there was a first time for everything. Wilfred Robbins was giving him an unexpected chance, a premature chance maybe, who could say? Of course, Harry Ross could never tell them any details. Yet it was the sort of thing that would make Harry's hard-working and very ordinary parents in Hendon proud. He was their only child. He had told them that he was 'working on security for the army'.

When they returned to their desks Harry felt that he should ask about Morgan's father. Personal matters were not normally discussed between them, nor between A

Group staff generally. But Harry could not help hearing phone conversations. Mr Janvir had been admitted to a care home. This had clearly caused Morgan distress. Earlier in the week, after a particularly lengthy call, the usually taciturn Morgan had told Harry more of the family background. He talked about his father fleeing Iran, shortly before the fall of the Shah. Settled with other exiles in London, at night he had been a refugee and political activist. During the day he had created a multi-million pound building business. Morgan's father had originally wanted Morgan to take that over from him, but Morgan had no interest in such things.

Morgan had added that his father didn't like him still being a bachelor. Like Harry, Morgan was an only child, so there would be no grandchildren.

Morgan had ended the conversation abruptly, as usual. He wanted no help from Harry.

Earlier, Sir Rory Armitage and Mr Wilfred Robbins had found more common ground.

'So Wilfred, I can sip my darjeeling and sleep more easily, to hear that you have this wretched Gilbey matter under control. I will show you my usual utmost confidence in transferring it fully from A8.'

When A Group of MI5 had moved to new offices, Sir Rory Armitage and his senior colleagues had thought to impress their staff by the choice of The Second Floor for senior staff and their assistants, draped as the rooms were by thick layers of net and plastic behind elegant fabric curtains – as if they, the senior management, were in the front line of all the battles. But both staff and visitors were more taken by the sheer size of the rooms. They had been created by knocking several planned rooms together, and by raising the ceilings. Then there was the mahogany furniture and the chandeliers. And, of course, the Modiglianis and Picassos. Harry had been told that these were prints; but Morgan had said that he was sure that some at least were originals – presumably surplus to the national collections, although (not that Morgan claimed to Harry to be an expert) some were 'unusual' and 'not of high quality'.

'In addition to what I have told you, Sir Rory, and that which is in A8's report, I have put Harry Ross on the job. I am sending him to interview Gilbey. A8 have agreed that Nicholson will remain on the case for a few days, as well. Ross will not be told everything of course, not yet. I retain a shadow file, safely under lock and key and in my sole control.'

Sir Rory smiled. 'I see the logic of all that, Wilfred. Best to send a sprat to catch a mackerel!'

'Or, at least, to send a sprat to find where the mackerel is heading, Sir Rory', who smiled again.

'Good, Wilfred. After what you have told me, I will feel confident enough to reassure the Prime Minister, and Sir Brian.'

Robbins gripped the sides of a commodious armchair and hauled himself up. But Sir Rory raised his hands and waved him down. 'Look, Wilfred, I will send my best wishes to Ross. But, do you know, I have the feeling, and I think Sir Brian and Mr Cameron might well agree, that this time the whole matter of July 1940 and the Irish demands, the so-called agreement, needs to be brought out.' Wilfred Robbins frowned. 'Yes, Wilfred I sense it. Perhaps it is time that it was all worked through? Sometimes, you know, things need to be brought to the boil. It is seventy years, after all. Is what happened to be concealed forever? Maybe, at this time of relative peace, we would suffer only a temporary and bearable embarrassment. It could well turn out worse for the Irish than for us, and it is to this country that we owe our sole loyalty…then, of course, there are other considerations, closer to home.' Sir Rory looked around the room as he spoke.

Robbins, who was in the middle of changing his spectacles, with his usual pincer movement around his neck, said nothing. He sensed that Sir Rory was testing him.

Sir Rory took Robbins's silence as encouragement to continue. 'Wilfred, if we do reveal anything, we will need thorough preparation at all levels, including public relations and the political. I know that you will cover all angles. I do not need to reiterate the importance of that. We need to remain masters of what can safely come out. Details that are not in our interest could surely be lost. There is no need for us to parade guilt about any aspect, even if we find to be true certain things that, well, we have long suspected.'

Sir Rory paused. Sir Rory smiled. 'You know to what I am referring.' Wilfred Robbins nodded. 'But, let me repeat, as this affair unfolds, I will sleep easily, Wilfred, knowing that you have mastery of the case, and that you will show your usual judgement.'

After a few moments thought, Robbins said: 'Well, yes, Sir Rory: maybe some parts can come out. I am not yet convinced, though, that we cannot keep at least a substantial lid on the story. There are still extremists ready to use new information, especially information that has been deliberately concealed. They would use it to inflame old passions. And there are surely matters which it could be useful to hold back, for the future. Using someone like Ross, who may not be the brightest of our people, rather than Janvir, should give us the necessary options. Janvir would be too independent-minded, too focussed on the rights and the wrongs. Ross will follow instructions.'

Sir Rory interrupted: 'It is an interesting decision to use Ross, but I won't question your judgement. You are probably right.'

Sir Rory paused and looked at his hands. 'I am an impatient man, sometimes, Wilfred. I like to plan, and to know the endgame. Maybe, in this case, we cannot do that. Mind you, that sense of impatience and that commitment to detailed planning is what has brought me to The Second Floor.'

Robbins ignored this. He replied as he stood up, and moved to the door: 'A lot depends, Sir Rory, on where Gilbey leads Ross, and indeed leads others. For our part I fear that we must be prepared for collateral damage. Good people have often suffered in the national interest.'

Sir Rory poured himself another cup of tea and spoke to a closing door: 'Yes, my dear Wilfred, that is the sort of judgement we have to make in A Group. It is a heavy burden for us, I know.'

# 3.3

As they closed their safe on Thursday evening, Morgan Janvir told Harry Ross that he was taking an unexpected day's leave the following day. He did not tell Harry why, but Harry assumed that it was something to do with his father and the care home. Robbins had given his permission.

Morgan suddenly said, 'Be careful Harry, be careful. I think Gilbey may be more dangerous than we know.'

Harry Ross did not know how to take this, but he thanked Morgan. Morgan shook Harry's right hand as they went into the office lift, using both of his hands: the first time, and the last time, for that gesture.

Morgan Janvir drove to Esher the following morning. He was reluctant to visit his father. It might become an unwelcome habit. But there were no other relatives in England. Morgan's mother was long dead.

So Morgan knew his duty. He was proud to be a man of duty and of conscience.

Morgan could not actually talk to his father about the work of A Group, so he was glad that the elder Mr Janvir never asked him about it, nor did his father ask about Morgan's personal life, of which he would certainly have disapproved. Instead, the conversation always harked back to the Persian homeland, how Mr Janvir had fled in 1979, how he had remained as active as long as he could in supporting resistance to the extremist ayatollahs; and how he had ultimately grown weary.

But the brave stories of intrigue and resistance that his father told Morgan now sounded stale. And they always ended on the same note: 'Morgan, my son, it was like this. In the Shah's time we begged for a revolution; but we got the ayatollahs, the wrong revolution.'

His father had used to add: 'The next time Morgan, you must get it right.' But he no longer did that.

So, as usual when they met, Morgan and his father ate and sat and looked at each other, Morgan taking in the new surroundings. His father was, as ever, in a formal suit and tie. His eyes were misty and far away.

Morgan attempted polite conversation. All the time, his father's mind wandered backwards and forwards in time. He would go from one story to another.

But today Morgan made no attempt to engage his father. He could think of nothing else other than Harry Ross, and how he might be handled by William Gilbey.

# PART FOUR

PART FOUR

# 4

## 4.1

*the mémoire of William Gilbey, posted to important persons, continued.*

I arrived early on Sunday for my second visit to the Bevington-Wards' flat in West Kensington. I wore a good suit, labelled Pierre Cardin. Like my other clothes, it had been dry-cleaned, by Mr Jeeves of Knightsbridge, while I was in prison.

I walked around outside the block of flats for a while, observing visitors and activities, noting that I was in a rough area, until I pushed the buzzer for the flat at exactly ten o'clock. There was no reply. I tried again. No reply. So I hung around, looking at my watch and inside my wallet, trying to be inconspicuous, until a teenage girl came out of the block, her face decorated with piercings and tattoos. Her ears were stuffed with headphones, out of which came tinny music. I held the door open for her and then kept the door ajar, my face turned away. She did not acknowledge me. I eased myself in.

I went up in the lift, now mended, and knocked on the flat door. No reply. I was impatient. I also had my criminal's sense that something was wrong. But I had not brought my holdall with me. A mistake. It contains some useful tackle.

I waited twenty minutes in the silent corridor. I knew that I had to force entry, however illegal and unwelcome that might be, yet the door was an old-fashioned heavy one. Breaking through the weak-looking lock would be noisy, even with my well-honed techniques. If I could get in, then I had a scenario to justify my forced entry, that I had smelled something burning inside – should the need arise. It had worked before.

But it was too quiet.

Just as I was starting to get angry, my fists useless and clenched by my side, someone started drilling in, or maybe near, the block. Once I caught the rhythm of the drilling, I was able to get the same rhythm into my shoulder charges. With three heaves I was inside, the wreckage of the lock dangling from the door. The shoulder of my suit was marked. But it was strongly made, as they were in the 1980s, so it did not seem to be seriously damaged.

I closed the front door as best I could. I went through into the kitchen. I found some musty bread. I put slices into an old toaster. When the bread had popped up I put the slices back in again for a second toasting, which created flames, quickly doused, and a hideous amount of smoke. The flat then filled up with a foul burning smell. I threw the burnt and mouldy 'toast' into a bin.

I sat down, reluctantly, given the smoke, the smell and the foetid state of the flat. It looked as though a tornado had been through, upturning a laundry basket and leaving a detritus of dirty shirts, multi-coloured socks and men's and women's soiled underwear.

I waited and waited. I was in, yes, but that was the limit of my plan.

Then I looked towards the bedroom, where Francis had said that the boxes of papers were stored. I went forward. What I could see alarmed me. Through the open door it was clear that two of the supposedly tightly sealed boxes had been ripped open.

I therefore abandoned my caution. After a quick look through all of the other shabby, disorganised bedrooms and the filthy bathroom, just in case there were clues as to what had happened, or even bodies, I began to sift the boxes.

The first box was business stuff: invoices, lists of payments, draft accounts, minutes of Board meetings, some dated in the 1950s, some from the 1960s. Various companies were involved. All their addresses were Post Office numbers in Piccadilly and Saville Row, London. One heading was Bevington Ward Associates Ltd. Another was Anglo-Irish Exporters Ltd.

I gave up on that box, for which I needed help, hopefully from Francis or his sister Gillian, to understand. I turned to the second. This was only three quarters full. There were torn papers and photos on top; then photocopies of deeds, mortgage agreements, property leases, and so on. I had been at the fringes of several frauds. I recognised the type of document.

Burrowing down, I came across the first item of interest for me. It was a black and white photo album, half torn open. It was a small album, a child's, with photos stuck in with little gummed corner tabs. On the inside cover someone had stuck down a label, Les Arcades.

I thumbed through the album. As I did so, my heart seemed to stop for a moment. None of the exterior photos could ever have captured my memory of the beauty of Les Arcades, the vividness of its setting, its bourgainvilleas and roses. It was of a rare beauty that I can still feel. The interior photographs showed antiques and art and dressing tables lined with Guerlain perfume bottles. Then there was the library filled with books, its walls decorated with prints of Roman and Greek scenes and framed pictures of men like Churchill and Eisenhower. All the photographs were equally grey and poor. But there was enough to conjure several wonderful mental images for me.

Two photographs showed a view down from the terrace at the back of the villa. I recognised the building where my mother and I had lived. I took one of the photos out of its gummed enclosure, and looked at the back. In childish, spidery writing were the words: *The garden and the shed.*

I put the print back in. I turned over more of the album pages. Page after page were anonymous views of the villa and the surrounding area. But, finally, some people appeared. I recognised them at once: Mrs Gloria Bevington-Ward on the terrace, Mr Andrew Bevington-Ward at his study desk, cataloguing, trying to look unposed, a lit cigar in his mouth. Both looked older than I remembered them.

I turned more pages. A little boy appeared in some of the photos, growing older as the album went on. Then a baby in a pram. Then other folks, in groups.

I found some loose photos, which might have come from a torn-open envelope that lay underneath them.

Several of these were formal portraits of my 'Uncle Andrew'. These were more the Mr Bevington-Ward, 'His Lordship', of my memory, with his round face, his balding head, his stern and confident, but not hostile, look. Some of the photos had embossed print in the bottom right-hand corner – Mr A.J.Bevington-Ward – with a Post Office box number, and telephone number. The numbers were not all the same.

I turned a few over. On one was written in the same childish handwriting as before: *logikly and therefore, my papa, Mr A B Ward.* I smiled.

I struck more gold: a series of group portraits, posed, but probably not taken by a professional photographer, more likely by a friend or a housekeeper, or Mademoiselle Prevert, using Mr Bevington-Ward's camera. The images were faded, but the faces familiar. Mr and Mrs Bevington-Ward featured in most of them. He was always in a smart shirt and tie, she in the cashmere cardigans, curvy skirts and pearls that were the smart uniform of that period. She also looked frail, confirming my memory that reclining or lounging were her favoured positions.

Then, all of a sudden, some even older photos. Here in front of me was my own mother, again so much of the period, just as I remembered her. In two of the photos she stood between the younger-looking Bevington-Wards. She was wearing flat shoes that accentuated her small frame. Her blouse was plain, of indeterminate vintage, and her skirt seemed to have a tartan pattern. Mother's face was blurred. But I knew that she was smiling, while the Bevington-Wards beamed. In a third photo my mother was alone with Mr Bevington-Ward, who smiled down at her.

At last it seemed that I, William Harrison Gilbey, had made an appearance. Here were photos of a scruffy, tousle-haired boy in short trousers and socks half rolled down, first standing in front of my mother; then alone with the Bevington-Wards, Mr Bevington-Ward pressing one of his large hands against the back of my head. Then there was a photo taken around the Bosendorfer piano. I was seated. Mr Bevington-Ward was standing directly on my right with his left hand ruffling my hair and Mrs Bevington-Ward was in the background.

I did not remember the occasion of these photographs; they did not help me understand the whys and wherefores of our presence at Les Arcades. But I was glad to see them. They validated me. They told me that there was a story to be found; and that there was more to life than my own, occasionally confused, memories.

On the back of one of the photos, the writer with the sprawling handwriting had put: *the boy from the shed.*

It was now approaching eleven thirty. I was nervous about staying longer in the flat. Anyway, without the Wards' help, I could make little sense of the business documents and most of the photos. I remembered The Duke of Connaught. I decided to leave a note at the pub for Francis and Gillian, with a duplicate in the flat, explaining, and apologising for, the broken door and the fire, and giving them my mobile number. I found some cheap paper and envelopes on the living room desk and wrote my notes. I manoeuvred the flat door back into position in a way that wouldn't attract attention. I left the building and walked out.

The only customers of The Duke of Connaught were three disreputable-looking men around a table, and a couple of workmen at the bar in overalls with a brewer's name displayed on their breast pockets, exactly where Mr Piercey had worn his name badge. I ordered a large brandy. When I handed over a note in payment I asked the polo-shirt wearing server, 'Have my friend the actor from the next block, or his sister, been in?' The lout's response was to turn away towards the till and to speak under his breath to the workmen at the bar. I think his words included 'must be that dirty bastard' and 'the one with the nails.'

The server then turned back to me to give me my change and said: 'If you are talking about who I think you are talking about, mate, they had better get back here quick, as they've got over fifty quid on the slate.'

I nodded. I took two fifty pound notes out of my wallet. 'That should clear your bills, and provide enough for a drink when my friends come in, won't it?'

The man, who I now thought to be Tony the landlord, described by Francis as 'an Irish sod', grabbed the money and nodded. 'So you won't mind giving one of them this envelope when you do see them?' The man nodded again. He pushed my envelope into the side of his till.

As I left, I heard one of the men at the bar say: 'I wish I had a poncey friend like that.'

## 4.2

At dawn the following morning, before setting off for Dublin, I dreamt of tattoos.

I have two tattoos, amateur and now faded. Both are on my upper arms. They are spiders' webs and signify years in prison and violent crimes. I noticed through taxi windows and in cafes how many people in London have tattoos compared to twenty years ago. Many of those on display are vulgar.

I read of a footballer with an angel tattooed on his back, his 'guardian angel'. If I decided to have one of those, who would I identify as my guardians? My uncles, I suppose: Swiss Joe, Artie and now the bossman Pete and Colin (although I still know very little about Pete and Colin). Maybe the bearded man normally following me was, in a way, a guardian. Being followed by him would perhaps keep me out of trouble. So some would say. Similarly Mr Piercey, a guardian appointed by the state.

The churchmen in prison? Miss Ingham?

Mr and Mrs Bevington-Ward? Were they truly my guardian angels as well as my pretend uncle and my pretend aunty?

My mother? My father?

I was in Dublin and in my suite at the Shelbourne Hotel, the best hotel recommended by the airport taxi driver, by twelve noon. I ordered a plate of sandwiches. I then called The de Valera Foundation using the phone in my bedroom. I was put through immediately. I arranged to call on Miss Canning at two-thirty. She sounded intrigued but happy to be in demand. She offered directions. I lied and said that I knew Dublin. In fact I planned that a taxi driver would take me to the

Foundation. I had no desire to walk through streets and shopping centres that looked, from the airport taxi, to be the same as in London.

When I got in to a taxi at the front of the hotel the driver said that the address was only two minutes away, however, I insisted on being driven there. I gave him a twenty euro note in advance.

The de Valera Foundation was housed in a smart terrace house, painted gloss black, with a green logo in a ground floor window indicating its tenant. An elderly woman opened the door. After I stated my business she said that the Director, Miss Canning, was expecting me. As we walked along a hallway to the stairs leading to the first floor we passed a reading room or library.

A bespectacled man, out of place given the formality of the building, in an open-necked checked shirt and wearing a bobble hat and a scarf despite the June heat, sat at a desk with an open file, in my direct line of sight. He was clean shaven. He smiled up at me. He reminded me of someone I knew or someone I had seen, maybe in a photograph in a magazine. The elderly woman said: 'He is a researcher visiting us from Spain.'

Upstairs my companion knocked on an ornate door, which was opened by a plain woman in her late thirties or early forties. She shook my hand and introduced herself as Eireann Canning.

Miss Canning's office was large and furnished in style, with bookcases, desks and tables on which rested open manuscripts, photograph albums and statuettes. There were classical paintings and prints on the walls, similar to those at Les Arcades. There was nothing garish, propagandist or modern. Certainly no statements by Ezra Pound!

The room was dominated by a full length portrait, behind what I took to be the Director's desk. I assumed that this must be a portrait of the man who had met Mr Churchill at Holyhead in my father's best story, the then Irish Prime Minister, Mr Eamon de Valera.

A tray of coffee and biscuits were quickly brought by the elderly woman and placed on the Director's desk. This was otherwise empty of working papers. The computer terminal, which looked to be a much older model than the one in Kensington, was turned off.

Then Miss Canning looked at me. She said how intrigued she had been by my message, and that they rarely had English visitors. How could she help me?

With a deep breath I told her the Holyhead story as related by my father. It must have sounded mechanical, this third telling in a week. But at least I completed it uninterrupted. I added that my father had died (I did not say how) before I had had chance in my adulthood to question him. Now that I had some time, and a fair amount of money accumulated over my lifetime of work and I was approaching retirement age, I said that it was my duty – I emphasised the word '*duty*' – to research the matter.

Throughout the telling of the story Miss Canning showed no emotion. But when I had finished she sipped more coffee, leaving the biscuits to me. She said that I had told her an extraordinary story, a fascinating story that touched on an enormously important episode in Irish and British history, especially interesting in the context of 'The Long Fellow's' life.

'We often call Mr de Valera 'The Long Fellow' or simply 'Dev',' she said.

Miss Canning said that what I had told her was entirely new and 'almost beyond, but not quite beyond, the bounds of possibility'. She thought for several minutes, and then said: 'I do not know quite what to say.'

I replied that I knew already from my own limited researches that the story was surprising and not, as far as I could tell, known to historians.

Miss Canning asked how many other people I had told. I said only my closest family and friends; but none of them had really understood it. This was not quite true. I had only started telling the story recently to Mr Piercey and the uncles. I had no family to tell my stories to. But I thought that referring to a family would impress a lady like Miss Canning.

Indeed Miss Canning then asked about my mother. But I said that sadly she was dead too. I said that one day I would tell Miss Canning about that.

Miss Canning said that she could tell by my message and confirmed by my presentation to her that I was a serious person. I was also, she thought, a conservative person, someone attached to old fashioned values. She said that she could tell from my manners and my clothes. I nodded. She said that it was a pleasure to see.

Miss Canning stood and looked round at the portrait behind her. Pointing to it she said that it was a matter of sadness to her how far Ireland had departed from the values, based on Catholic principles, which Mr de Valera had lived for.

'Maybe this economic crisis will make us turn back to where we should be, back to those old values. That is one of the reasons why I value this job so much, and why I am so careful in what this Foundation does, because we have to hang on to the values which created us. I have to be careful not to take us on wild goose chases!'

We both laughed at that remark. But I added nothing, hoping that she might answer her own doubts.

'Mr Gilbey, there are many unanswered questions about that period. We were neutrals and came under great pressure from both sides, you know. The Taioseach, as we call our Prime Minister, was criticised for his condemnation of Hitler when the Germans invaded the small countries, Belgium, Holland and so forth. He had been the last Chairman of the League of Nations. He cared passionately about small countries. Well, the new Ireland he had created was a small country. But many of the Irish people were not as internationalist as him. They attacked him for failing to take up German offers to arm the nationalists in the north. At that time, of course, we were fully and actively committed to a united Ireland. There was great resentment at the state in which Britain had left us. There were calls in the 1930s for reparations, for the British to pay for all the damage they had done to Ireland and particularly to restore the wealth and possessions that had been taken to the north or to the mainland after independence.

'Equally, Mr Gilbey, many brave Irishmen volunteered for the British cause. There was much sympathy in the Irish establishment for Britain after the fall of France when Britain stood alone. However most people now think that The Long Fellow played a clever game that benefited us later, and that we were right to remain neutral. He was a great diplomatist was Dev. Although some say his touch failed him at the end of the war.' I knew what she was referring to. There had been a famous visit by Mr de Valera to the German High Commission in Dublin in 1945 to register condolences on the death of Hitler. This had caused outrage in Britain. It was always mentioned in any article about de Valera on the internet, even those that I had read in prison.

I said nothing, however. I was focussed on Miss Canning's remarks. There was nothing to distract me from them. Miss Canning was not an attractive woman. Her hard features were not softened by make-up. An over-sized green brooch was pinned to a lapel of her grey suit. I could see that the brooch was costume jewellery, not an emerald. Miss Canning's face was also scarred in several places, as if she had suffered a severe illness in her childhood.

'Well, I must not go on too much into the detail of history. But the other main point to make is that, as with the British negotiations with the Germans through Halifax and Butler, and the Swedes and so on in 1940, there are many documents still missing or kept secret, even so many years after the events. I am sure you know that, Mr Gilbey.'

I nodded.

'Of course, I have many contacts in the state archivists, who might help. Also you know the relationship between your Mr Churchill and our leader was always intriguing. It is, dare I say, a romantic thought that they could have met, as you described, on a hill in Wales.'

'At Holyhead.'

'Yes, at Holyhead. Although Mr Churchill and Dev had met several times during the various stages of the Irish independence negotiations, I didn't think that they had met again until they were both Prime Ministers in the 1950s.' Miss Canning sat down.

'You know, I suppose, that Dev had been close to Churchill's predecessor Chamberlain, who in 1938 negotiated with him changes to the Independence treaty, returning our Atlantic ports. He also respected the other British leaders such as Lord Halifax, Mr Eden and Mr Attlee, also your King George, the Duke of Windsor and the Royal Family. He very much liked Mr Malcolm Macdonald, your Colonial secretary in 1940. I have read documents about that. But it is generally said that he disliked and distrusted Mr Churchill as so many in this country did.'

We were both silent for several minutes. Then Miss Canning asked me if I had anything else to add to my story. I said not. Miss Canning said that I had given her material to think about, matters indeed of great importance. Maybe I could leave it with her. She would contact me – hopefully 'within a week or so'. She said that she would treat the matter with 'the utmost discretion'. She would not relate the story in the form I had given it to her, certainly not in any way that might mention mine or my father's names.

I thanked Miss Canning for her reaction. After a few moments' pause, as she drank some more coffee, I said that I knew I was being forward but that I would really like to talk through with her more of the whole context, while I had this opportunity on my first visit to Dublin. I said that, unfortunately, for business reasons I could not stay long. Might it be possible for me to take her to dinner that evening, nowhere extravagant but somewhere typical of Dublin, and good, that she would enjoy? Again I apologised for being so forward; then, looking down at the floor, I added that otherwise I might have a dull and wasted evening, which had not been my expectation on my first visit to Ireland.

Miss Canning spoke about her mother, Bridie. She said that she generally stayed at home with Bridie most nights, save one night a week when she went to the Catholic League meeting, and one night a month when they both went to play bridge with friends. She would certainly have to tell 'a white lie' to her mother, if she accepted my invitation! But she then said that Bridie didn't really need constant attention. With a little glint in her eye, Miss Canning said that she rather suspected that her mother liked to look at a few television programmes of which her daughter would not approve on the rare occasions, such as the Foundation's evening meetings, when she was left on her own. Why not? She was only eighty and in good health. So Eireann Canning's answer was: 'Well yes, why not Mr Gilbey?'

Miss Canning said that she would be failing in her Irish duty if she were not hospitable to a visitor. She thought for a moment. She then said that we should go to a branch of Fearneys, who served old-fashioned French food 'touched with the Irish' at various locations. She would book a table. She would meet me at seven-thirty at my hotel, which was? 'The Shelbourne.' My mentioning that glamorous hotel's name brought a glint to Miss Canning's eye.

## 4.3

Back at the hotel while changing for dinner, I turned on my mobile phone. There were three voice messages, the first two from Gillian, Francis Bevington-Ward's sister. Her messages were rambling but her voice was nice. In the first she thanked me for the note and the money. I wasn't to worry about Francis, as he often 'went off' and he would be back 'like the proverbial bad penny'. She also said that she was sorry about the mess in their flat, and that she was always keen to meet 'friends of her Ma and Pa'. Then in the second message she said that she'd forgotten to say that she'd love to meet me. I could come and talk to her anytime. She read out her number carefully. She said that it would be best to ring back at lunchtime or in the evening, as the lady she worked for as a secretary didn't like her taking personal calls during the working day. I decided to call Gillian after getting back to London.

The third recorded call was from Mr Ross of the government, following his message. He said that Mr Piercey had given him my number. He said that he wanted to meet me to talk about the letter that I had sent. Mr Ross's voice was outwardly friendly, but I did not like it. Voices of authority always trouble me.

I left a message suggesting a time and location for a meeting on Wednesday morning after my return from Dublin.

I then made another call to the Bond Street investigators' office. Two calls made from the airport taxi had gone to an answering machine, and had not been returned.

This time the phone was answered with a 'Yes?'

I gave my name. There was some muffled noise. But I caught the words 'It's that Gilbey again'. More muffled words. Then Charlie, one of the investigator's sons whom I had been introduced to, came on the line.

'How can we help you, Mr Gilbey?'

I said that I wanted to know how their inquiries were going.

'Oh, very well, very well. My dad is pleased.'

'So, what have you found out?'

Charlie said that I must ask his dad, who would 'bring everything together'.

I said that I was in Dublin. I was making progress on the story that I had told his father about Mr Churchill and Mr de Valera.

'OK,' said Charlie. Then after more muffled noises, he added: 'Yes that's great Mr Gilbey, thank you for letting us know.'

'While you are on the line,' I said, 'can you not tell me something of what you have found out?'

'I've got my notes in front of me Mr Gilbey, but only mine of course. It's dad who brings everything together, that's his job, Mr Gilbey.' A pause. I coughed. 'But in my notes, Mr Gilbey, I've got the names of Harrison and Lee, I've got Post Office robberies, I've got *Daily Express* and *Daily Mail* extracts, I've got judges' remarks, I've got prison records, I've got lists of shooters.'

'Yes, I see.'

'So, it's all coming together, Mr Gilbey.'

'What about saggermore?'

'Sagger who?'

'That was a name I gave to your father.'

There was more shuffling and muffled talk.

'Yes, Mr Gilbey, we are on to that too. I'm sure we are. It will all be brought together by my dad. He's good at that. That's his job.'

I was unhappy. I had expected more. My fists clenched white. Compared to the progress I was making on my own in Dublin it seemed that the people I was paying might be letting me down. But I kept my temper. I said that I would ring again.

Dinner with Miss Canning began smoothly. She didn't seem to have changed, or maybe she always wore the same type of dress. But there was just the tiniest hint of shading underneath her eyes which to be frank (and rather ungentlemanly) made her look older. The scarring on her face was also more apparent in the shadows of the low lit restaurant. However, I did the expected thing. I complimented her on her appearance.

Our conversation was polite but dominated by Miss Canning's devotion to The Long Fellow, Mr de Valera, to the Catholic Church and to Bridie, her mother. Bridie had lived at number 3 Moor Place since before Eireann had been born. The house was worth a lot of money now, even with the recent property price falls, Miss Canning said. But they would never leave it.

Miss Canning then asked me about my hobbies. She

seemed pleased when I mentioned twentieth century poetry. Miss Canning had read the poems of T S Eliot and William Carlos Williams; but not those of Ezra Pound. She said that she would. Miss Canning was impressed that a man of my age could cook. I told her about my piano playing.

But I could see that Miss Canning was asking about these things through politeness. She was soon talking again about her Dublin background, her traditional education and her work. Thus she didn't pursue anything about my past (other than my father's Holyhead story); nor did she ask in detail about my own career. I told her I was in 'import and export', using Francis Bevington-Ward's words about my 'uncle'. I thought that she could think about these and my other interests later, to appreciate what I had accomplished and what I could have become. One day I might tell her the full truth. I hoped that she would understand the bad things. I knew that they were bound to come out, if my father's story was verified and published in any form.

The food at Fearney's was not good. My lamb cutlets were overdone and the choice of puddings limited. After two glasses of wine Miss Canning's conversation turned harsher, focussing on the decadence of contemporary Ireland and the fellow diners as examples of that. She raised her eyebrows as a mobile phone went off at a nearby table. She shook her head as two girls came in with low cut dresses. I don't think that the other diners noticed her antagonism. I remained relaxed. Once again, Miss Canning complimented me on my clothes, my suit (double-breasted) and my green silk tie (double-knotted, Duke of Windsor style). She said how much she disliked fashion.

Why had I taken her out? Sex with a woman like Miss Canning was out of the question for me. Such dullness could not excite me; and any long term friendship was not an option for me. But I decided to value her, for the time being, as an acquaintance with a common interest, someone legitimate that I could trust.

The way to Miss Canning's knowledge was, I thought, to take her seriously and to respect her values. She reminded me of the maids at Les Arcades, forever at devotions, presenting themselves starched and upright against the reclining Mrs Bevington-Ward. Or the occasional women working in French prisons, yelped at by the male prisoners, clutching the crosses around their necks in devotion. Such people preserve their beliefs, and their dignity, however much the world changes.

I suggested to Miss Canning, without giving the idea much forethought, that if need be she might come to London to help me with my researches, once her inquiries in Dublin were on their way and maybe revealing something.

Miss Canning said that she had only once been to London. It had been a trip arranged by her convent. And, yes, it was an ambition to go again. There were things she would like to see and contacts made through the de Valera family that she could pursue. And even if the trustees of the de Valera Foundation couldn't fund the trip she could take time off, making provision for her mother of course.

Dinner was over in an hour and a half. Miss Canning then walked with me back to my hotel. With the help of the bellboy I put her in a taxi, with instructions to take her to Moor Place. I gave the driver a fifty Euro note. Miss Canning repeated that she would be in touch soon.

As I turned to pass into the hotel I caught the gaze of a bearded man sitting in the lounge, a whiskey and soda or something similar in front of him. He didn't flinch. He continued to stare. That is an old trick I know well. If you want to put people off the scent the watched person assumes that you'll do everything possible to look away. But hold the gaze and appear amused, embarrassed or indifferent. That is what unnerves most prey.

The bearded man's gaze eventually broke. He smiled at me. He knew he had been caught by someone who knew the game.

On the flight back on Tuesday morning the same man boarded just after me. Like me, he was in business class. He took a seat a few rows behind me.

I waited until the fasten seatbelts sign went off. I then asked the stewardess if I could move seats, as I preferred an aisle. She said that my preferences would be noted in future and that of course I could move. So I moved to a seat where the bearded man was directly in my line of gaze, one row forward, on the opposite side of the aisle. I watched the man throughout the journey. He did not glance around until he rose from his seat after the heavy breakfast, about forty minutes into the flight. He smiled at me. I smiled back.

I remembered that I had once strangled an Israeli man in an aircraft toilet. It had been a spur of the moment trick. He had offended me at the check-in. It also became a successful frame-up; a Pakistani unfortunate was arrested. I left the airport unimpeded. My uncles had for a while held this murder and frame-up as examples of good technique. At least, that is what my memory told me.

## 4.4

The only new email waiting at my apartment, on my return from Dublin, was from Swiss Joe, with a booking for me to eat that night at Honfleur in Mayfair.

I had wanted to see Gillian Bevington-Ward as soon as possible, hopefully that evening. Now it appeared that I would have to squeeze in such an important discussion. However I managed to reach Gillian at two thirty, during what she said was her late lunch hour. Calling herself only Gillian Ward, she seemed delighted to hear from me and said that we could meet immediately after her work, at five thirty, at The Duke of Connaught pub. I said that this was fine as it would leave enough time for me to keep a dinner engagement, which was in Mayfair. The idea that I had such an appointment clearly impressed Gillian. She also said that Francis was still missing, but that I was not to worry about that. In fact, she said, it would make sense to meet at The Duke. Her brother would be much more likely to go there than their flat, if he did reappear. He would then be in a great mood when he discovered that I had paid off his slate, as the landlord had apparently already told her. She also said that she had 'some stuff' to show me.

I have to admit that I felt tired that afternoon. I was trying to be exhilarated by the search. But I was also beginning to feel the pressure.

I therefore took an early taxi, so that I had time to walk around the area near the Bevington-Wards' flat and The Duke of Connaught, for maybe half an hour, to refresh myself. I had spent too long indoors in the previous few days, in taxis, in airports and on planes. It had been like being back in prison.

At about five fifteen I walked down a back road, behind The Duke of Connaught. The road was lined with flats shaped like squashed-down tower blocks, of the sort that my mother had talked about in our past life in Burnley. She always talked of the grime there. Indeed, West Kensington seemed to be like Burnley in my own limited memory. It was a poor area, with overflowing bins of litter, boarded-up garages, and battered and rusty cars. I began to regret being there.

I heard racing steps behind me. I was off guard. Two, or maybe three, youths grabbed me from behind, one by the arms, another put a hand across my eyes and started to pummel me. I knew how to deal with this, of course. These boys were rank amateurs, given their general flailing around. But I didn't want to engage too hard. I was wearing one of my 1980's Next wide-lapelled suits, with a yellow shirt and pink tie. I didn't want to spoil my look.

I therefore hit out with my open hands rather than with my fists. One youth, who for a fleeting moment I thought was Colin, my skinhead helper, clung to my left suit lapel. He tried in vain to get his other hand on to my wallet. But he had no technique. He wasn't to know that I was a professional. I hit and kicked him back. I felt waves of adrenalin: first signalling danger, then victory; and then the humiliation of opponents scattered.

Within a few minutes I was at The Duke of Connaught door, in safety. There were a few men and women hanging around outside, smoking. They must have looked the other way during the scuffle.

A door opened. A woman came out and lit a cigarette. I knew instinctively that this well presented woman was Gillian Bevington-Ward. She, even more instinctively, recognised me, even though I was bent over and coughing.

'Mr Gilbey, William,' she said, 'oh my God.'

'There are people who don't want us to meet,' I managed to say, between coughs.

'Local yobs,' volunteered one of the indolent smokers. 'It happens all the time.'

'No,' I said. I then stopped myself, before I shared my suspicions. Best not to say anything more, best not to give the game away, that I was someone special, that I was a target. Otherwise awkward questions might be asked.

Gillian looked around outside, after first puffing fiercely. She then put out her half-smoked cigarette. She led me by the hand into the saloon bar of The Duke of Connaught, an even more repellent place than I remembered. Despite the early hour, it was busy. Badly-dressed men, with poorly shaved faces like Swiss Joe's, clustered at the bar and around dirty tables. Over made-up women of indeterminate age, with legs hanging off plastic stools, were sipping yellow and green drinks decorated with little cocktail hats.

I wanted to leave. But my inner voice told me to stay.

'Get the man a double brandy,' commanded Gillian Bevington-Ward to the polo-shirt wearing server, apparently the landlord, the same man who had insulted me on my Sunday visit. 'And I'll have another double Tony. Oh, look at your suit, Mr Gilbey, it is scuffed all over. Maybe you had better go to the mens and wipe yourself down a bit.'

Actually I was pleased to find in the mens that another of my well kept suits had stood up. There were some shiny spots and the imprint of a boot on my trouser seat, but I wiped the area clean and adjusted everything. I had Honfleur in mind, rather than my appearance to the hoipolloi in the pub.

When I went back into the main body of The Duke of Connaught, Gillian was sitting with a group of dreadful looking men, whose faces I would have preferred to see only in blurred outline rather than to be introduced. I wanted privacy. But she insisted on introductions. She went round the table: 'Cecil, Ray, Larry.'

I was able to sit at an angle to their little table, in a way I hoped conveyed to them that Gillian and I had intimate conversation to share. They ignored me, anyway.

'Oh, Mr Gilbey, William, I am so sorry, what a to-do. Well, at least I've got some interesting things to show you. That'll make it up to you.'

Tony brought over a double brandy and a double whisky, asking for fifteen pounds. Miss Bevington-Ward told him to put it on her slate, which I assumed was going to be mine.

'Yes, Mr Gilbey. May I call you William or Bill, by the way?'

I said that my friends knew me as William.

'Well, William, do call me Gillian. I know that the time of people like you is always short, so I'll come to the point. I'll show you the things that you might be interested in. It's really quite exciting isn't it?'

I must have looked puzzled, a feint of course.

'Well, for me, William, it's so exciting, for Francis too, since that man came round on your behalf a couple of weeks ago. That friend of yours, was he called Artie? We thought at first that he might be a policeman in disguise, or a private detective, you know, as he asked so many questions. But I guess, from what you told Francis, that he was just a friend looking out for you. It *was* Artie, wasn't it? Not a well-dressed man, like you. Quite the dandy, aren't you? But I can tell that you are a nice man. You are easy to talk to, and generous.'

I didn't interrupt. I noticed again that, while Gillian's tone was voluble and nervous as she sipped her neat whisky, she was well made-up, not too clumsily or overdone, as so many women I had seen on the London streets were. Her clothes were of a good quality. To be blunt, she was attractive to me. Her face, turned to me at certain angles, had a cherubic quality. She was also the sort of direct woman, with a naughty streak contrasting with a pretty face, who tended to like me.

'Well, anyway, Francis had started a while ago to sort out the old boxes of papers, as I guess he told you. But, to be honest, he has been drinking more lately. We looked at the boxes again and had them some of them open, as you must have seen, when you came round and thought we were burning down. Anyway, here are some photos we found.'

Gillian took several photographs out of a used manila envelope. Most I had seen at her flat. But I didn't say so.

I smiled. She smiled back.

There were three photos that were new to me. They were all of a smallish boy sitting in the grounds of Les Arcades. His legs were too short to reach the ground from a canvas chair. In one the boy was bare-chested. In another he was wearing a dirty t-shirt. In the last one he had changed into a bathing costume.

'That is you, isn't it William?' said Gillian. 'It must bring back happy memories, although I didn't know you then, of course.' She looked at me, her lips puckered. 'Yes, William, it is you. I can see the resemblance. You were quite a catch even then.'

One of the men, Cyril I think, interfered. 'Oh yes, it's him all right, he's just as filthy now!' Gillian laughed, and waved him away. Even though I was offended by this coarse humour and intimidation, and my fists clenched, I laughed too. Cyril was not a person for me to be troubled about.

In truth, I didn't remember any of the photographs nor the specific occasions. Yet Les Arcades, in all its beauty, was again called to my mind. Of course, I had so many mental images of the Bosendorfer piano, just then.

'Even better, though,' Gillian continued, 'what we found out, Francis and me, just a day before you came, was that our Pa, a year or so before he and Ma were killed in that dreadful crash, had started to put together some notes about his own background, his wartime experiences, you know the sort of thing. Our Pa was in the Second World War. His firm was requisitioned. I think that's the word they used. All his business vans and cars and all his employees were put into the government service.' Gillian paused for a moment and swallowed all her whisky. 'Yes, many of Pa's men were quite high up, supervising others, because all his team were professional drivers. Whatever he did, Pa was always a very professional man. His work was in this country. He never went overseas in the war. He was always in England, and a bit in Wales and in Ireland.'

'That's how Mr Bevington-Ward must have met my father, Herbert. He was a driver in the war too.'

'Oh isn't that interesting! But I don't see any Herbert Gilbey, though, in this list, William.' Gillian produced a smartly typed, but faded, piece of paper from the manila envelope. It was a list of seven names, to which had been added, in several hands, phone numbers and addresses. There were numerous crossings out as well. 'I guess Pa wanted to get back in contact, like a lot of wartime people did, for reunions, old times' sake, you know.'

I glanced down the list. The name I instantly honed in on, which had also been underlined in red ink and had an address and phone number next to it (these additions looked more recent than the others) was Roy Harvey. A very important name to me.

'You see, after you came round, Francis and I had another look at this list, hoping to find a 'Gilbey' on it, but we couldn't, as I said. Maybe your Pa had passed away long before my Pa started his researches.' I nodded, but I didn't say more. 'Anyway, Francis, well he is a bit of a boy, he gets ideas in his head, enthusiasm you know, doesn't last long, like that idea of being an actor.'

Then a buzz came from Gillian's handbag. She took out her phone. 'Well, talk of the devil, lads!' Gillian turned to Cecil and company. 'It's a text from His Highness himself, my brother. It says 'All well, back Saturday or Sunday'. I suppose I should ring him and find out what trouble he's in this time.'

'That fucking waster!' said Cecil.

'Now, now. Anyway I'd better get on, as my friend William here has a date to keep.'

Cecil laughed.

'Anyway, William, most of the numbers were wrong, and the addresses. No reply on most of them. But, to keep a long story short, we traced two of them. First a Mr Moore, in Australia. We got hold of a woman who turned out to be his widow. Mr Moore died years ago. His widow was stuck-up and very bad-tempered on the phone – well, we had to do reverse charges.'

I smiled.

'But then, we found Roy Harvey, who we couldn't speak to, as he was asleep the two times we phoned. But he is in a care home in Esher, in Surrey, south of London.'

'You say that Roy Harvey is alive?'

'Yes. A snooty woman told us that Mr Harvey had resided there a long time. She wouldn't give out any personal details. She said that Foxdale Lodge was a very particular and private establishment about things like that. She said that only on application did their guests receive visitors. She really was a snooty cow. Our country is full of them, William. That is the address, though.' Gillian pointed it out. She then called Tony over to top up her drink. I declined a second drink. 'Francis left our number. He said that we would call back. But I'm not sure that he did.'

I noticed that the rest of our group had fallen silent.

Gillian continued: 'I want to keep this piece of paper, William. But I took a photocopy for you while madam was looking the other way this afternoon. Not all of it has come out well. But you can see the details about Mr Harvey. Maybe that's some use to you.' Gillian opened her handbag and gave me the copy.

Again I said nothing for a few moments. I then thanked her formally. In my head I was agitated. I was waiting for a voice to tell me what to do, as has often happened at key moments in my life. The voice came through. My duty was clear, it said. I must go the following day to present myself at the home in Esher. I must immediately see Roy Harvey, my father's superior and friend, a man who had been named every time he told the Churchill story and was in other stories too. I must find out what Roy Harvey still knew.

But it also meant, I knew this as soon as it happened, that, with such a critical lead, I might have little more use for the Bevington-Ward children. I had not known either of them well before. I had sensed that neither knew anything much about me. I had cared nothing for them until I had met Gillian. Francis was a waster. Even his drinking companions said so. Yet, the unopened boxes and papers in their flat might reveal additional stuff. So I didn't want to offend. And seeing Gillian again had its clear attractions.

I had just one more question for Gillian. 'Does saggermore mean anything to you? I remember my father mentioning it several times.'

Gillian concentrated. Then she said: 'No, William, sorry. But I'll remember that name. I'll think about it. If anything comes to mind, I'll let you know.'

I wasn't sure whether to give Gillian something in recognition of what she had told me. But I didn't want to be too showy, nor did I want to appear too focussed on money. I therefore slipped her a fifty pound note under the table, once more to settle her slate.

As I left, the noisy talk around Gillian Bevington-Ward resumed.

## 4.5

At Honfleur, I was agitated and ate more quickly than normal: a meal of smoked halibut, calves liver, and no dessert. I was out of the restaurant by eight thirty. I had drunk little, not even an armagnac to conclude.

A taxi was nowhere to be seen. So, I walked down Marylebone High Street, which was full of drinkers and late night shoppers. I recognised no-one, and could see no followers. As if caught in a circle, I walked again past the restaurant. The maitre d' looked out at me, and then beyond me, even though he had surely recognised a recently departed customer. Why was he so rude?

I had to snap out of a growing mood of irritation and nerves. Finally, I pushed aside a young woman and grabbed a taxi, from which a couple of young men had descended, arm in arm. I gave the driver my Twickenham address. He seemed startled and reluctant. Our journey was a slow one.

As we turned into the terrace, it was my turn to be startled. There were lights on in my house, as well as in the house next door. I decided to be bold. I turned my key into the inadequate lock, without knocking on the door, or calling out. There in front of me in the hall, under a white light, was Mr Piercey, and beyond him another man. They were moving something up the stairs. They were both casually dressed.

The other man was white, and older than Mr Piercey. He looked alarmed to see me. But Mr Piercey was calm. 'This is my friend Rob,' Mr Piercey said, looking at me. 'Rob, this is William Gilbey.' Apparently nothing more needed to be said. Mr Piercey and Mr Rob went upstairs. I thought that I heard a woman's voice as well, but I wasn't sure.

So I moved into the main room and sat down at the piano. I didn't take my jacket off, nor make any refreshment. All I wanted to do was to make music and to lose myself in the joy of piano playing, hopefully recovering some of my unused skills. I sensed from what Gillian had told me, and what I had thought about her, that I could be on the verge of life-changing deeds. Maybe, I could now gain entry into the maze of knowledge of my own past and my father's past. Playing even this upright piano, with its construction largely hidden and its tone uneven, unlike the wonderful Bosendorfer at Les Arcades, might help me see this in perspective.

To keep calm I started on my version of the piano part of the Beethoven fourth piano concerto, the opening where, in a manner revolutionary for its day, the piano soloist enters before the orchestra.

But, within a few moments, the inevitable happened, whenever good music is heard. Someone from next door started banging on the thin wall that separated my house from theirs. No doubt it was the curtain twitcher. I assumed, correctly as it turned out, that I had an old woman, a bitch, as a neighbour.

I played louder. I ignored the noise and the shouting, the shouting of a hysterical female. I played as loud as I could, not more of the Beethoven concerto, but basic scales and arpeggios in several different keys. I played them louder and louder. I dug into the sustaining, or 'loud' pedal. I thought of the choral music that my mother had loved, and the older 78s and her newer 33 rpm long playing records. I heard those in my head, as I played with growing confidence and fervour.

Then I sensed that I was being looked at. Had someone from The Duke of Connaught followed me to Honfleur and then to Twickenham, and had then broken in? Was it perhaps Colin and Pete standing behind me? Or the bearded man? Or had the neighbouring bitch come into my house? My nerves became stressed.

I rose from the piano and looked around. Of course, I should have known. It was just Mr Piercey, and Mr Rob. No-one else. They may, possibly, have been there for a while, or maybe they had just come down. But, once they had my attention, they made clear that, whatever my feelings, whatever my desire to play, they were not interested. They sat down, but I could tell that they were in a hurry. Mr Piercey said that it was nice to see me and that I looked OK. 'It is good to see you dressed up, by the way.' Of course he hadn't seen me dressed properly before. 'As you look good, and as I'm pretty busy with new cases and court work, I suggest we cancel our appointment for Friday morning.' He said that we should meet up the following Friday.

In fact, I had forgotten that I was due to see him each Friday, so this was welcome news. I said nothing. Mr Rob looked uninterested.

However, they had a responsibility to me, at least Mr Piercey did. So I told them, in some detail, about my dinner at Honfleur. I then said loudly as they stood up, ready to leave: 'You need to know more about me. You need to know about my qualifications to comment on food. I have a story to tell you. I like telling stories. They can teach us. They can give us a link to the past.'

Mr Piercey knew that he owed me a favour, after I had let him cancel our interview. So he smiled. He gestured to Mr Rob, to sit down. He said: 'OK William, tell us your story.'

I said that at the age of fourteen I had run away from the English college in Toulon chosen for me by my guardians. There had been no emotional scenes between me and them, nor me and my mother at my departure from Les Arcades earlier. I did not know whether the college told her later that I had run away. I never contacted her again. 'I hitched lifts, for favours, to Paris. There, I found work, initially as a kitchen porter. But, within a few weeks, hard-working and clean lad that I was and passing for sixteen, I was filling in as the most junior of sous-sous-chefs, earning a few francs. Most of my fellow workers were ravenous, alcoholic wasters. I certainly acquired a taste for pastis, and for good brandies quickly. I knew that I was different. Unlike my co-workers, I was involved in my work. I was fascinated by the techniques and chemistry of cooking and how the bones, carcasses, carrots and herbs I stirred into the vast copper pots were transformed by successive tiers of chefs into elaborate roulades and golden sauces. They were matched with partridges, pheasants, beef or veal fillets and then decorated with bright green creamed spinach or broccoli rosettes, in the fashion of the time, to be approved by the Master himself, the great chef, Guiseppe Carnarolo. They were then sent up to the private dining rooms of his restaurant Grand Carne, on the Boulevard Raspail.

'I learned about the freshness of foods, and how some combinations do not work or can be dangerous to health, or even poisonous.

'One day, I dared to approach Carnarolo as he adjusted one of his special dishes. He only ever involved himself in this way if it was for a president, a prince, or a duke. The rest of the time he would sit on a stool, at the far end of the cellared kitchens, and yell. His words were incomprehensible to me, as I was too far away: but they terrified his senior brigade.

'Carnarolo had caught sight of me from the corner of his eye, as I approached him. I backed off. He had appeared to ignore me. But a few days later he touched me on the shoulder: I was promoted.

'Successive promotions followed quickly. But I overreached. I challenged the accepted order of things. I began to experiment, with my colleagues' apparent encouragement, on the preparation of entirely new dishes, especially at the two lunch and two dinner sessions that Carnarolo, becoming an obese and easily-tired sixty-year-old, took off each week. I created my signature dishes on those days when he was absent, so that Carnarolo could not spy and claim credit. With the help of a head waiter, who admired me, I served them off-menu in the private rooms to a growing personal clientele, including a direct descendant of one of France's greatest generals, the Duc d'Enghien.'

I said to Mr Piercey and Mr Rob that I had often thought that one day I would like to supervise the recreation of those dishes, and to invite all my friends and acquaintances, possibly even the Duke's family.

I said, 'I would certainly invite you Mr Piercey, and Mr Rob, and even all my enemies and all the people who follow me, to a celebration of my lost art.'

They both laughed and agreed to come.

'But, to continue, my career was cut short. Guiseppe Carnarolo came in on one of his supposed days off. Neither the other chefs, through jealousy of my talent, nor the head waiter whose advances I had finally rejected, alerted me. I was at the premier station of the vast kitchen, focussing on an original sauce I was devising, to accompany a tart sweetbread and pepper concoction. I knew that this would appeal to the Duke's mistress's jaded palate. Then, there was a pressure on my shoulder. I recognised the squeezing hand. I turned to look into the Master's face. He shouted abuse. I took up a long, thin knife. I stabbed him repeatedly. His clothes were padded and his fat deep, so I could not kill him. But his severe injuries put an end to my second chosen career. The first had been to be a concert pianist.

'The incident with Carnarolo thus marked the end of my two true 'metiers', as the French call careers.

'Mr Piercey and Mr Rob', I said, 'I was left only with crime.'

The two men nodded. They got up and spoke quietly to each other as I turned back to the piano. Then they wished me well and left without further comment. After I had heard them close the front door, I played for just a few minutes more.

Before going to the taxi rank I knocked on the front door of the neighbour's house, long and hard. The bitch wailed from inside to 'leave me alone.' I shouted through the letter box: 'I'll be back for you, you interfering bitch.' Then I found a taxi. I returned to the flat.

My worries, lifted only temporarily by the meal, the piano and my memories, had returned. I thought about calling Swiss Joe or Artie, or even skinhead Colin, to chat and to report on progress and to take their opinion. But, maybe they would not have opinions? I thought of emailing Miss Canning in Dublin. But I did not want to be pushy. I was still unsure, anyway, how far she was truly interested in me, and my story. My visit to Dublin seemed to have gone almost too well. But then I thought that, if I could get a successful interview with Roy Harvey, my mood must change. There was just the challenge of Mr Ross of the government to get through first. I did not believe that he would help me. I had decided that he would obstruct me. I should give him the benefit of the doubt though, at first. That would be the honourable thing to do. No inner voice advised differently.

I went to bed and slept fitfully, with no consistent dream.

In the morning I had a simple breakfast, very early. I took out another smart suit, again broad-lapelled, a blue tie and a white shirt. I wrote up this mémoire, as best I could, for an hour, bringing it fully up to date.

I rehearsed inwardly my stories and my aims, before setting off: first to meet Mr Harry Ross of the government, and then to go to Esher, to see Roy Harvey. I asked myself 'Is today to be the most important day of my life?'

# PART FIVE

# 5

## 5.1
### *Twickenham*

Harry Ross had finally managed to pin down William Gilbey to a meeting, at a cafe near Twickenham station. 'It is nice to meet you.' Harry held out his hand. But Gilbey was holding a coffee cup with his right hand, while his left hand remained clenched under a table. He did not get up.

'You are Mr Gilbey, aren't you?'

'Yes, yes, indeed so. My father, Herbert Gilbey, known as Bert Gilbey, was the last man to be executed in England, by hanging, at eight in the morning on the 18th of July 1964. He is buried in the precincts of Pentonville prison, London.'

'Yes, I have heard that.'

'Does Mr Piercey know that?'

'Yes, I think so. He told me...'

Gilbey ignored this. 'Mr Piercey knows a lot of things. But, he is not what he seems, you know. Anyway Mr...?'

'Ross, Harry Ross.'

'Oh, yes, your name was mentioned by Mr Piercey. And I am rude. Yet, I was taught good manners at an early age in France. Would you like a cup of coffee? It is not good coffee here, to be frank. I like nice coffee, nice food, nice wine.' Harry laughed. Gilbey did not.

'I wouldn't mind a coffee. I had to leave…'

Harry Ross was going to say that he had left his office without coffee. It had been seven in the morning when he had called in. There had been no time to get the machine cleaned and the coffee on. Gilbey had insisted on meeting at eight o'clock. William Gilbey stood up and said: 'Better, Mr Ross, if we walk to my second little place, the one that Mr Piercey has found me. It is nearby. No need for a car or anything.'

'I came here on the…'

'Perhaps you came on the train.'

Gilbey was already on his way to the door.

Harry Ross was following Wilfred Robbins's instructions to the letter. His first job, now being carried out, was to assess Gilbey. There was to be neither anonymity nor disguise in this. Harry was to offer William Gilbey help if necessary. He was to befriend him and find out how much Gilbey knew, and what lines of inquiry he was following.

The picture that MI5 had of Gilbey's character and his activities was incomplete. Even the material they had on file did not seem, to Harry Ross, to add up. Gilbey's activities had started and stopped over many years. But now he was in full swing, in search apparently of his past and his father's history. It seemed extraordinary that, after all these years, he should do this. Was someone leading him? Was someone pulling strings? Had he found out something new, a critical clue that MI5 ought to have as well? What documents did he have? Were his documents complete? As a matter of protocol (indeed a legal requirement since Gilbey was out on licence) Robbins's instructions were that Harry had to call, and at least nominally remain in touch with, Lloyd Piercey, Mr Gilbey's probation officer. But Robbins wrote that no-one in the probation service knew of, nor must be given any information about, any matters other than were apparent from the prison and other custodial files. Copies of those were held by A Group. Robbins also reminded Harry that, in MI5's experience, probation officers were defensive about their clients. They were not people naturally sympathetic to the work of A Group. Harry must deal with this diplomatically and seek – without compromising anything – to keep Piercey thinking that he was an ally. However, if such approaches failed, and if there appeared to be any risk of Piercey being 'unhelpful', Robbins said that there were 'matters known', that could be used against Piercey. They would ensure that Ross's mission was not interfered with, nor compromised, at least not by the probation service. The main matter against Lloyd Piercey was described, in detail, complete with dates, lists and other evidence, in one of the appendices to Robbins's instructions. Robbins wrote that, as Gilbey was a serial criminal, he would probably think of himself as skilled in deceit. However, while there was no reason to expect him to be open and honest with Harry – that would be against his nature – it was some years since Gilbey had committed a crime. Even serious recidivists did sometimes reform. Unlikely, but possible, even in Gilbey's case. Such people often suddenly took a detailed interest in their past and their parents' past, to absolve themselves of responsibility for their own crimes. That was at least the beginning of an innocent explanation of William Gilbey's behaviour.

Robbins had written that whatever Gilbey's motives Harry's duty was to sell him a set of ideas to keep him quiet. If such an approach satisfied Gilbey, whether he knew or not that he was being misled, and would take him out of MI5 interest, 'all well and good'. Robbins gave Harry authority to spend up to ten thousand pounds to deal with those circumstances.

But matters were likely to go in a different and more difficult direction. Gilbey's personality was described as more erratic than most. This was where Harry's judgement and skills were to be tested, and where there had to be absolute discretion and information shared only on the strictest need to know basis. John Nicholson, the A8 seconded policeman, whose contribution Robbins had previously dismissed to Harry and Morgan Janvir, would stay on the case for a few days, to assist and to advise.

Harry was permitted to keep such hours as necessary, with special pay and supplements authorised. He was relieved of other matters for three weeks, or until he could report a 'satisfactory closure', whichever came first. He was to destroy Wilfred Robbins's, instructions after he had memorised them. Robbins had reminded Harry that he was authorised to take whatever steps were necessary to protect the interests of the state.

Gilbey said 'sorry' as he let Harry into his house behind Twickenham station. He clicked his fingers.

He had no coffee. 'I forgot. I am yet to move in here fully. My main apartment is in Kensington.' Harry knew from Nicholson's notes about Gilbey's rooms in South Kensington. He didn't say so.

There was a beige sofa in this living room. It was streaked: something had been spilled. The room was otherwise pristine, decorated conservatively and carefully. Harry was a little envious. Harry's shared flat in Pimlico was jumbled and dirty. It was difficult to be one of three sharers. Harry imagined that his colleague Morgan Janvir's flat would be rather like William Gilbey's.

Gilbey waved to Harry to sit down. He looked tired. He said: 'Do you think you can help me? Mr Piercey said you would.'

Harry took out a card from his wallet. It had a Cabinet Office logo on it and Harry's address, telephone numbers and e-mail. It was headed 'Harry Ross, Administration Officer'. William Gilbey looked at it intensely.

'A very useful thing, but please tell me – can you help me? Others are helping me. I am much in need of it.'

'We had your letter.'

'Yes.'

'That is why I am here.'

'Yes.'

'Of course your father's service was a long time ago. So, we need to know more before we can properly focus on the records. It is the 1940s that you are interested in.'

'Yes, although I also want to discover more about the hanging.'

Harry nodded.

'I would also like to tell you some stories, if that is acceptable to you, Mr Ross. My father was a great story-teller, and so am I. The first I have told to Mr Piercey and others, since I was released.'

'The one about Churchill and de Valera?'

'Yes.'

Gilbey then told that story exactly as it was told, from different perspectives, in the file that Harry had read. Without waiting for comment – Harry had been keen to start a proper interview but he could hardly interrupt and lose Gilbey's interest – Gilbey then told another story. It was a story, he said, that his father had told him two or three times. But he had not recorded it. It was not a political story, Gilbey said; yet it was important.

'My father told me that his mother, my grandmother Charlotte, was what they called in those days 'in service.' She was a maid in a big house in Flint, in Wales, which belonged to the owners of one of the big steelworks there. They had come from Ireland originally. They had made money through their own efforts. They were, thus, what used to be called 'trade', rather than 'old money' or 'county'.

'According to this story the master of the house was a marvellous businessman. His methods were known throughout Europe and even America. People flocked to see him. Among the visitors in the 1890s was a young man called Theodore Roosevelt, who became President of the United States at a young age, after the assassination of his predecessor, a Mr McKinley. Mr Ross, my father said that Americans have always been fond of assassinations. They are a cheap way, he said, of getting rid of politicians. He said that it would have been better had some British politicians been assassinated.'

Harry Ross smiled.

'Anyway, according to the story told by my grandmother, the master and the mistress tried to make a lot of their Presidential connection. For a time they even renamed their house after Mr Roosevelt's country house.'

Harry Ross smiled again. He was trying not to show impatience. None of this meant anything to him. But there was no great hurry was there?

'According to the story at one time the house in North Wales boasted over thirty staff. My father's mother, my grandma, was one of the most junior when she went in service there, at the age of twelve. She met my grandfather at the house. He was the master's chauffeur. Grandma learned to read and write. She was a feisty one, my father said. At first she got on well with the mistress. But she did not get on with the long-serving housekeeper, who had come from Ireland, and who treated everyone like scum. She claimed to have worked for a 'genuine Lady', one of the aristocracy, or 'ascendancy' as they liked to call themselves. Actually, according to my father, my grandma thought that the mistress was as fearful of this housekeeper and her brutish husband as the servants were.

'Then one day, according to this story, a diamond went missing, a big diamond that the master had bought at Boodles the county jewellers in Chester, ready to be set in a ring for his lady. It had been set on a little presentation pillow on a table in the dressing room. Now the servants had seen thefts happen before, because the mistress left her windows open. She encouraged the birds to come in. She hadn't minded what they took while she was feeding them. If she had to explain how an object had gone missing she would tell the master and the housekeeper that she had dropped it while out walking, and that rough local people had kept it.

'Among those that flew in to the dressing room were magpies, which are known to all to be especially thieving birds, and without any fear of bigger objects. Indeed, a magpie had taken the big diamond, as birds had taken other things before. But nothing anywhere near as valuable or noticeable. The magpie had flown away. He had then put the diamond into a nest. The diamond was, in turn, taken from him by a cuckoo. And it was in a nest some weeks later that the jewel was found by one of the boys from the house, out looking for birds' eggs, although he never admitted that. Taking the master's birds' eggs was forbidden, like so many things were in those days. The boy said that he had spotted the diamond glistening in a tree.

'Anyway they could not disguise such a great loss. Someone had to be blamed. Fortunately, it was not grandma, my father said. The housekeeper disliked another girl more, a small girl from Anglesey, the most Welsh county of all Wales. Most of the staff came from Chester. But this girl was true Welsh. She could hardly speak English. She had been taken on by the mistress on request from an Anglican curate. The girl hadn't learned how to curtsey properly and how to behave to important people – to the nobs, as my father called them.' Gilbey sneered as he said this. 'I haven't learned that either, I am proud to say.'

Harry Ross smiled, a little guiltily.

'This young servant girl was marvellously musical, with a gift for the harp and the piano. So the devil's mate of a housekeeper and her devil of her husband, who was only fit enough to polish boots, indeed fit enough really only to lick boots, decided to make a lesson of the girl. They said that they would beat the girl until she produced the diamond, 'even if you have to sick it up' they said.

'So they flogged the girl and beat her until she fainted, and she would have been near dead had my grandmother, God bless her my father said, not thrown herself forward, stopped them and ran for the mistress. But, before she could be fetched, that bitch of a woman and her cruel husband – they really did act as though the devil himself was in them – they ripped the clothes off the poor girl. They cut marks on to her back. So that when the wounds healed, by which time the diamond was returned, you could see a shape that was said to be the devil's mark of 666 scarred into it. You know Mr Ross that devil's mark remained on the poor girl's back for life. It always does. There is no escaping such a mark. The housekeeper said that the symbol of 666 was a sure sign of guilt and of sin. She said that the girl must have given the diamond to the magpie, which she had summoned, by Welsh witchcraft, on her harp. The devil had rewarded her by taking her for his own, she said. The housekeeper's husband said that he knew the girl to be responsible for every type of devilry in the house, including the temptation of him and other men. Then...'

Gilbey looked at Ross, who was yawning. Obviously this man did not understand, nor appreciate the story.

So Gilbey stopped and said: 'I will tell you a different story, something more relevant to you perhaps, as you are in the service of the government.'

'OK,' said Harry Ross.

'This is a story, Mr Ross, that my father told me about Anthony Eden, who was Foreign Secretary during the war, and later Prime Minister.

'Eden was outwardly elegant and assured, a typical upper-class man, my father said, but, in reality, he was a nervous wreck. On even a short journey to make a speech, or to Parliament, Eden would be sick. He, or his assistant if he was not travelling alone, would reach forward into the driver's section. My father would pass back a brown paper bag.

"Yes William, a small brown paper bag, that's all we had,' my father said, 'and Eden would try to retch into it, but more often than not he missed. But he never got the sick on himself.'

'My father would then describe the colour and texture of the sick in detail, which made me laugh and my mother cross, but the more I laughed the more detail he would go into.'

Harry Ross laughed.

Then, to Harry's alarm, Gilbey began to breathe more deeply. He seemed to be concentrating ever harder. He began to speak in a different voice, a raspier lower voice with a more pronounced northern accent. It was his father's voice, thought Harry. Yes, he is imitating his father. More than that, he is *becoming* his father.

'Then William, Eden would say something like 'it must have been the lobster, or the foie gras,' a sort of liver paste William, 'or a bad oyster', but more like it was having two gins too many, or maybe just nerves, I don't know what. Anyway what was he doing with that fancy stuff when all we had had, even for drivers like me doing demanding work, was potato and parsnip pie, on the rations?

'Anyway, one day, in 1941, Eden was so bad I had to keep driving round and round Parliament Square. I daren't stop to let him out. He was retching so much. He was saying things like 'I can't go on, we can't go on, we should have stopped it when we had the chance, all this bombing, all the property lost, all the young men killed. We should have made that agreement."

William Gilbey's voice returned to normal. 'Do you know, Mr Ross, my father said that in those wartime days people used to wait all day in the square right up to the Parliament gates to wait for a glimpse of their hero, Mr Churchill, or one of the other nobs, especially Mr Eden. He was a dandy, a brilliantined dandy Hitler called him in a speech. Politicians here in Britain called him a glamour boy. Women used to swoon over him, like he was Clark Gable.

'Anyway, on that day, according to my father, Mr Eden kept on saying to go round again, and he even went up Victoria Street and round the back lanes there. So, all in all, they were fifteen minutes late, and Mr Eden was late for his Parliamentary statement.

'It was in all the papers, my father said. Mr Aneurin Bevan, he was 'a big noise' in the Parliament then, he got all aeriated. He 'played Hamlet' about it, to use an expression of the time. Bevan said that it was contempt of the House and a danger to security and all sorts of other rubbish, as if Corporal Hitler or Mussolini, 'Old Mussy' they called him, were bothered because Mr Eden gave his statements a bit late.

'But, do you know who got blamed, Mr Ross? My father. These were the exact words he used: 'I, Herbert Gilbey, was blamed. That posh fraud Eden never admitted what really happened, never spoke to me privately nor thanked me, though I drove him many times afterwards. I took the blame.'

'It was said in the official report, Mr Ross, that my father had asked the Foreign Secretary if he could 'detour' for a minute (that's the word they used 'detour' – now, my father, unlike me, he would never have used a French word!) to deliver some papers to one of the Ministries, 'and then we got stuck in a jam'.

'Yes, I remember my father's exact words: 'we were supposed to have got stuck in a traffic jam, son, in those days, a jam when there were no private cars on the road, who were they kidding?'

"Yes, I got the blame son,' my father said: 'I got docked a week's wages, and taken off the government cars for a week. They all knew of course, Roy Harvey, my boss, and all that lot who sucked up to the nobs. But they had to cover up for Anthony Eden, and not allow that he was a nervous wreck who couldn't hold his drink. It was 'bad for morale', you see.'

"But the truth is,' this is what my father told me, Mr Ross, 'the truth is son, in those days you did as you were told, and didn't expect thanks. The 'stiff upper-lip' they called it, and we were all supposed to have it. Really, though, it was more that the high-ups despised us, the common sort: one law for them, and another law for us."

Gilbey turned to Ross. His own voice had come back fully and consistently. But he was red in the face. 'My father used to get really mad when he told that story. He would say 'son, has it changed? No. That is what this country is, and always has been, the despisers and the despised. We should have had a revolution when we had the chance. We should have listened to Moseley, or the Communists. Anyone other than the so-called establishment: Eden, Churchill, that miserable sod Attlee, now Douglas-Home, Harold Wilson, George Brown and all their sidekicks, they're all the same.'

'When my father had finished, I think I heard those ideas in one form or other many, many times, Mr Ross, with the list of cursed names getting longer, my father's threats to them becoming more personal and more violent, his sweaty face turning even redder. I remember my mother coughing loudly, saying things I could not hear and might not have understood had I been able to hear. I remember all this so clearly, Mr Ross. It is stories and memories like that which drive me on.'

'Your father was a man of strong opinions,' said Harry. He now wanted to move on, quickly. No reply from Gilbey. 'That is not uncommon for that period of the nineteen thirties, and even after the war. There were extremes everywhere. Surely things are better now.'

Gilbey did not speak for what seemed to Harry to be several minutes. He seemed dazed, tired no doubt by the effort of so much story-telling. Harry was becoming uncomfortable. He was thirsty.

'I remember, Mr Ross, my father Herbert and my mother Marjorie saying, at different times, that people had to look after themselves. Personally I think it is important for people to have friends, or groups, or family to look after you…'

'You mean…?' But Gilbey was talking to himself, thought Harry. No point my adding anything.

' …having a group around you, as well as having your own inner voices – that is what keeps you going, especially in times of trouble, when the world doesn't want to hear you. I have been in prison a lot. There is a sense of community in prison, Mr Ross. I also have a community looking after me now, the Uncles.'

Another long silence. Harry was getting hotter. He was very, very thirsty. Harry had to say something, something blunt. 'Do you believe your father's stories, Mr Gilbey? I mean, the Churchill and de Valera one especially.'

'I hope that no-one would ever expect a son to say that his father was a liar, Mr Ross.'

Harry saw that Gilbey's left fist was clenched. It was pure white. Gilbey's determination was clear. He was staring at Harry, an unrelenting stare.

'Why do you think…?'

'Listen to me, Mr Ross. I have met people who are helping me, who believe what I was told to be true, who will bring all the evidence: some of the best historians in Ireland and England. I have a lot of money, a lot of, let us say, muscle and, dare I say it, a lot of firepower.'

Harry, tired and thirsty though he was, saw Gilbey stroke his inside jacket pocket, as he spoke. Was he really carrying a revolver? The seconded policeman John Nicholson – who was in their car, outside the cafe, using an electric shaver to trim his beard – had told Harry that Gilbey had been given one by his helpmates. Nicholson had said to Harry that he would intervene: 'if there's a problem, speed – text me.'

'I know people – do you know Mr Ross, maybe even more than you with your office card! I know people whose names would surprise you. There are people everywhere, in all walks of life, people who will break their life pattern, who will do the extraordinary to protect people like me, to ensure that truth is known. I read that in prison many times. It is what people pride themselves on. We live in a democracy and a country founded on truth. I was told that by a chaplain. And, after all, what is the value of anything but truth?'

So Gilbey went on. Harry could only listen. There seemed no point in interrupting William Gilbey.

Gilbey talked about his reading, and about Ezra Pound. Gilbey talked about his father and his mother, and about the Bevington-Wards, his guardians in France. He described the cars, the gardens and the flowers at the villa Les Arcades. Gilbey talked of art, of chandeliers and crested porcelain. He talked about food – about meals in prisons; and Michelin-starred food in restaurants in France and in London.

Gilbey told Harry that he had trained to be a chef, and that he had studied with a great master in Paris. He still thought of the career that he had missed. Yet, he was not so old was he? Gilbey said that he was in his late fifties. He couldn't remember his exact age. Age had been confusing after he had been taken to France. Years had been lost. What did age matter anyway?

Then, Gilbey talked about pianos. He talked of a 'Bosendorfer' grand; he talked of a piano teacher; he talked of his failed careers and his time in borstal. He talked again of prison, of how he had been blackmailed and buggered and double crossed. He talked about the iniquities of people of all classes, and of a world that lived on hypocrisy. He talked of 'civil service parasites', 'aristocrats and public school boys', 'those ponces sponging on others'.

Gilbey talked of his determination, to do 'whatever it takes' to get his story heard.

Gilbey, his eyes cold, his back straight, walked across the room and opened double doors to the next room. Gilbey sat on a stool. He began to play an upright piano, set against a wall. At first Gilbey played some simple chords. Then he played something more complicated. But even to Harry's unmusical ear it was wrong – the melody wayward, the accompaniment distorted. Harry could sense Gilbey's frustration and anger at his own incompetence.

Suddenly, Gilbey stopped playing. Harry stood up, nervously.

Harry said: 'Well, Mr Gilbey, William, I know that you must have faith in your father and his wartime stories. Whether there is anything I can do depends on the details that you have. But I can confirm, at least, that your father saw service as a government driver in the war. I have checked the staff records already. They are on-line now, to us in the service. But the records are pretty minimal from that period. You can understand that, I am sure.'

Harry was now gabbling, just as Gilbey had done. Despite the importance of this case to his career, he really wanted to leave, as soon as possible.

'So, William, do you remember any other names or details?'

Gilbey laughed. 'The word 'saggermore' keeps coming to me.'

Harry Ross took out a notebook and wrote 'saggermore' down, while William Gilbey started playing disjointed chords again on the piano.

'Anything else? I mean: did your father leave you any documents, for example?'

Gilbey shook his head, but continued playing, in a softer tone than before.

This seemed to Harry to be a good time to leave.

'Look, William, we attach a lot of importance to recognising people's service, and also to getting the history of our people right. Your stories are certainly fascinating. I have a few ideas as to whom I might talk to, and where I might look. Leave this with me. I'll get back to you soon, certainly within a week. We'll arrange to meet again. I'll keep Mr Piercey informed.'

William Gilbey stood up and said: 'Of course you will, Mr Ross.'

Harry moved towards the door: 'I'll show myself out.'

Gilbey said 'thank you', and again returned to the piano. Harry could hear the piano chords getting heavier as he closed the door and went down the path. There was also a strange twanging noise. It seemed that Gilbey had broken some piano strings.

'Any luck?' asked Nicholson. 'What's he like?'

'He's mad, well half-mad at least. Get us out of here, please.'

Nicholson started up the engine. 'So, no new clues?'

'He talked non-stop. Him and his wretched stories. The only new thing was something, or someone, called 'saggermore'.'

'Really?'

'Does that mean anything to you?'

Nicholson was focussing on the road, and thus had an excuse not to reply for a few moments. Anyway: why should he, a comprehensive school educated policeman who was being taken off a case, help a young Uni-educated, case-grabbing whipper-snapper like Harry Ross? Let him do his own research.

'Nothing relevant comes to mind, no.'

## 5.2

An hour later, Ross reported to Wilfred Robbins, who looked irritated as soon as Harry entered his office. He did not stand up. When Harry began to speak Robbins shushed him. He then slowly changed his glasses, using the sinuous movements that Harry knew so well. Harry laughed in nervous reaction. Robbins looked more annoyed.

'Well?' said Robbins.

Harry gave his report – although, as he thought to himself, it was a 'non-report'. Harry set out in some detail his conversation with William Gilbey, which had produced no new material or conclusions.

Robbins reacted sharply, lifting up his hands as Harry rambled on, re-telling Gilbey's stories: 'So, Mr Ross, you have found out nothing of value?'

Harry did not know what to say.

'I suggest, Mr Ross, that you return to focussing for a few days on reading the files. That may give you greater insight into why we are pursuing this matter. I suggest you look particularly at the notes made in 1940. You will see references to the possible Irish viewpoint, and, tellingly, to Irish demands. Then, maybe, you will begin to understand the importance of your mission. I do not have the time to spell it all out for you. Meanwhile I will arrange to keep Nicholson or one of his other colleagues from A8 on observation. I will contact you if I need you to intervene.'

Then, Wilfred Robbins added in a kinder voice: 'I wish you well, Mr Ross. There is still time to make a contribution to this case.'

Harry went to his own office. Morgan Janvir was on the phone. Harry opened up the Gilbey files again. This time he would concentrate even harder.

Amy Moynihan called by, but not even she could raise Harry's eyes from the files. She left, offended.

As for Harry and Morgan Janvir, they exchanged only pleasantries for the rest of the day. Harry did not seek Morgan's advice, nor even ask him about 'saggermore'.

Harry felt humiliated enough. He did not want to get another dose from 'know-all' Morgan Janvir.

# PART SIX

# 6

## 6.1

*the mémoire posted in London to important persons,*
*continued*

I will not dwell on my meeting with Mr Ross, the agent of the government.

I had wasted time. I had met Mr Ross in Twickenham. I think he or Mr Piercey had suggested that; Mr Piercey always wanting to lure me back there.

I had dressed down for the meeting. That meant that I had to take a taxi back to Kensington to change, before going to see Roy Harvey in Esher.

Despite the delays travelling across London four times in one morning, I managed to arrive at the front door of the care home at twelve-thirty, precisely as I had planned. I had been obliged to take a taxi, then a train, then a taxi again, to get there from South Kensington. I had not used a train in England, unsupervised, for over thirty years. It was a strange, unpleasant experience, despite my travelling first class. I sensed that people were looking at me. I was surely being followed. But this time the bearded man was nowhere to be seen.

The taxi driver from the station at Esher rubbed his hands when I mentioned Foxdale Lodge. It was fifteen minutes on the other side of the town, and a twenty-pound fare. He was another talkative driver. He said that Foxdale Lodge was the best retirement home in the area. He said that it was exclusive and very private, that many of the people there were well-heeled, although they had, he said, quite a few terminal cases as well, as they 'never turf anyone out'. The driver said that if he or his wife 'ever win the lottery', they had promised themselves that Foxdale Lodge was where they would both end their days.

Although I disliked his chatter, the driver's information calmed my nerves. Roy Harvey must have done well for himself. This appeared to put him into the Bevington-Ward category of people, rather than state employees like Lloyd Piercey and Harry Ross. Hopefully, Mr Harvey would have good memories of my father, Herbert, and thus he would help me.

On being buzzed in, I announced to a receptionist dressed in a nurse's uniform that I was at Foxdale Lodge to visit Mr Harvey. She looked puzzled.

I lied to her. I said that I had telephoned a few days earlier and that I had been told I could visit him. She asked me to sit down in a small area of easy chairs and low tables covered with magazines and newspapers. Glitzy chandeliers hung from the ceiling. I liked Foxdale Lodge.

A notice read: Cameras are placed for the security of our patients and the comfort of visitors and staff.

Several well-dressed people glided through the reception area, carrying files, nodding to each other. A woman in real fur and real pearls came out of a lift and asked for a taxi. The nurse receptionist said, 'Of course.'

One elderly man, who I assumed was a consultant or patient, came in through the front door, without having to press the buzzer for entry. He was over-dressed, as if fearing an arctic storm, even though it was a humid June day. Like all the others who passed through the waiting room he looked at me and smiled. For a moment I thought that this might be Roy Harvey, who had been sent for from a walk. I found myself swallowing in excitement. But, on closer look, his face had a Middle Eastern aspect. He walked on. Perhaps he was the man now following me. I was not sure.

Fifteen minutes or so later an older woman, also dressed as a nurse, came to me and said that they were not expecting visitors for Mr Harvey. Was I a relative? I said I was not, but that I had called well in advance. Then, when she looked disturbed and went to the front desk, as if to check, I corrected myself by saying that it was my 'representative' (that is to say, I made it sound as though I meant a solicitor or a secretary) who had called. Also, I said that I was the son of a dear friend of Mr Harvey's and, surely, he could have visitors whenever he liked and why were they, or she, being so difficult?

All the time, smart people came and went. The woman asked me to speak quietly, 'For the benefit of the patients.' Finally she said that she would consult Mr Harvey's doctor. I said, 'Why not consult Mr Harvey himself?' She walked away.

A tall young man then came, dressed like me in a good suit, although his was slimmer cut and shinier than mine. It was a smart outfit. It reminded me of the man outside the private detective's building.

This man said that he was the 'executive assistant'. He was called David. He said that he wanted 'to assist'. Then, when I tried to explain, he accused me of being argumentative. He said that, without Mr Harvey's express permission, I could not visit him.

We went around the same discussion several times, until I said that, since I was not allowed to speak with Mr Harvey, how was this permission to be obtained? He agreed that Mr Harvey would be asked but that I should have called first and made an appointment, after Mr Harvey had been consulted. 'David' either did not know, or chose to disbelieve, my earlier statements on that matter, as I pointed out. He then said: 'Please take a seat, Mr Gilbey, since this could take some time.' I thought that he must need instructions from higher up to deal with me, so I agreed.

I decided that, despite his smart appearance and ingratiating manner, this 'David' was the sort of person I had known working in prisons, who only wants an indolent life and who relies on instructions from others. David cared nothing about anybody or anything.

Finally, after hushed telephone calls and conferring, at about one fifteen I was taken by the older lady nurse into a lift, then up three storeys and into a suite of rooms, in which at the far end was a man in a wheelchair, with tubes up his nose. He was tiny and wasted, with sharp and penetrating eyes that I could see from ten yards away. I think that I was supposed to only acknowledge Roy Harvey – that he might then acknowledge me, and then his keepers would make a proper appointment. A compromise.

However, on an impulse which I regret (but this was an extraordinary moment), the tension within me burst. I unclenched my squeezed hands. I pushed back the nurse. I ran forward, almost throwing her to the floor. I shouted out: 'Mr Harvey, Roy Harvey, tell me all you know about Herbert Gilbey, my father Bert Gilbey, why was he hanged, tell me about him and Winston Churchill, about him and Mr de Valera!'

The face of the man in the wheelchair froze for a few moments. Those other parts of his body that I could see turned puce, and then red. He lunged forward, choking. He tried to wrench his hands from his wheelchair, where they had been tied with protective rubber straps. His arms looked as if they might break, so thin were they, like those on the Edwardian dolls that Nicholas Prevert used to carry and point at me as he grimaced from the corner of the room, during my piano lessons with his mother.

The nurse steadied herself and brushed herself down. She said to the bent body: 'Now then, now then.' Then she turned to me: 'We warned you, we warned you. I'm fetching Mr Alexander.' (Whoever that was.)

'No, you didn't warn me,' I said. 'Why is my friend in this state?'

'Leave now!' she said. 'Leave him be! Leave the poor soul with his memories.'

And, for twenty-four hours, I did as she asked.

# 6.2

I found an empty first class compartment on the return train from Esher. I was still shaking with a mixture of anger at my own conduct, and anger at Roy Harvey, and those who were guarding him. They had asked me to leave 'as quickly and quietly as possible'. A taxi had arrived for me at Foxdale Lodge, with remarkable speed. I had to focus my mind elsewhere. I called the private investigator in Bond Street from the train. This time, the man himself answered. But all he would say, in a cool and annoying voice, is that that I would have a report 'soon, hopefully next Monday'. He said that I would find it 'conclusive'. His boys had been 'hard at it'.

I said: 'Is that all you can say?'

He said 'Mr Gilbey, I know my job. It is best that you are patient, and that you read my report. Believe me. Believe me.'

Now, it was clearer to me, than ever, that the events of 1964 had changed everything, for me, as well as for my father and my mother. I hoped that I would soon know whether my assumptions about those events were correct. So I kept repeating to myself the words of my investigator, that I must be patient.

I have gone through the Manchester scenarios numerous times in my head, even though neither my father Herbert, nor anyone else, had ever described them to me. I imagined my father waiting outside the Post Office. My father would have been nervous, but confident in his gang. Maybe they would have been made up of old driving colleagues from the war. I suspect that some of them were worried about money, and not being able to feed their families. So many brave people were abandoned in that way after the German and Japanese war, my father told me. Some of that was their fault, but mainly it was the fault of the government.

I am sure that my father must have been reluctant to accept that he must carry a gun, like the others. He was only a driver, after all. I remember his occasional fits of anger, but I think that, like me, he was a gentle man, at heart.

Maybe my father had been stroking his gun. He would have been waiting for a signal to start up the getaway car. Cars were less reliable in those days. My father was a good driver, I believe. He told me that, anyway. He would have planned the route; where to accelerate, and where to drive off the main roads.

Then the two women approached the car. Why? Maybe it was parked somewhere, for example on a pedestrian crossing, that interfered with their business, or where they wanted to cross. Who were these women, Miss Maeve Harrison and Miss Dora Lee, what sort of relationship did they have? Was one what used to be called 'a companion' to the other? Were they lesbians, 'ladies of Llangollen', or 'bad women', as people of that sort were known? Llangollen is in North Wales, where my father had been born, and where my grandfather had been a chauffeur in service at a big house. Was that something to do with it? Was that the saggermore connection again, as in my father's stories?

Were those women busybodies, or nobs, the sort of people my father hated? Did he know them? And, above all, why did he wind down the window and talk to one or both of them, at exactly the wrong time? It was just at the time he must have seen or heard movement in the Post Office, and his comrades running out. Then, mayhem. My father was said to have shot twice. Maybe he only intended to warn. Maybe he misfired or the angle of the shots aimed into the air was awkward, through the open windows of the car? But there certainly were two shots.

One could be explained as a freak. But two?

There were also my mothers' jewels, gifts she always said she had had from my father. If he had not been involved in crime, where did they come from? He had not been employed properly since the war, as far as I know. We did not live well, but we were better off than most. So father said. He always seemed to be relaxing at home, or in one of his favourite pubs.

Was the jewellery connected with the Post Office murders? Maybe they were a gift from someone who had got away, when my father took the blame. Or, maybe they were my father's actual share of what was stolen.

Thinking about the jewels, I became anxious about money, even though I still had plenty of ready cash. So I called Swiss Joe. He said that Pete had said that he would have a definitive date for my visits to the bank vaults, to see my money and my jewellery, 'within a few days'. The Milky One said: 'Our bossman has promised that, and I believe him. And you must believe him, William, my friend.'

As the train came into London Waterloo station I called Gillian Bevington-Ward. I knew that it would be a pointless call, because Gillian would be working.

I regretted trying, as soon as I had selected the number from the phone's memory. But, despite my anger at the world, I managed to leave a polite message, saying, among other things, that I hoped that Francis was well, and that we must all meet up. I said that I would ring again later.

Then, as if on cue, a call came into me, just as I was getting into a taxi outside the station. 'Mr Gilbey, William?'

'Yes.'

'It is Francis, Francis Ward here.'

'Francis Bevington-Ward?' I said.

'Oh yes, that's right.'

I explained that I was in a taxi. But he said: 'No matter, this is urgent.'

I asked Francis if he had thought any more about 'saggermore' as it was very much on my mind.

Francis said, 'Well, no, actually William. But, look here, old boy, what I have to say is important.'

'So,' I said, 'is saggermore; or it could be. I am not sure.'

'Maybe so.' Francis sounded annoyed. 'Look, William.' In fact Francis also sounded a little drunk. It was what I should have expected, I suppose. I wanted to ask him if he had seen his sister lately. But the phone connection was not good. So, I thought, I had better just let him speak.

'Look, William, I have been thinking a lot about this. You are a nice man, old chap, but I don't think you know what you may be in to. I mean this is a wicked world. It is not the world you described to me, or that we talked about.'

'You mean the world of Les Arcades.'

'Well, yes, the world you talked about, and I have looked into for you, that world in the south of France. Fifty years on, you know the world in London is more complex. Anyway, I have things to tell you. But, most important, I want to say to you: just be careful, William: please be careful, they are not.' The phone line went suddenly dead. We were going through an underpass. I tried to call Francis back a few moments later. But there was no reply.

I entered my apartment. It was just after three-thirty. Reluctantly, I looked at the computer. My mood, so down, tired, blocked and confused, suppressing images of things that had happened as recently as that morning, and worried by both Francis and Gillian Bevington-Ward, was immediately lifted. There in the email inbox was a pleasant and most unexpected message from Eireann Canning, timed at ten o'clock. She said that she was using a terminal at an internet cafe at Dublin airport to send me a message, as that 'in the light of developments, and new information' she had decided to come to London straightaway. She had reserved a hotel near me, in South Kensington. She would call me at about four o'clock, after she had settled in. At exactly four o'clock Miss Canning rang. I asked her to come round. I gave her directions to do so.

## 6.3

Eireann (we decided on this third meeting that we could be on first name terms) said that she was overwhelmed by my apartment, its luxury and 'sense of being modern and being well-equipped' while having 'a traditional character'. She said that it suited me. I did not say that it was only loaned.

For Eireann I had quickly changed into another good suit, a light green shirt, and a spotted tie. She wore an outfit of the type that she had worn in Dublin at both our meetings. She took some notes out of her black handbag. She said that she had typed them the previous evening, so as to put her thoughts into order, after the research and inquiries she had made. Eireann had brought me a copy. This has been very useful in writing this part of the mémoire.

Eireann had a lot of history and a lot of ideas to share with me. She took me through the notes, in a teacher's manner. She had first listed a number of people, historians and the like, that she had consulted, one of whom, a Professor, she said she had spoken to only on the telephone. She was due to see him, later that day, in London. I must have looked worried by this. But Eireann insisted that my privacy was fully protected. I had no need to meet anyone myself. Eireann said that she had simply told the Churchill and de Valera story to those she had consulted, as coming from an 'impeccable' and 'truthful' source. She had had their reaction on that basis. No names had been mentioned.

Eireann continued by telling me, apologising for her bluntness, that the literal truth of my father's story was not so far accepted by anyone. Some, she said, wanted to believe, especially those who were admirers of de Valera. The Long Fellow, she reminded me, had fallen out of favour in the permissive Ireland of recent decades. Now he was again appreciated, as people looked back to a more community-focussed and traditional society, one less obsessed with money, one where politicians were selfless public servants like Eamon de Valera, and Sean Lemass, his protégé. They were not the corrupt self-serving villains like Charles Haughey, who had followed them. Such villains had sold out Ireland's interests.

Eireann looked down at her paper. But I interrupted her before she could resume our shared lesson, to ask about saggermore, which still weighed heavily on my mind. Without pausing for thought Eireann said that she did not recognise the name. Instead she continued: 'Personally, I think this: what could be bolder than Mr de Valera travelling, with apparently only one other person, across the Irish Sea, to meet with his enemy and rival Churchill, at the time of greatest danger to their countries?

'Was that not,' she said, 'the equivalent of Neville Chamberlain's heroic, if fruitless, flights to Munich in 1938 to see Hitler? Those missions had failed too, but they were missions of courage. And if Mr de Valera had been willing to abandon neutrality and to place the Republic's ports and their limited forces at British disposal was that not also courageous given that Mr de Valera was one of those heroes who had led the Irish people in arms against the British? At any time the Germans could have landed troops, from U-boats, to devastate the Irish land and people. Mr de Valera would have been placing great trust in Churchill, whom no Irishman trusted at all, with good reason.

'And the price that Mr de Valera and Mr Churchill had apparently agreed on, the unification of Ireland, was something that everyone in 1940, the British included, felt was inevitable anyway, whether or not Britain won the war. It was not a large price for them to offer, whatever Churchill's public stance.

'So Mr de Valera's behaviour was not only that of a man of courage, and of principle,' which Eireann said that she already knew; 'but also that of a man prepared to take a risk in his relationship with the Irish people. That sense of risk balanced with duty had never been so clearly revealed in his character, in any story told about him. Until now.'

I nodded. I was trying to follow and to understand.

Eireann continued, saying that there would have been many people in Ireland who would have resisted a deal with Britain, even if it had achieved reunification. On return to Dublin Mr de Valera would have had to use all his moral authority to have the agreement recognised. He would have placed himself in the opposite position to the one he had adopted in 1923, when he had decided against the treaty with Britain that had led to the separation of north and south. His resistance had led to a civil war. It was virtually impossible to imagine any terms brought from the British that some in Ireland would have accepted. They would have wanted to see Britain humiliated. So, Eireann concluded, Mr de Valera in 1940 was a selfless man indeed.

No-one she had spoken to, Eireann repeated, had produced anything definitive that could determine whether or not the meeting my father described had taken place. But there were still large gaps and unedited materials relating to the history of the period. There had been no central state archive in the Republic until after the war. She reminded me that, as she had said in Dublin, some British documents relating to the period remained sealed. Not even famous historians could see them.

Maybe, Eireann said, the clue to the lack of knowledge and recognition of the meeting might lie in the failure of the Churchill/ de Valera agreement. Who would have benefited from such failure? Which side had failed to deliver?

Eireann said that everyone she had spoken to was intrigued that Mr Churchill's companion in the story was General Brooke, later Field Marshall Lord Alanbrooke. Brooke, she said, was one of the greatest soldiers of the war. Had he not been passed over in favour of Eisenhower as commander of the Allied D Day forces he would be far better known to history. Brooke was, however, an Ulsterman and a determined Unionist. Maybe he had blocked Mr Churchill's agreement – just as, her correspondents had told her, with his control of the army, he had blocked many of Mr Churchill's wilder schemes during the war.

'So that led,' Eireann continued, 'to another idea that has been suggested, given the difficulty in believing that Churchill and Brooke were involved.'

Was my father sure about the identities of those he had driven on that extraordinary night? Was he sure that it was Winston Churchill and General Brooke? 'Might one have been Malcolm Macdonald, the British Colonial Secretary', a man, Eireann said, who was highly regarded in Ireland and admired by Mr de Valera. Eireann said that in early July 1940 Macdonald had circulated a plan to the British Cabinet to encourage Irish entry into the war and thus, inevitably, re-unification of the whole of the island of Ireland. He had been allowed by Cabinet to pursue it in correspondence with the Republic.

The historians that Eireann had consulted had attributed Macdonald's failure to the intransigence of the Northern Irish, and the lack of will on Churchill's part to make the Unionists see sense, despite the clear danger faced by the whole of Britain and the whole of the island of Ireland. In contrast, the Republic had given the Macdonald plan as much encouragement as they could. Perhaps, Eireann said nervously, my father had altered the story to include Churchill and Brooke 'to increase its importance'.

'No.' I had to interrupt at that point and say: 'No, my father never wavered in talking about his driving Mr Churchill. That was the key part of the story. That and your Mr de Valera. He also told me other stories about Anthony Eden, for example, so I would have remembered the names. The names of Churchill, De Valera and Brooke I gave you were on the tape.'

'Well,' said Eireann. She paused and thought. She looked at her notes and I looked at my copy. There was a line towards the bottom 'The End of the War'.

'This is so important, William. Let us say, for the moment, that your father was right. But there is one further idea, a really extraordinary idea.

'It seems hard to believe to the people I have spoken to that so much energy, from then until now, should be put into suppressing knowledge of two leaders meeting especially as the meeting apparently achieved nothing and thus was just a footnote in history. Anything involving our two countries has problems, but – this has been put to me forcefully – why should such a meeting and its discussions about reunification, constitute such a dangerous matter that they have had to be kept secret for seventy years, when so much else has been revealed?'

I shook my head.

'William, I share my friends' doubts. So what if there was something else, of even greater importance, that had to be hidden.'

'You see, it has been suggested to me that Mr de Valera, the last Chairman of the League of Nations, a neutral and a democrat, may have been bringing to Churchill other, even more significant, proposals. 'Dev' may have been acting after contact with other neutrals such as Sweden and Switzerland, or Vichy France. Some of Mr De Valera's entourage admired and were in contact with President Petain. In short, Mr de Valera may have been bringing definitive, well worked-out proposals to end the whole war, not just to deal with Ireland's involvement and to satisfy our demands, but wider proposals to make peace, proposals that may have been transmitted with some encouragement from the Germans, from Hitler himself perhaps. Or if Hitler was the obstacle and was intransigent, maybe Mussolini, or the other fascists like Franco of Spain, or Salazar of Portugal or even the Pope, Dev's spiritual leader were involved. Or maybe the ideas came from what were sometimes called 'good Germans' such as Goering or Hess.'

I nodded at the mention of Hess's name.

'I see you know about Rudolf Hess, William. The year after your father says that he saw a meeting between Mr Churchill and Mr de Valera, Rudolf Hess flew solo to Britain to pursue peace. That is how determined some Germans were to make peace with you. Anyway we know that Mr de Valera tried to keep those contacts and those routes of information open. He remained active throughout the war in the quest for peace, which he regarded, as all good Catholics would, as a religious duty. So, let us suggest this, William. Mr de Valera secured Mr Churchill's agreement to the outline of a plan to end the war. Your father saw Mr de Valera and Mr Churchill sign the documents. Then there was stalemate as Mr Churchill reneged in London. Attempts continued. In frustration, Hess came in 1941 to tell the British about what had been offered, and what had been refused. There was for a long time the suppression of the truth, the determination to portray Hess as a madman. After the war, Hess was kept imprisoned, with no access to reporters or historians until he killed himself.

Eireann paused and then concluded 'What an extraordinary story we are putting together, William! What a tribute to your father!'

I said nothing. Then Eireann offered to make tea. I said that I would prefer a glass of armagnac. Eireann nodded. She said that she would have one too.

After I had poured the armagnacs I did not want to hear more history. There had been enough to be absorbed.

So I told Eireann about my visit to Roy Harvey. I did not say that I had lost my temper, just that Harvey had been startled. I said that I had not been able to communicate with him. But, at least, Roy Harvey was alive. He was there, waiting to talk to us. I also told Eireann some of what I had discovered about Roy Harvey's links with Andrew Bevington-Ward.

Those stories led me, in the glow of the armagnac, into wanting to talk about something more personal, something that would give us both time to reflect; and that would also stress to Eireann the sort of man I was.

I could still not tell Eireann about my father's hanging. I felt that story might fatally prejudice her, or indeed anyone else, against any words of his or mine. I wanted her to continue investigating the meeting at Holyhead. I did not want her to know that it was a story told by a convicted murderer, the last man to be executed by hanging in England, at Pentonville Prison, on 18th July 1964. I had to walk a careful line in telling my stories. So I ventured quietly 'Tell me about your father, Eireann. I have told you stories about mine.' Swilling the armagnac in her glass, and looking over her notes again, Eireann simply said: 'There is time for that. You and I have more important matters in hand, William.' I nodded. But I would not be discouraged. I wanted no more history. I wanted to get back to what was real for me and what had made me the man that I am. So I decided to tell Eireann, who I thought would be a sympathetic listener, about my mother's death, the second most important death in my life, which is not otherwise described in this mémoire. I said that I had been in some minor trouble and had been sent to  a young offenders institution, Hollesley Bay in East Anglia, in 1974 (in fact I had been deported there from France for a series of assaults and, my eighteenth birthday approaching, I was awaiting transfer to an adult prison.)

I was called to the Governor's office. Mr Spratt, a distant, moon-faced man with rimless spectacles, who I had not seen since my admission, looked up at me when I was announced by my escort: 'Gilbey, William Harrison Gilbey, well Gilbey, I have some bad news for you.' This squat, intelligent little man, who I saw kept books of poetry and plays on his desk, had then looked up at me as if I was supposed to supply the news myself. The escort coughed. The Governor remembered himself. 'Yes, Gilbey, I am very sorry to have to tell you. It is my sad duty to tell you that your mother has died. Of course, this is very sad news indeed. It would be for anyone.' Mr Spratt had then reached down into his lower desk drawer, and had fondled the top of a bottle, whisky, I think. We were not supposed to see this. I shared the escort's embarrassment. I smiled, not out of any pleasure at the news, although I had given my mother very little thought since I had left home. I had wanted a complete break. I had wanted to get away from her, from the Bevington-Wards, from Les Arcades, from their son Francis I was meant to grow up with (and have only now met again, to discover that he is a wastrel alcoholic) and from the other children like Nicholas Prevert. 'You see, Eireann, my life had not worked out since I had run away from college, not as I had planned anyway.' Eireann laughed. She said: 'life rarely works out as we plan it, William.' I continued describing how the Governor had caressed the top of his whisky bottle. Mr Spratt then said: 'I am sorry. There is one more thing, Gilbey. She died in a way that means that she could not be buried in hallowed ground, you know, in hallowed ground.'

I said to Eireann that I must have looked puzzled, although I think I knew immediately what he meant by those words, just as I had understood what was meant when Mr Bevington-Ward had told me that my father had been hanged, by 'bastards.' 'The Governor means that your mother killed herself, Gilbey,' my escort said. Eireann sighed. 'Quite,' I remember Governor Spratt saying: 'Quite, well that's all, oh and this news is not so new, I am sorry to say. It has only just reached us. Of course everything happened, was taken care of, four or so weeks ago. It has taken a while for the French authorities to contact us, and your mother was an Irish woman, of course, so that complicates the whole thing. Ireland always complicates everything. Anyway we can tell you, William Gilbey, that there is no point in planning to go to a service for her, or anything like that, as it were.' The escort had then intervened to spare the Governor further embarrassment. Also, I suppose, to let him get on with his whisky.

'Thank the Governor, son.'

'Thank you, sir.'

'And, Eireann, that was it.' Eireann slowly drank the last of her armagnac. She had listened. I hoped that she had understood. She smiled.

Eireann broke our silence and said: 'There must be something we can do about Roy Harvey. It is our only lead isn't it?' Eireann looked me up and down. 'I know that you are really a thinker, not a man of action, William. This is not a nice position for you. I believe that you are used to dealing gently, and carefully, with people, in a way that does you credit, given what has happened to you. But, I am sure that, if we could speak with Mr Harvey, we would make him understand the importance of the situation and of his position, and the need to act quickly while we still have his testament.'

I wondered then whether to tell Eireann about my dealings with Harry Ross. Yet what was there to tell? If she knew that I was in touch with a British Government man it might have embarrassed Eireann, given her position at the de Valera Foundation. It might have put her off completely. I did not know, for certain. I liked and admired the way that Eireann had pursued my case, and I felt trusted by her. As you can read in this mémoire my life has been founded on a series of trusted relationships. I guess that is how the best lives proceed. I did not want to break trust by admitting that there were other people on my case.

Eireann insisted, again and again, on the importance of Roy Harvey. She was sure that he would understand, and that he would respond. We might then get the crucial, independent confirmation that we needed, the statement that could persuade historians and politicians to take up my cause.

I said that I doubted that. It might be that I was going too far in opening up unpleasant memories, and old wounds, for a man like Roy Harvey. I also suggested that, if he was as ill and as sedated as he looked, it might be impossible to get through to him.

'But, get through to him we must, William. He is the only man alive who can bear witness to the important story your father told you. Time is not on our side. What a pity that your father died so young, and then your mother.'

'Of course,' I said, wishing again to avoid talking to Eireann about my father's death. 'But Mr Harvey may simply not remember. He may suffer delusions and twisted memories. He might have come to hate my father. He might say terrible things about him which would upset me, for no purpose. Maybe I should just accept matters as they are.'

'Courage, mon brave,' said Eireann. She patted me on the knee.

I was becoming nervous about Eireann's attentions and intentions. I knew from our dinner in Dublin that alcohol had a quick effect on her.

Then Eireann took a deep breath. 'You may think I am mad, William. Indeed, I think I may be mad myself. But I did not come here to London to give up, not with the information I have discovered, and the ideas that have been put to me. Now, did I tell you that I trained as a nurse? My best friends are nurses. The Foundation has not always seemed a steady job. You know, a charity is often short of money. So, I have kept my hand in with temporary nursing work. There's mother to look after too.'

'Bridie,' I said.

'Yes. What a good man you are, William, to remember her name. Well, why don't we pay another visit to Mr Harvey? I can make myself up to look like a nurse easily. I don't need a uniform. I can just pull my hair back in a bun and wear my coat tight. You know, nurses are a type the world over!'

I looked at her. I thought: *Yes, she is the image of a plain, old-fashioned nurse; but of a good type, not one of the thugs who had treated me in prison hospitals.*

'I could assess Mr Harvey, then we could wheel him out, into the grounds or something or even take him out in a car for a few hours, and get to talk to him properly.'

I was astonished. I had worked on kidnaps before. I knew that a kidnap takes weeks, or even months, in planning. The obvious and immediate objection to this one was not having a car to take Roy Harvey away at all, still less one to take a wheelchair. But now was not the time for a true Gilbey to be fainthearted. I thought of Pete the bossman, Swiss Joe, Artie and Colin, and their insistence on being able to do *anything* for me. At that moment Eireann Canning's confidence and courage transferred itself to me.

'Yes. I think I can get hold of a car or a van which could take a wheelchair. I have friends for occasions such as this.'

'Well, that's perfect.'

'When shall we aim for?'

'Why not tomorrow? Oh, let's not delay, William. Let's make it tomorrow. I've worked in such places. They use agency nurses any day of the week. I am skilled enough not to be recognised.'

I smiled, but I was wary. I knew that as soon as I appeared at Foxdale Lodge the staff would call the police. 'Eireann, I have to be blunt.' I told her that it would be best for her to go in alone. 'You know, if Mr Harvey sees me, I don't know what might happen.

I'm sorry now about my behaviour. But I wasn't at my best.'

'I understand, William. Of course I do. Oh, I am quite excited by this, William. May I have another glass of armagnac?'

'I don't want you tipsy when meeting your friend the professor, Eireann,' I said.

'Oh yes, you are right.' Eireann laughed. In fact we both laughed. 'And I mustn't give any hint to him about this little plan. I should get back to the hotel now. I am meeting the Professor near there at seven o'clock. There is so much to talk about. He has been filling me in on things I mentioned – you know the background of the meeting that your father witnessed. I had no idea that there were so many efforts to stop the war in 1940, after the fall of France and the invasion of Holland and so on.' I nodded. I knew most of these facts. I had researched them in prison. It is therefore easy for me to remember them for this mémoire. But she then said something new. When she had left I added it to the notes Eireann had already given me. I hope I have recorded her words correctly.

'It seems that Hitler never wanted to attack England, as your Mr Churchill claimed. At least that's the theory. People like our Mr de Valera wanted to stop the war with minimum damage to your country. That would have left Hitler to deal with the Communists in Russia. That is what the Professor said on the telephone. If it could be shown that the German peace ideas were sufficiently good for Dev to risk his prestige and maybe even his life to present them to Churchill, then that would be an extraordinary new thing to add to his achievements, even if everything turned sour later. It would change everyone's ideas of what happened wouldn't it? There would be much blame to be attached to Churchill, if the peace terms, and the terms for Ireland especially, were now thought to be reasonable. '

I nodded, although I did wonder if Eireann's admiration for Mr de Valera, a man, and a reputation, to whom her life appeared to be devoted, was clouding her judgement.

'Yes,' Eireann continued, 'it might well destroy the reputation of some of the British 'nobs' your father talked about. Anyway, I can extend my stay in London until, say, Sunday, if they have a room. I'm sure Bridie will be okay. And the Foundation can get along without me. Jane will see to that. This is exciting isn't it?'

Having made the arrangements for the pickup with Swiss Joe, I spent the rest of the evening writing this mémoire. I rose early. Then, at nine in the morning, Artie, Swiss, Colin and I pulled up outside Eireann's hotel in Knightsbridge in a smart modern people carrier, stolen to order by Swiss and specially modified to take a wheelchair. Swiss had not hesitated for a moment when I had made my strange request. The name Swiss Hospital Services with Swiss flags was on stickers displayed on three windows.

I admired The Milky One for this speedy response, and Artie for his art. 'He can't write, but he can't half draw!' said Swiss.

Artie was dressed in a chauffeur's uniform, Swiss in his track suit and trainers, Colin in a patch-decorated jacket and bleached jeans.

Artie drove us to Esher. By ten-fifteen we had drawn up outside Foxdale Lodge. Eireann then went in alone. Swiss muttered to me that he should go in too, but he was too dressed down in my view.

Colin, Artie, Swiss and I sat in the people carrier, while Eireann carried out her role, perfectly. Only ten minutes or so after she had gone in, the front doors to Foxdale Lodge swung open. Eireann appeared, complete with wheelchair and in it the unmistakeable, squatting, bird-like figure of Roy Harvey. He looked pale, his face a true death mask. He was asleep.

No-one was following. Swiss calmly got out to help Eireann. Within a few minutes we were on our way.

'How did you manage that, Eireann?' I asked.

'By simple Irish smiles,' she replied, to laughter from Swiss and Artie. Eireann said that she had taken my directions to Mr Harvey's room, smiling at everyone she passed. Roy Harvey had been unattended and asleep. She had made a quick assessment by looking at the graphs and notes. She had then woken him. She had given him a sedative, mixed in the glass of water that he had at his bedside.

'You see, William, I had some tranquilisers prescribed for Bridie. I always keep a few in my handbag. Mr Harvey swallowed quite happily. He fell into his slumber, which will last quite a while. I don't think he is seriously ill, by the way. He is just very old and tired. I couldn't see anything in his notes to suggest that he is in any danger. I suspect they keep him deeply tranquilised. It is easier, and cheaper, to look after the elderly that way.'

'Shocking,' said The Milky One. 'Disgusting,' added

Artie, 'no respect for the punters.' Colin opened the back window and spat out.

I wasn't as sure about the situation as Eireann and the others. Roy Harvey looked like a pallid imitation of a man to me. Was he ever going to be awake enough to tell us the truth? Or would he play the madman like Ezra Pound, when they captured him and took him back to America?

I sat back to think about what I would ask Roy Harvey.

Our car came to a long halt, in traffic, in Esher High Street. As we waited at a crossing for the useless elderly, hobbling with their Zimmer frames, I looked through the car window directly into the face of an attractive woman, her face made up behind large sunglasses. Her manner was calm, her shoulder-padded clothes cream and elegant.

With emotions of both pleasure and fear, I realised that this woman was Gillian Bevington-Ward. She was beautiful, as I had never seen her before. Gillian was hesitating, deciding whether to cross the road in front of us. I could not see the reaction in her eyes behind the sunglasses, but at first I thought that she must see me. Then I remembered that the vehicle we were in had tinted windows. Gillian went out of view as the traffic began to move.

I said nothing. I had realised, with a lightning strike of feeling, maybe exaggerated by a sense of triumph in having captured Roy Harvey, that I was very attracted to Gillian Bevington-Ward.

# PART SEVEN

PART SEVEN

# 7

## 7.1

*the mémoire, posted to important persons in London,*
*continued*

At three o'clock in the afternoon, back at the Kensington apartment, I removed the gag that Eireann had applied to Roy Harvey's mouth on the journey from Esher. Eireann and I were ready to begin the interrogation of the man who was, probably, the only living figure from my father's history. Swiss Joe, Artie and Colin had left.

Roy Harvey was distressed, not knowing where he was. He began to cry. He said things about pills and drugs; although Eireann, who had taken what she said were the main notes next to the bedside in Foxdale Lodge, insisted that there was nothing medical he needed. She said that she was reluctant 'yet' to give him another of her mother's tranquilizers she had brought with her from Ireland.

Harvey then pulled against the bands we had placed across his chair. His face became contorted. He began to cry louder, although Eireann managed to control that by putting her hand over his mouth. She said something in a foreign language, religious words I believe; then something more soothing: 'Mr Harvey, please be calm. You will come to no harm. I am a trained nurse.'

I decided that there was then nothing to be lost by telling Mr Harvey my own story: straight, but looking away from him, so that I would not be distracted by his reaction.

I paced the room. I explained who I was, and who I thought he was. I explained about my father, without referring to the hanging. I gave the full Churchill/de Valera story, as I had told it in the previous ten days, augmented a little by the ideas that Eireann had given me.

I said that I wanted to find the truth. I said that I was not a violent man, but that I could be angry if pushed. I said that I was a rich man. I said that telling the truth in my world was always rewarded. I looked at Roy Harvey as Eireann relaxed her hold over his mouth, so that we could hear any response. Eireann laughed and said: 'He's only got a few good teeth you know, that's typical of the English.'

But, as soon as he could, Harvey was wailing again, demanding pills.

I was becoming impatient. I asked Harvey if he had any family. He didn't reply. Eireann said that she had seen that there was 'no next of kin' stated on his medical notes. I asked Harvey if he was hungry. Again, he didn't reply. But Eireann said that we should give him something. Eireann untied his arms. She forced water and crushed biscuits down his throat when he refused to swallow.

Eventually, Harvey stopped resisting. He slumped back.

'What shall we do?' I said. 'This is pointless.'

'We can't give up now.' said Eireann. She said to think of the risks she and I had taken. She said that, of course, if I insisted, then my friends could smuggle Harvey back straightaway without problems, as no alarm might yet have been raised. After all he was in a care home, not a prison. He was free to go where he liked.

'No, it isn't a prison,' I said.

'Look,' said Eireann. 'I will go to a pharmacy, while a local one is still open. I passed a branch of Boots on the way here. I have an idea that I can get some over-the-counter drugs, which will help to calm him down, and to make him a little more cooperative. I know about these things. If there is a friendly pharmacist on duty, I might even be able to get something a little stronger. I have an Irish Nurses registration card with me. I've also these medical notes, although I'll be careful not to display a name. It's just possible I can get something that will make him talk. While I'm out, I can get some more food as well. I don't see much in your kitchen. All three of us will need something.'

I nodded, although I was surprised by Eireann's confidence in being able to get more medicine.

'It could be a long day and a long night. If nothing emerges from him by morning, your friends should take him back. But I'll be sorry if it's been a wasted effort.'

'So will I.'

I could see sense in what Eireann planned – and no alternative, short of taking Roy Harvey straight back: which is what we should have done, of course.

Eireann left, saying that she would be back within an hour, or maybe two. She also said that she would pop into her hotel to get some things. She gave me one of Bridie's tranquilizers. She told me to give it to Mr Harvey, 'if he becomes agitated again and disturbs you.'

I turned on the television in the apartment, for only the second or third time since I had been in London. I had felt very little connection with the news or entertainment that it offered. I managed to find the main news channel; then the more local news for London and the South East. I watched a bulletin. But nothing was said about a sick man missing in Esher.

I called Gillian Bevington-Ward on my mobile. I so much wanted to talk to her. When she answered, there seemed to be pub noise in the background, The Duke of Connaught, no doubt.

'Oh, Mr Gilbey, William, how are you?' She seemed happy and relaxed as soon as she had confirmed that it was me; which showed, as I had thought, that she had not actually seen me observing her earlier in the day in Esher. I asked Gillian if she and Francis might be free to meet later, maybe somewhere near my apartment, for a change. I didn't mention that I had spoken to Francis.

'Oh, William, what a nice idea. I can't speak for Francis as he's out, maybe with some of his old chums. I'm not sure when he will be back. But, why not?'

I said that I had an early evening business meeting to go to. I couldn't resist adding: 'I guess you have been relaxing, shopping and so on, or maybe had a few drinks with friends in The Duke.'

'No. I have been a working girl, William.'

I had thus given Gillian an opportunity to explain about being in Esher. She hadn't volunteered. But I wanted to believe the best of her.

I said that we should meet near Harrods, next to the Knightsbridge tube station entrance (a landmark I remembered from my taxi travels), at about nine-thirty.

I turned back to Roy Harvey. I sat and looked at him. I began to feel a strange, and new, mixture of feelings. Anger and resentment certainly, that someone who might know so much was keeping silent. But also I felt pity for him – and also maybe for myself. Roy Harvey and I were the only ones that were truly affected, weren't we?

For Eireann Canning, her involvement seemed to be part adventure story, taking her away from her narrow life in Dublin, and partly serious academic and political research, cementing her obsession with her hero Eamon de Valera.

For the Wards (the Bevington-Wards, as I knew them) their involvement was a chance to make peace with the history of their parents. Maybe they also thought that they would get money from the long lost boy 'from the shed' that Francis had known in his childhood.

For Swiss Joe and Artie, I guessed that, without saying it, they were repaying a debt to me for all the years I had spent inside, much of it for jobs in which I wasn't involved, or for jobs I wanted to forget.

For the newcomers Pete and Colin, the same I suppose.

You see, in our own way and within our own community, however they may appear to more conventional people, the

Uncles are worthy men. But I feared that I, William Gilbey, was just a tiny part of their world. I was a piece of nostalgia, of no ultimate use to those still active. The sooner that I was satisfied about my past, the sooner the debt to me would be paid. Then, they could walk away and return to their true business. And I, hopefully, would be at peace.

As I write up this part of my mémoire I can see more clearly what I felt that afternoon. Only me, together with my late father Herbert Gilbey and his old friend Roy Harvey, – the sad, sick and very old man in front of me – really counted in this story.

## 7.2

Roy Harvey woke after about forty-five minutes. He stretched his loose arms down. He shook his upper body. Freed from the effect of medication he came alive. He looked at me with his piercing eyes, which followed me round the room as I spoke. I began repeating what I had already told him. But this time, Eireann not being present, I was able to talk more freely about my father. I talked to Roy Harvey about the hanging, and about my stay in Les Arcades.

Harvey didn't react immediately. In fact he seemed to be listening, and thinking.

'Is this a bad dream?' he said, eventually, in a weak and high-pitched voice.

'No, Roy Harvey.' I started my story again. I wanted him to know first and foremost who I was, and who my father was. I said that it was important to me, to my father's memory, and to Mr Harvey himself, that I should have his account. I wanted him to relive his part in my father's and my life, there and then.

'Bert Gilbey's son?' he interrupted, his voice stronger. 'Yes', *at last,* I thought.

'Son,' Roy Harvey said quite loudly, 'son, you are talking a load of cock.' Then he slumped back, as if the effort of those words had finished him.

'No,' I said quietly, 'no, Mr Harvey, please.'

'Son, whoever you are, take care of an old man. Be a good boy. Just give me my pills. Let me go back to the place I was before.' Harvey was pleading. But I could tell that undrugged, in his light frame, this ninety-odd-year-old was a fighter. They made them tough in those days: to think that my father, his near contemporary, his friend, had been dead almost fifty years.

'Please tell me the truth, Mr Harvey.'

'Who knows the truth, son?'

I said that I was sure that he knew the truth.

'No, son, you don't want the truth. Too many people, too many people always suffer when the truth gets told; and what you're asking happened a hell of a long time ago.'

'Please, please.' Yes, it was me pleading. For me, it was my best, possibly my last hope. Roy Harvey might die, and all that he knew die with him.

I untied the restraining bands from around the tiny, angular wrists. Harvey leaned forward. He tried again to shake himself from the waist up. His short-sleeved silk shirt was stained with dribble and mucus. He would have been entitled to shake his fist at me, but he didn't. He seemed to pity me, as I pitied him. He continued, in a calm voice. 'Son, I will tell you things if you promise to let me go, and then to leave me in peace. I'm only asking you to do what the others promised.'

I stopped myself asking about the 'others'. I wanted to let him go on, uninterrupted.

'I'll keep it short son, I'm bang tired, anyway, without my medicine.'

I told Mr Harvey that my friend, the nurse, had gone to get him something.

'A nurse, son? I know all about nurses. Well, ok, yes I'll tell you this, I'll tell you what I know. So, you are Bert Gilbey's lad are you, well, well, well. Your father, yes, he worked with me in transport in the war. He did trips around the country. Like me, he drove some real high-ups. Yes, he might have driven Churchill. I certainly did, regularly. Churchill was a bastard, by the way. He never stopped smoking and drinking. He never had a good word to a common man like me, whatever the history books tell you. So, yes, your dad might have driven Churchill to Ireland.'

'You mean Holyhead, in Wales?'

'Or Wales, son. I don't know, son, it's so many years ago, isn't it? I'm ninety-four; or is it ninety-six? I'm so messed up, who knows how old I am? And after the war, anyway, what you should know is that your dad worked for the Bevington-Wards. Andrew we knew as an army lieutenant. He had a business before the war in haulage. Anyway, we had met His Lordship – as we called Andrew – through his dad. They were both officers. His dad was ok. But Andrew was a real stuck-up bloke, he got a double-barrelled name and all. He had a posh wife. She had an Irish background. But you'd never know it from the way she talked. In fact they both talked all la-di-dah and French and by the way…'

Roy Harvey wheezed badly. His voice was becoming hoarser every minute.

But he drew himself up and managed to continue: '… and, by the way, now you ask me, I heard that Andrew Bevington-Ward did your mum. She was also a Belfast girl. Somehow, your dad got into a lot of trouble as well, something to do with that I suppose, I don't know. But he was never hanged son, he was *never* hanged son, not your dad. He was not that bad a man, your dad. He never murdered no-one.' Harvey could hardly speak now. 'Son, your dad Bert Gilbey was a lazy bastard, who whored and drank. He was a charmer. He told a good story. But he never did anything to get hanged, son. Oh, never, never son. Oh, my God, son, never that!'

Roy Harvey fell back exhausted. I stood up and put my hands on his shoulders, unsure as to whether I should shake him, to stop him talking nonsense. He was as fragile as porcelain.

Ten full minutes passed on the clock displayed on the television screen. Then I said: 'You said that my father wasn't hanged.'

Harvey reared up to make one more effort to be convincing, even though at no time did he fool me: 'No, for God's sake son, who gave you that idea? I don't know what happened to Bert Gilbey. He disappeared. Yes, it must have been about fifty years ago, never came to any of our meets after the 1960s. So he must have died then, maybe later. Did nobody ever tell you? I heard your mum died though.' Harvey's voice faded away. He croaked: 'Oh, my God, son, can I have a drink?'

The effort of speech and of the drugs must have made the man delirious. My father Herbert was the last man to be executed by hanging in England on 18th July 1964. He is buried in the precincts of Pentonville prison London. This is public history, on the internet, on wikipedia and so on. An investigator employed by me was at that moment preparing a report on the crime that sent him to the gallows. A death is a death. A crime is a punishable crime. A hanging is a hanging. A guillotine is a guillotine. An electric chair is an electric chair. Even if all those executions, those state murders, are now carried out in private. In 'civilised countries' at least. They are all on the record. For the executioners they are a matter of pride. They cannot be concealed.

My fists clenched white. I could see that it was useless carrying on trying to talk to a man whose brain had gone. I gave up. I went to the kitchen to fetch water, and more armagnac.

The apartment entry buzzer sounded as I returned. It was Eireann. When she came in, she saw that Harvey was awake and untied. 'He's talking,' I said.

'Is he now?' said Eireann. 'He's a strong one. I didn't think that pill would have worked off yet.'

'Who the hell's that bitch?' said Harvey after he drank the armagnac I held for him. He swallowed it neat, straight down, followed by a large glass of water.

'I'm a nurse, Mr Harvey.'

Harvey's tetchy, high-pitched voice came back: 'The hell you are. I know your sort of voice. You're just an Irish whore. I can tell. All of you Irish women are bitches. There's been more of them coming in on me recently. Don't let her near me again, son. Please son, please you're Bert Gilbey's lad. Bert was my friend.'

Eireann said: 'Now don't be rambling Mr Harvey, disturbing William, our Mr Gilbey. He's your friend, yes; and I'm your friend. Look, I've brought you food, and some stuff that will calm you. It will help you through the night.'

'Fuck to that, and fuck to you. But, well, I am tired.' Roy Harvey's eyes closed, involuntarily.

Eireann turned to me: 'What has he been saying?' I told Eireann the bits that I knew would interest her: the confirmation that my father had been in transport, that he had known the Bevington-Wards.

'Well, that's half a story I suppose.' Eireann spoke to me as if Roy Harvey wasn't there. She then said that she had had 'a good chat' to an Indian man in the pharmacy. She had told him that we had an elderly relative staying, who seemed not to be doing too well on the drugs he had brought with him. The pharmacist had given her me some stronger pills, and something to inject later, if needed. So Eireann said.

Harvey jerked awake, or maybe he had been awake all along. Again he was proving himself a strong man, worthy perhaps of working alongside my father. He said: 'I'm not being injected by an Irish bitch.'

'Now, now, Mr Harvey.'

'Eireann, I want him to keep talking. He might get back to sense again.'

Eireann said that it was more likely that Mr Harvey would talk better after he had had some proper sleep.

Roy Harvey shouted: 'No, no, I ain't got nothing more to say, nothing more I'm going to tell you, nothing more in front of a pockmarked bitch. People will be harmed. There's stuff that belongs a long time ago, and shouldn't be raked up. Oh, I'm dog tired, I'm starving, I need my pills, I need my doctor, I need a real nurse. Please let me go.'

Roy Harvey tried to continue. But his voice broke back to being pathetic and weak. His screams now came out like whimpers.

Eireann spoke with confidence to me: 'Yes, you see William this reaction was predictable, a sudden confrontation with his past and with the truth. That's why we had better take it slowly, in stages. I'll give him some of the sandwiches I've bought. Also a few glasses of your armagnac won't harm him, or indeed either of us. Then he can take a pill, so that when he wakes up in the morning' – Eireann was now talking to Roy Harvey as much as me – 'Mr Harvey will feel right as rain. He will want to help us. So that, when we have the full story, we can get him taken back to his comfortable life in Esher.'

Roy Harvey groaned. He shook his head. But, this time, he didn't resist the food being pushed into his mouth, followed by more armagnac. Almost a whole bottle of brandy had now gone between us. I was tired as well, but I hoped, against hope, that Harvey would tell me the truth. So far, he had talked in delirium. He had said that my father had not been hanged; that my mother 'logically and therefore' had been involved with 'His Lordship' Andrew Bevington-Ward. What nonsense was all that!

Eireann took out another tranquilizer from her handbag. She pushed it down Harvey's throat. Then, before I could say anything, or he could object, she injected him. She said: 'You might like to sleep on the sofa or a bed.' It wasn't a question, but Roy Harvey nodded. He was half-way to dreamland. Eireann said some more words, in what I think was Latin, and some in a language which again I didn't recognise. But I guess it must have been Irish, or Gaelic, as I think they call it.

I was dumb with fear. Maybe we were losing Roy Harvey? However, we lifted him, according to Eireann's directions, and put him on the sofa. I saw how withered the lower body was. He could go nowhere without others. Roy Harvey was like an elderly polio victim I had seen in a prison hospital, who was a human being in name only, living a worthless life.

Harvey was soon asleep, and snoring.

I told Eireann that I wanted to have a bath before I rested for a few hours. I had to go out to meet 'a contact', a lady friend, at just after nine. I might then not be back until eleven, or even later. Eireann said that she would gladly sit vigil, while I bathed and rested. She would wake me up in time. She would stay in the apartment until about eleven. If I wasn't back, she would ensure that Mr Harvey was settled, and she would give him another sleeping draught, if necessary.

Eireann asked if she could use my computer to look at the news, in Ireland as well as England, also maybe to do some more research, just to keep her mind occupied. But, although she had brought some personal things, she said that she wanted after that to return to sleep in the bedroom in her hotel. She would come back to my place when I called. We could continue our work if necessary, and decide what to do.

Eireann said that she would leave me a note for my return from my 'date'. She said again that she would have Roy Harvey 'sleeping like a baby' for my return. I said that she could, of course, use the computer, but that it had been adapted for me: so I must make some adjustments first. I opened the e-mail account. I deleted all the old e-mails (there were no new ones). I checked the settings. Eireann said that she understood how important privacy was.

Eireann smiled and said that she was sure we were on 'the cusp of discovery'. Maybe what we learned from talking to Mr Harvey might not all be good news. But, at least, we knew that my father's story was in some part credible. Eireann said: 'We will be left with something to build on.'

## 7.3

Eireann woke me at eight forty-five. She said that Harvey was still sleeping soundly, as indeed he was; and as I had.

But I was a little late getting to Knightsbridge, even though a taxi picked me up outside the apartment. The traffic was bad.

Gillian was waiting for me, as we had arranged. She was alone. Her hair was up, her face well-scrubbed and made up, as it had been in Esher. Gillian was wearing a sweater and skirt that looked expensive, but not as high-class as earlier. I complimented her. We found a table at a wine bar opposite Harrods, a couple leaving just as we went in. They looked back at me – spying, I suppose.

We began by talking about Gillian's brother Francis, and his drinking. Again, I did not mention his call.

Gillian told me about her boss, her 'madam'. We looked through the wine list together. She said that she was 'famished', so we ordered some of the buffet-style food the bar served. During the meal, Gillian read several texts on her phone, saying that they were from friends. She also drank wine. Gillian's voice took on the timbre of one affected by alcohol.

I wanted that. I wanted her to be receptive, so that I could confide in her at least as much as I had confided in Eireann. With Gillian Ward, I wanted to find signs of love – or, more accurately, lust.

A borstal chaplain had told me about the distinction between 'agape', true Christian love; and 'eros', pagan and devilish passions. I believe that that distinction is true. I have enjoyed the temptations of eros on many occasions, sometimes to extremes. Whether or not I have enjoyed the benefits of agape, spiritual love, save perhaps the love of comrades like the Uncles, with their sense of duty, I do not yet know.

But I had to move on. With an eye on the time, and in the hope of finally making her a real and useful ally, I asked Gillian straight out about her trip to Esher. For a moment she looked at me blankly. Then, yes, she admitted that she had been to see Roy Harvey at Foxdale Lodge. She had heard, she said, that 'someone answering your description William' had already been and had 'messed things up'. So she had gone there very early. She had been at the home by nine o'clock in the morning; but they had refused her entry. She said that I must have seen her later, after she had walked around a little to collect herself, to look at the shops and to get a drink. She would have been on her way back, to try again, as she had been told that a more senior person – a Mr David Alexander – would see her at midday. But, when she had returned to the home the staff had been even vaguer.

Gillian said that she had then given up. She also said that she had to admit that the motive for her visit was 'money rather than curiosity or research'. She hoped that I would forgive her for that. My pursuing Roy Harvey had convinced her that there was 'lots of money in this business somewhere'. She reminded me that she and her brother had been left with very little by her father, 'His Lordship', 'your so-called Uncle Andrew'.

I was at that point determined, really against common sense and all evidence, to forgive Gillian; and to believe her. As she had been talking I had brushed my knee against hers. She had not withdrawn it – not noticeably, anyway.

I therefore decided to tell Gillian Bevington-Ward about Eireann Canning. I talked about her warmly, perhaps a little too warmly. Gillian laughed and raised her eyebrows. Then, because I wanted to offer Gillian hope that we might together find something, I told her about the kidnapping of Roy Harvey, which also didn't seem to alarm her.

I said that Eireann Canning was still with Harvey.

'With Roy Harvey, where?' Gillian's voice was

suddenly sharp. Any romantic or even alcohol-induced haze had gone.

'Well, at my flat. You can come and see if you like.'

'You say that Eireann Canning is there now, with this man Roy Harvey – for God's sake, for how long? I thought she was with her gentlemen professor friend?'

I told Gillian about my agreement with Eireann; and when I was expected to be back in the apartment.

'Oh, my God.' Gillian's tone was cold. 'We thought he would be left alone, that he would be too conked out, that's what we thought. So she has been alone with him, for almost two hours? Oh shit. Nobody said. I bet the boss doesn't know either. He's still at that hotel with those Arabs, him and those stoned gamblers. I've got some calls to make. We must get back there fast.'

*Writing this up a day later I find it hard to set down exactly what then happened in detail, to set events out and to recall the changes in my emotions.*

I remember that Gillian returned to a state of calm, looking at me with a sensitive face, not unlike the face that Eireann had shown to me and to Roy Harvey.

Gillian told me not to worry. Then she settled our bill in cash, and made more calls.

Twenty minutes later, too impatient to wait for a taxi, and walking there at a superfast pace, silent, and ignoring the rings on both our phones, Gillian ahead most of the way, we were at my block. I opened the front door. I went up to the apartment. I turned the key to the door. But it was opened from within as I did so.

'Eireann', I said 'still here Eireann?'

'No, William, my son, she beat us to it. Missed her by ten minutes, I reckon. Anyway she has scarpered, *comprende?*'

Pete, the bossman I had first met near Hatton Garden, was sitting on the sofa. Swiss had opened the door.

Someone came in behind me. I looked. It was Artie. He must have slipped in when Gillian had opened the door to the block. He was a silent operator, was Artie.

'Come in, William. It's your pad after all, make yourself comfortable. Come in Artie.'

I looked across the room. In the corner Roy Harvey was in the wheelchair. His body was pushed back, his mouth was open, his face white. Roy Harvey, the last link with my father, was dead.

'Well, my dear William, my son, you need an explanation.'

Pete's voice was as cool as Gillian's and Eireann's had been. But his jowelled and lined face was flowing with rivulets of sweat. Swiss and Artie meanwhile were standing rigid, as was Gillian. The smell of fear was everywhere.

'And we will need an explanation on certain matters from you, William. So, sit down next to me. You tell me your side, and I'll tell you ours. But we had better make it snappy. Because there's something like five, ten, maybe twenty million quid resting on our finding this woman, this Miss Canning, to whom you introduced our sole source of real information. I'm assuming that she got that out of Mr Harvey here, or at least enough information to take her to the next little clue in this mystery hunt.'

I asked what the bossman Pete meant.

'Just sit down next to me, and listen, son. First, let me introduce ourselves properly. You know me, Pete your bossman. You know Swiss 'The Milky One'. You know Artie. You have met Debra, although to you she has been 'Gillian', Gillian Bevington-Ward. Debra here and her poncey friend James Loughlin, 'Francis Bevington-Ward' to you, who has gone absent without leave…'

Artie laughed.

'Well it sounds as if Artie found him! Tracing the calls on your special phone has proved useful once again.'

Artie laughed again, as did Swiss and Debra.

'Well, James and the delightful Debra here, are what we know as small-part actors, a bit down on their luck. Such folks love the drink, the drugs and the high life. There's several of them who do a bit of work for me from time to time – escorting, whoring, stealing whatever. It helps their acting skills – so they say – these guys getting into the criminal world, the '*demee-mond*' these ponces call it!'

I looked at Gillian, now 'Debra'. She looked away.

'So James and Debra here have been happy to play the role of your long-lost friends, Francis and Gillian. But the nervous poof James took fright and went on a bender. You asked him too many good questions. There's no depth to that man at all. He could never remember his lines. So Artie was sent to him after he called you, *comprende*?'

Artie grinned.

'Now, that's the introductions,' Pete paused. 'Save there's one player missing. Where is Colin, our tecky wizard? Debra, you don't know? Artie, Swiss, you neither? Where the fuck is that boy?'

Artie and Swiss said that they hadn't seen Colin since three o'clock. They had been sharing 'surveillance'. But Colin had said that he had a cold and that he 'wasn't much use anyway' at watching people. Artie said that Colin always 'preferred action'.

'Skinheads don't get colds son, they're too tough for that. Their shaved heads are like leather.'

Swiss and Artie laughed. Pete didn't.

'And not much surveillance was it, that you allowed this Eireann woman to have so much free time? We now have Mr Harvey sat dead in his wheelchair here, poor bugger. She not only murdered him, uninterrupted. She tortured him.'

I looked over at the wheelchair. There were deep red marks on Roy Harvey's face and neck.

'You have a nice, efficient electric iron here, William. No wonder your old clothes are always crisp.' I then saw the iron itself, propped on the floor next to the wheelchair. Its light was still on. I walked over and turned it off.

'But you told us, Pete, to follow William here all the time. Never to leave him. Never do anything even when those kids beat him.'

'Don't argue with me, Swiss. Don't argue with me.'

The Milky One blinked.

'But ok, ok yes, if that's the way you want it Swiss, I, Pete, must take the blame, as ever and always, 'logically and therefore' as a certain dead gentleman used to say. I am the bossman after all. Yes, I guess that, if I employ monkeys, they can only be expected to bring me peanuts? And I know, before you say otherwise, that I told you not to bother me at the hotel across the road, where I had a nice little session going on. But I said not to bother me, unless it was 'life and death'. There again, to quote our friend William's guardian Mr Andrew Bevington-Ward, 'logically and therefore', a life and death situation is what we clearly now fucking have!' Pete laughed and turned to look at me. No-one else laughed or moved.

Pete squeezed my knee. He was calm. He was thinking things through. He was in that state which I had always wanted when on a job, but had not always achieved. That is why I had been caught and had spent so many years in prison. I suspect that Pete had never seen the inside of a cell.

Pete said that there would be time for full explanations later. 'All I want you and the others to understand now is that this here corpse, when it was still breathing, Mr Roy Harvey, possessed the key to a large sum of money, jewellery and precious objects. It has been our plan that you, William, would have got that key from him, that vital clue, as your father Herbert's rightful heir. Then you would, willingly I hope, but if not, how can I say it to such a good bloke, well **unwillingly**, pass that information on to us, or more precisely to me, you understand, son?'

'Of course I would Pete,' I said. I chose my words carefully. 'But I don't need money, do I? I've got plenty just waiting for me. You told me. It's been there building up all these years. Then there's the jewellery, my mother's jewellery box. Swiss told me that you had it all sorted. You told me yourself too.'

Pete took a deep breath. 'No, no, son. Let's get that straight now, William. You must take a deep breath like me. In fact, you must take several deep breaths, son. You have been the victim of a long-standing and, though I say it myself, well-constructed deception. You ain't got no money son. You ain't got no jewellery box. You ain't got a two pound piece to aim your piss at. Do you *comprende*?'

I felt sick. I looked at my friend, The Milky One. Swiss pursed his lips. Pete continued: 'In fact you, William Harrison Gilbey, you owe me an awful lot of dough. What with all those meals and taxis cruising around London half the day and half the night looking for you; business class flight to and from Dublin; people carrier hire; bribes to restaurants to let you in; bribes to hospitals; bribes to your prison friends; not to mention keeping Debra in the manner she likes, just for you. And you haven't even done her, have you, son?'

Debra (or 'Gillian' as I knew her) laughed. 'Is there any whisky here?' she said.

Pete ignored her: 'Did you even fuck your bit of Irish, Miss Eireann, by the way?' He didn't wait for a reply. 'Surely you at least got that pleasure? Oh my God, think what this nice apartment has cost for two weeks! He hasn't even fucked anyone in it!'

I said that I didn't understand.

'*Non comprende* eh? Well, son, there's time for that. What we must do now is to find that Irish lady, because it's obvious that she's on to the same thing that I've been looking for for a hell of a long time. I am not going to let some clever Irish piece get there ahead of me.'

I had to be helpful. What else could I do? This tragedy, like all tragedies, had taken on a momentum of its own. I said that Eireann would have gone back to her hotel before coming back to my apartment.

Swiss Joe called out the hotel name. We had picked Eireann up there earlier.

When Debra rang the hotel we could all hear the receptionist say that 'Miss Canning' had checked out in the morning. In between her gulps of whisky Debra pressed a little. After the receptionist checked with the porter's desk she said that she had come back for her luggage later. But she wouldn't say when, 'security'.

'And you said she had a companion in London, a professor?' asked Pete.

I said that I had never seen him. I didn't know his name.

Pete looked up in the air. He was quiet for a while. He then said, 'Where the hell is Colin? I'm missing his smell.'

'He's not answering his phone,' called out Swiss.

Pete shouted back. 'He knows the rules. I'll whip that boy... Now I suppose, don't you William, your friend Eireann will be heading back to Ireland.'

Pete took from his pocket a fancy mobile phone. He tapped into it. 'But the last plane to Dublin will have left way too early for her.'

I had an inspiration. But before I could say anything Pete was searching his phone again.

'You said that this Canning woman was from the *'de Val-aer-reeyar* Foundation'. How are you spelling that?' I called out the letters.'

'D.E. gap V.A.L.E.R.A?, you say William? I can't get that on Google, where did you find it?'

'On that computer.'

'Oh yes, the one that Colin rigged up for you, the one we told you to use to the exclusion of all others, which you did, kept away from temptation by taxis cruising just for you – unless you ate your meals too quick that is, like the other night?'

'Yes.'

'I'll try the lady. She should be here if she's so high–up and well known. What did you call her?'

I spelled out the name, 'E.I.R.E.A.N.N. C.A.N.N.I.N.G.'

Pete Googled that. 'Nothing for her, neither. I guess her name was on that computer too?'

'Yes.'

'Oh yes. Yes. Yes. The computer William that's yours, with a whole set of programmes and Wikipedia and Google entries designed by our wizard Colin. Thinking again about Colin, Swiss: please enlighten me where do you think the fuck is our friend, the one you introduced us to?'

The Milky One looked around the room, pausing to cast his eyes slowly over me. He then said with emphasis: 'He might be with that Irish bint, William's piece.'

Pete paused as well. Then he slapped himself, hard across his forehead: 'Swiss, you are a mastermind. Yes, of course he's with her. I worked that out some time ago. Where else could he be? Sipping Lemsips? But why is he with her? That boy's not Irish. He's not a Catholic. He's got an Iron Cross tattooed on his neck. This is the biggest turn-up before the Second Coming. I didn't want to believe it until, Swiss, you said it. I couldn't say it myself. But is our Colin a fraud, a traitor, pushing his cock into some Irish pussy?'

There was a long silence. None of us dared to speak. Then I had an idea.

'Do you want to know something?' I said.

'Give me more bad news, son. But make it snappy.' Pete pressed his hands together above his head.

'I think I saw Colin in disguise. I hadn't until now realised where, but his nose gave him away.'

'Yes, a Yiddisher sort of nose, oddly enough – a bit like mine'.

Swiss Joe, Artie and Debra laughed loud at this. Debra poured more whisky for herself. But Pete wasn't laughing. The others' faces tensed up when they saw this.

'I'm picturing it, bossman. I saw him in Dublin. He was in the library at the foundation, the de Valera foundation. He was wearing a hat.'

'What a great disguise for a skinhead William! So he's an actor too, like Debra here. The world is full of fucking actors. And we sent him to Dublin to follow you. But he never mentioned no foundation.'

'There was a bearded man following me, as well.'

'Popular, aren't you William?'

There was a slow and steady silence, broken only by a sudden swoosh. The upper body of Roy Harvey had slumped forward, the lower section held back by straps on the wheelchair.

'Oh, hell,' said Artie and Swiss Joe together.

Debra and Pete laughed.

I had to offer an idea. I needed to get myself back in Pete's good books. Otherwise, I might have faced Roy Harvey's fate then and there.

I said that I thought I might know Eireann's mind, and her plan. 'They'll be driving to the ferry at Holyhead, to cross by sea to Dublin, to recreate the scene I described to her, and she believed me, when my father was Mr Churchill's driver and took him to meet Mr de Valera.'

'Yes, yes, William Gilbey. You're a clever fellow.' Pete gave me a gentle punch on the shoulder. 'Now, silence folks, while I think this through.'

For five minutes, judging by the time shown on the television screen, the silence was total. No-one dared distract a bossman.

## 7.4

Pete spoke: 'Oh, one thing, while I think this through. As you are the lady here, Debra, just go over there, kneel and take a look at poor Mr Harvey. You're a tough bitch. Don't be embarrassed. I want to know exactly how he died. See if there are any injections, or whatever.'

Debra walked unsteadily across, whisky glass in hand. She kneeled in front of Roy Harvey's wheelchair. She began to push his upper body back up.

Pete then hauled himself up, slowly, from the sofa. He signalled Swiss and Artie to join him. The bossman walked over to where Debra knelt by the wheelchair. He pushed his fat right thumb and fat right forefinger forcefully into the back of Debra's neck, pressing her down onto Harvey's lower body. At the same time he put his huge left hand around Debra's mouth and nose, squeezing them hard. His grin widened as he applied pressure with both hands.

The Milky One and his comrade Artie pulled up Debra's arms. This was a textbook group killing manoeuvre that I had been trained to carry out, years ago.

After twenty seconds or so Pete let go. Debra breathed a short sigh of relief. But Pete, having had his fun, slapped his hand over Debra's face harder than ever. After a few moments of pressure and muffled squeals from the defenceless woman with grunts of appreciation from Swiss Joe and Artie at a job well done, Pete let go. Debra, my Gillian Ward, my Gillian Bevington-Ward, a woman I had begun to love, was dead.

Calmly, Pete took Debra's mobile phone out of her skirt pocket. 'OK, that's got rid of one problem. It will also help us to solve several others. I never liked women in this business, anyway. Too independent, waltzing off to Esher this morning. Strip her!'

Swiss smiled.

'But, no wanking, Swiss. Do that in your own time, and into your own sheets.'

Pete looked at me. 'Artie got rid of her so-called brother. Well he shouldn't have rung you should he? So, Roy Harvey, James and Debra, three corpses today already! A red-letter day, indeed.'

*To my shame, I said nothing. I told myself that Debra had deceived me about everything. She had had her just reward.*

Then Pete's words accelerated, as he came up with his plan. He told Swiss Joe to get the syringe 'the Irish' left behind and to inject Debra. Then he was to wash everything that might have fingerprints. Also, to get Debra's prints on the syringe, while they were still moist. Artie was told to call 'Jack and his boys' and 'get them over. We've got time, the police would have been here by now had the Irish bitch called them, although we've got shooters if it comes to it.'

When Artie had done this, and while Swiss started the clean-up, Pete sat back on the sofa and lit a big cigar.

'Look, boys, this is what I want. I want it to look, after you have finished your tasks, as if she, that is, this bitch Debra, also known as Gillian, and he, Mr wartime Hero Harvey here, died in some drug mix-up. You see, the bitch has been to Harvey's fancy and security-tight care home, Foxdale Lodge, a few times, only the last time was without my say-so. It's all there on camera.

'So we spin a story to one or more of our friendly newspaper hacks that this poor old war hero of a man, Roy Harvey, a hundred years of age or whatever' – Pete jerked his thumb at Roy Harvey – 'well, he desperately needed a mercy killing. But when Debra done it for money, we can do that in her account tomorrow, bank transfer from Switzerland to Debra, of course we can get it back later, this crack-ridden alcoholic addict ex-nurse and bit-part actor turned the syringe on to herself, overwhelmed by guilt. You all *comprende*?'

By the time he had finished giving these directions, Pete could hardly speak for laughter. Such cleverness! Swiss and Artie laughed as well. I thought that Pete might ask for a round of applause.

'Now, who said, William, that we Uncles aren't

creative? Just like you, with your cooking and your piano playing. By the way, the piano's one thing we never thought of here. Well, you banging away might have attracted unwelcome attention. But we got Piercey to supply one, to satisfy one of your addictions.' Pete looked at me and grinned.

'Now, boys, when everything has been cleaned up, get everything you can out of here, give it a total fingerprint sweep. Then pour a few bottles of brandy around. Fire it up near the bodies. Make it look as though they'd both gone bonkers. Open the windows at the back, the ones that look over the courtyard. But keep the ones over the square closed. We'll give our Met plodder mates a real mystery, a Miss Marple one to solve, rather than the run of the mill, hoipolloi policing the pigs usually get. Well, you wouldn't want it any other way, would you, William? Of course, none of this will stand up if they get full forensics. But that assumes some hired-in technician in the police lab is doing his job properly. Fat chance of that. Anyway, by then we should all be sorted and far, far, far away. We'll be down the proverbial yellow brick road, counting our money.'

Pete, back in his element as an all-commanding, successful bossman, puffed on a cigar.

'What about the geezers at the home in Esher, Pete, where we've been?' asked Swiss. The Milky One gestured at the dead body of my father's friend Roy Harvey. 'Won't they be already on to the law and, as you said, we'll be on the cameras?'

Pete gave Swiss a look that was at once condescending and supremely confident. 'Swiss, have you, or any of you, including William heard of David Alexander?' No-one spoke. 'Why you, William, you met the poor boy. You shouted at him so much that he almost burst into tears. You others have seen him in my car once or twice.' Swiss and Artie looked blank.

'You say 'no, no?' Oh, you blind bastards, so you don't remember the good-looking guy in a thin tie, the recently appointed executive assistant at Foxdale Lodge, that luxury care place in the stockbroker belt, where even the cabbies speak posh? Well, let me tell you that my friend Mr David Alexander is cut from the same cloth as William's Mr Lloyd Piercey. He's a poor guy earning shit, who likes luxury. He will do anything for a thousand quid. I mean *anything*, understand? Well my young David is holding the fort at Foxdale Lodge now, turning cameras off and on, wiping tapes and so on, ensuring no discoveries are made and no questions asked, until his Uncle Pete tells him so.' Pete's grin widened. He puffed away on his cigar.

'You see David's like all of us in this room. He's not one of the hoipolloi. He's seen the way the rich old folks live off the backs of ordinary folk, and he wants some of what they've got, what we've fought to get. I like David. I can see him as my replacement Colin, the odd-job well-educated clever boy, good at the techie side of the business: like you two, Swiss and Artie, are good at the rough stuff. There has to be a clever feller as well, in any gang. It's just happening quicker than I expected, now that skunk Colin has absented himself.'

I caught a worried look from Swiss. He had introduced Colin to Pete.

'Now, I've told young David there's a lot more

pleasures to come and a lot more money. And David, like us, he gets off on all this naughtiness. He loves the rubber and the leather. He's an innocent boy, as yet, compared to you, Swiss and you Artie, and even when compared with you, William. But he loves pussy. He loves the poker tables and the backgammon, the coke and the ket. So David will say, as per my new instructions, that our friend Debra told him that she was Harvey's granddaughter and took him out for a treat. Not that folks in that place with their five star living want much for treats. But maybe Mr Roy Harvey wanted a better quality of caviar, a vintage champagne, say a 1990 Veuve Clicquot, or a lady-boy tart, or a trio of Brazilian trannies with white powder up their arses. But when David's patient, and the woman he had entrusted him to, didn't come back after twenty four hours he gets alarmed, as a good carer should. He phoned the number she gave him, which is the mobile phone over there, and he gets no reply. So then he calls the police, terribly concerned. They trace the number here, *comprende*?'

Pete waved Debra's mobile phone in the air. 'We'll wipe it, see. Then we'll put it somewhere in the apartment where it won't get damaged. Of course the bodies will be dutifully recovered, reflecting in full the terrible agonies of their deaths. Makes a good romantic story doesn't it? They could make a film about it.'

One by one we all nodded. It was, I admit, a great plan, apparently thrown together on the spot. Pete seemed a master of detail at that point. 'I'll call now, just to cheer up David. He's expecting me. He likes to hear from me. The boy likes his Uncle Pete.'

Yes, I thought, and a man like that can grow up to be a master and a bossman; and a masochist can become a vicious sadist overnight. I know. I have seen it. So maybe David's time would come. Maybe sooner than he or Pete expected.

Then, as Swiss and Artie laughed and Pete made his call, the flat buzzer went. I half-hoped it was the police or even Mr Lloyd Piercey or someone, anyone, to get me out. But instead 'Jack, with Charlie and Frank' were announced over the intercom.

As Pete, the bossman, was distracted by the new arrivals, I noticed at the computer terminal a sealed envelope with 'For William' on it. I crossed the room. I picked up the envelope. I put it into the holdall where I keep this mémoire and other personal items and equipment for my profession. No-one saw me, as far as I knew.

Jack came over and put out his hand to shake mine. He was, in fact, my Bond Street 'private investigator', with his two sons.

Gang members. Frauds. Actors.

## 7.5

Forty-five minutes later Charlie was driving me and the bossman Pete on to the North Circular Road, heading to the M1 motorway out of London. We were in a big Mercedes. Charlie had changed into an over-tight chauffeur's uniform. I still had on a good suit. I had asked Pete if I could bring my bag of notes and papers with me on the drive. He had nodded. After we reached the M1 approach road, Pete began. He said that he would explain everything. He wouldn't stop until 'a nice little place we have off the M6'. Refreshments would be provided 'just like your dad's passengers, in the story that he told you'. Pete said that it was best not to interrupt him, as 'like all leaders' he didn't like interruptions. He said that I could ask any questions I liked 'when you have the full picture'.

Pete gave his mobile phone to Charlie. 'That's a special one, Charlie: so, if it rings answer it and say nothing. Only if they say the code 'Ingham', then pass it back to me.' Charlie nodded.

'Good. William, let's talk about your dad's story first. You've already got some Irish history. You've had the lady's version, I guess? So you need to know more. You need the real truth, the things your dad didn't tell you, or you have forgotten, and that the Irish folk certainly wouldn't have wanted you to know.'

Pete re-lit a cigar. He took a swig from a hipflask. He said that there were a lot of cars of the sort my father Bert Gilbey drove, and vans that went between London and Ireland in the war. It was a complicated set-up, Pete said. I knew much of the history, but I listened.

Northern Ireland, Pete said, was with Britain, but the Republic was neutral. And there were people in the south who were Nazis. They hated the Brits so much, they had become Nazis. And many that were not Nazi, but just Irish, saw the war as a chance to kick the Brits out of the north. Many Brits also wanted that, sooner or later. 'To be frank, William, most of us Brits have never cared a fuck about Ireland, north or south, have we?'

True, I thought. That is what the Irish in prison had often told me.

'So many of those better off people in the north, who hated the southern Catholics, were scared. They thought the Nazis would invade, helped by the south. But the Brits wouldn't help, because we couldn't.'

Pete the bossman said that, added to the black market trade of food from Ireland, butter and meat mainly, there was a trade in arms, guns and stuff for the northern Unionists. Many of them were well placed in the British Army. Then people started sending jewellery and art to England. A lot of this had already crossed one border from the south in the twenties, when it gained its independence and became the Free State. Most of this wasn't paid for, Pete said. It went into storage in England.

Pete said that, 'Army officers organised the caper, men like the one you knew as 'Uncle Andrew', Lieutenant Andrew Bevington-Ward. His father was a Colonel by the way. There was a whole family of the bastards. One of them was even a bishop.'

Pete stopped for a moment. But I did as I had been told. I didn't speak.

Then Pete said that all the barriers went up again after the war, and all the customs officers came back 'better fed and a lot nosier' so a lot of that stuff couldn't go back. 'I mean, you remember that art on the walls of the villa they had, Les Arcades?'

'Yes.'

'Where do you think that came from? Yes, a lot of stuff disappeared from Ireland, my son. But nobody could say much, because it should never have been moved. And when people died, they would have had to pay taxes and death duties on it, with Attlee and his Labour lot in. Their families didn't have the money after the war. But, can you blame those good people for panicking in 1940? Do you know who the biggest Irish Nazi was? Well, it was a man called Adolf Mahr. Adolf, yes, Adolf, Mahr. Would you believe that name? A lot of this was filled in for me by a good friend in a high-up government department, by the way. He says he's been working away at this, off and on, for twenty years.'

The mobile rang, interrupting Pete's flow. Charlie answered it. I caught the word 'Ingham'. Charlie passed it to the bossman. Pete held the phone as far away from me as he could. I could hear agitated mutterings at the other end, and Pete's response.

'Yes, yes, all under control. This is one of the best chances we've had in years. No, it won't slip away this time.' The call was over. 'Well, that was a nice touch William. There I was, just talking about my hig-up friend, and his voice just pops up out of nowhere. Anyway, William. Yes, Adolf Mahr was the director of the biggest museum in Dublin, believe it or not. But he was such a Nazi that he lost his job. Early in the war, though, he was licking his lips at all those paintings. You know all that classical stuff, all those golden vases, little chairs and candlesticks, that he could get for his museum. Like that fat bastard Goering grabbed for his castle in Bavaria. You can get the caper, all the stuff he'd get, if the Germans won; or at least if the Republic could march up north.'

Pete drew deeply on his cigar. 'Now, from what we worked out, your dad Bert Gilbey seems to have been one of the cogs in that machine. He did regular runs. Roy Harvey was another, a bit higher up. They had access to cars and to petrol stores. Of course, Bert Gilbey and Roy Harvey would have been paid something. But maybe they did it mainly for excitement, as they couldn't get to the real war. Or maybe they were fed up with being ordered around by what they called 'the nobs', the men from the gents' clubs, the Churchills and the Edens of this world? Who knows? Perhaps they did it alongside legit trips.'

I had to speak now. 'Are you saying that my father was a liar? That he told me stories which were lies?'

'Now, quiet, son, I'm loyal to my dad too. So I know where you are coming from. But I told you to wait and to hear the whole story. Don't rush me.'

I coughed. It was the cigar smoke. The bossman opened a window briefly.

'To be honest I don't know, William, if that story he told you was true; whether he saw Winny and the Irish geezer, that's politics, not my thing at all, or whether they were other people, army sorts, or whether they were just another pair of gun and money runners, and your dad Bert decided to tart up a story a bit, to make a bash of it to you, to show how important he was. We all do that, son. You've done that yourself, haven't you? Haven't you?'

I said, 'Yes.'

'And I think your dad was one of those story-tellers who liked to come at a thing in a roundabout way. Me,

I'm blunt. What you see and hear is what I am, and what you get. *Comprende?*'

I nodded.

'What we do know,' said Pete, 'is that there's a hell of a lot, a hell of a lot, of fine art, jewellery and money gone missing and has stayed missing for seventy years. Millions worth of it, son. So it's been the aim of every Irish gang, every political group, north and south of Ireland, to find it, even if they've never let on. We know Bevington-Ward took some. We know Roy Harvey had a share. That's how they lived the expensive lives they did.'

I thought, does this relate to my father? Yes, we were comfortable and he didn't work. But we were never rich. There were the jewels, of course.

Pete the bossman continued: 'But you might ask: what happened to the rest of the art and the dosh? Is it in some Swiss bank? Is it down a Cheshire salt-mine? That's where they put some of the official stuff in the war you know, once all the cellars in central London were full. They also used cellars on the country estates the nobs had in those days, many of them knocked down and built over now, of course. That's a problem, a real problem by the way.'

Pete said that if the Irish loot could be found I should have a share, if my dad turned out to have been involved. But, what he wanted to know was this: did I have any clue as to what happened to dad's share? And why did my dad get killed? Pete paused. This time he wanted me to answer.

'Bossman, you know that my father was hanged. He was the last man to be executed, by hanging, in England at eight in the morning on the 18th of July 1964, for the murder of two women, Miss Dora Harrison and Miss Maeve Lee. He shot them outside a post office in Manchester. It was a robbery that went wrong, like the job I did and got sent down for, my last job, although I didn't kill anyone. But my father did kill two women, and they hung him for it. It's all being investigated again. Well, I thought it was.'

Pete relit his cigar. He spoke slowly, and in a sad and sympathetic tone of voice. It was the first, and the last time that he spoke to me that way.

'No, no, listen son, listen. Take a deep breath, again. You must take several deep breaths if you have to. What you were told was a lie. Your dad never killed anyone. Your dad wasn't hanged in prison. The last people to be hanged in this country, poor sods, were in August 1964. They were called Peter Allen and Gwynne Evans. God help them. If they could have waited another six weeks to have done their robberies, and the old geezers they murdered, they might still be alive as the Labour lot stopped hanging in October 1964.' Pete laughed. 'Bloody bleeding-hearts Labour, they've got a lot to answer for. Son, it's all on the internet, save the one you were using at our apartment was fiddled by skinhead Colin. No, son. Your dad was executed all right, maybe even hanged, but not after a trial. I guess, and it sounds as if you know no different, he was disposed of on the orders of Bevington-Ward, your mother's lover, one of the bosses of the whole shebang. Maybe His Lordship Andrew got fearful that if your dad Bert was going to spin stories to you about Winnie and de Val-aer-reeyar, the running up and down to Holyhead, in front of you and your mother, who the fuck else would he be talking to? Yes, your dad was a great story-teller. We all know that. Maybe you are also. I don't know. But he was also a drunk your dad, wasn't he, whatever you say, whatever you tell others, or fantasise. You remember that don't you?'

I remained silent. I swear that I remained loyal. I can hardly write this. But I must record what I was told, then set it out in this mémoire, this record of truth.

'Maybe your dad just couldn't be trusted. Your mother was Irish, wasn't she, from Belfast in the north, from a good working class Catholic family, good Fenians. Theirs looks to me as if it was what they used to call a 'shotgun' marriage, when she got pregnant with you. She couldn't have you aborted, because she was religious. Anyway, in those days abortion wasn't legal. So she was stuck with marrying your dad, and having you. Maybe she reacted against your dad when she realised the truth of what he had done, the crimes, the robberies, especially the robberies from Ireland. Anyway, your mum never missed your dad after he died. She never talked about him afterwards, did she?

'But, there again, whatever she thought, and he promised her, she wouldn't have been good enough for a Bevington-Ward; he was a pretend double-barrelled aristocrat who wanted to be a man of the Ascendancy. I guess that when your mum threw herself at the lieutenant he arranged the travel, and kept her and you in a shed at the bottom of their garden of that fancy house in the south of France. It was out of the frying-pan and into the fire for both of you. I will say this, though, his wife Gloria, your so-called 'aunty', wasn't such a bad woman. I think she just needed company. There was plenty of money, plenty of jewellery and art, but no company. Just you Gilbeys and a few other bastards he flung out later – his 'extended family' they call it nowadays. There, you see son, it all fits, as does the jewellery you said your mother had.'

How did Pete know all this? But I thought I had caught him out: 'You said, bossman, the jewellery didn't exist.'

'No, son, I said it doesn't exist now. The stuff you took when you ran away from home was fake. A lot of people like your mother had fakes made up, to guard against theft. They kept the real stuff locked up. Nobody had the heart or maybe even the nous to tell you, when you passed it into the care of our friends. Of course me, with all my background, I saw it straight away. The real stuff would have been given by your mum to Bevington-Ward until it was safe to fence it. The real stuff was never under your mum's bed. Bevington-Ward, the bastard, kept it. But he would have had to wait many years after the war to sell it. Maybe he never did. Maybe it's buried somewhere.'

This was nonsense, a ruthless criminal's nonsense, I was sure.

'But you, my son, you ran away, you wanted freedom, you thought you were better than them, and you never checked anything. And, when we went to look a year ago, and after I had a chat with Mr Andrew Bevington-Ward and his family, they sadly met their deaths in a car accident. So we never got your jewellery.'

Pete smiled. He lit the cigar again. He muttered: 'Well that fool Bevington-Ward wouldn't give me anything.

He said I had no rights, so 'logically and therefore', what a pompous git, he would remain silent!'

That at least sounded like truth. I felt sorry for Francis and Gillian, even though it was only their acting doubles that appeared in my mind's eye as Pete spoke.

'After we had used every piece of equipment I had – he was a tough and stupid old nut Bevington-Ward – I invited him, after we'd guided his hand over certain documents, to take his wife and his stuck-up family for a drive along a mountain road. It was not the Grand Corniche by the way, that was an invention of James the actor, the man you knew as Francis. It was somewhere a lot less public, in a new car we supplied. Most annoyingly, believe it or not, the brakes failed going downhill. That was caput for them. We were driving behind them. Actually we had to finish Gloria, the old bird, off. She got out of the back seat. She was a game one!' Pete laughed. 'But there was compensation for us. Bevington-Ward finished up with no other relatives or friends, being a miser. Nobody missed them. He was a warning to us all. Look where you and your mum lived, in a shed.'

I didn't speak.

'So using the documents he signed, and a nifty French lawyer, the son of your piano teacher, a man called Nicholas – maybe he was a Bevington bastard, by the way, in fact maybe you were as well William, perhaps I'm wrong about your mum? – well, Nicholas was thrown out when your Uncle Andrew and Aunty Gloria caught him with their gardener's cock up his arse.

'Sorry to say, William, that Nicholas remembers you well. He doesn't like you, my son. He thinks you were

Bevington-Ward's favourite. He was jealous, all those special lessons and so on.'

I smiled. The lingering jealousy of Nicholas Prevert was good news, at least.

'Anyway, from our deal, Nicholas got twenty percent in cash, and your old German piano. Worth a bit, I was told. No good to us. Too expensive to move.'

I retched inwardly when I heard the fate of my beloved Bosendorfer. I could have been spared that news. 'We got Les Arcades and the smaller treasures, some good stuff. But Bevington-Ward had sold a lot over the years to keep his wife and children in the style they liked, and to keep them quiet. That's when we found those photos that Debra, known to you as Gillian Bevington-Ward, showed you. But there's a lot of secrets still hidden, a lot of money still to be claimed, rotting away somewhere. It is really most annoying!' Pete paused. Time for me to ask a question, however unwelcome: 'And Roy Harvey?'

'It took us years to find Harvey. Anyway we didn't know he was that big, until you saw him on that list and recognised the name. The hard old bugger never gave anything to us. But I guess we were too soft with him, as you turned out to be. You failed there. You let in Miss Eireann Canning and her gang.'

'Gang?'

'Yes, gang; bloody mob, terrorists, William. As I said, we have never been the only ones interested in the lost hoard of art and money. Some on the Republic side believe it's theirs by right. You fell in with them after that toe-rag traitor Colin – God I was tricked by him – wormed in with us. Swiss Joe, by the way, was the one that told him about your release. They planned a job together. Not that Colin did much other than draw diagrams, now I think what Swiss told me. I should have sussed him then. Of course we never thought they would let you out.

The whole thing seemed lost. But, when you did get out, telling everyone you were going straight, and when we found Roy Harvey, what a golden chance, wonderful ser-en-dip-ity, we had to restart. We fixed up an apartment. Colin said he could fix your computer. We gave you high class meals to keep you happy. We got you over to see the so-called Ward children, to see if you'd cough up anything. We had it all sorted. But then Colin, the scumbag, took all that Churchill and de Val-aer-reeyar stuff a stage further. I don't know why he cottoned on to that. Maybe he's some sort of amateur historian or something. Anyway he fed you all that nonsense about the 'Val-aer-reeyar Foundation', a set-up. He must have been in with some of the Irish all along. As I said to you in London, there ain't no such place as a Val-aer-reeyar Foundation, just, I guess, a plaque in a window, and a few posh desks and chairs.'

I didn't believe half of what I had heard. I tried to work out why I was being told these things. It was torture.

'Now, despite what I said to my friend on the phone earlier, I think it is only a half chance that Miss Eireann Canning and that piece of skinhead trash, Colin, got anything from Roy Harvey, anything about the money anyway. Whether they found out anything relevant to your Churchill story I don't know. Maybe we'll find out later today. But Roy Harvey was a disappointment to us. It seems that he's been half a corpse for twenty years, living off the fat of the land and the cunt juice of young nurses wanting ready cash. It must have tasted like Royal Jelly to Harvey, I guess. So maybe this is just another dead end. But, given the amount we've invested, it is worth a punt.'

The car had turned off the motorway and was slowing down.

'Otherwise, it's like you seem to be, son, my dear William Gilbey, up another blind alley, involved in another of life's many disappointments. Oh, I've had some of them, William, on this Irish palaver!' Pete shook his fat jowls.

The car had stopped. 'Time for a break, my son, like I promised you. By the way, I know you are carrying a revolver. The Rossi 38, I think. Artie last had it. But he lost it, left it in our apartment, I suppose. It's a great shooter. Don't use it, unless I tell you.'

## 7.6

It was three-thirty in the morning. As our car pulled up, several men emerged from the shadows. Two of them opened the car doors. I followed Pete inside what seemed to be a farmhouse.

A silent woman came from a kitchen. She gave us a smelly breakfast of eggs, bacon, black pudding and baked beans. Pete ate most of mine as well as his, drinking brandy from his flask as he did so. I looked at the greasy food and the bad, weak coffee, which, I guess, was probably no better than the powder of crushed acorns and chicory my mother said that she had been given to drink in the war.

Charlie, the driver, gulped down everything that was offered.

The bossman's monologue in the car was churning over in my mind. And the food had brought back another memory.

It was about the one breakfast I had taken with Uncle Andrew Bevington-Ward.

Early one morning, just before my fourteenth birthday, the maid walked across the lawn from Les Arcades. She told me that 'the master' wanted me.

In our little place my mother and I always breakfasted on bread with dripping and tea, just as we had in Burnley. The crockery wobbled on a tray on our bed. But His Lordship, my 'uncle', was sitting alone at a table in his ornate dining room, with separate little dishes of eggs, bacon, sausages, tomatoes, mushrooms, croissants, little pains au chocolat, brioche buns and various shapes of toasted bread in front of him. As I was ushered into the room, Mr Bevington-Ward was dipping a piece of a croissant into his coffee. The sight and the smell were extraordinary to me.

The maid took out a chair from under the table, so that I could sit down. Mr Bevington-Ward then put food onto a plate for me. I ate all that he gave me, but I left the two mushrooms.

Uncle Andrew Bevington-Ward glared at me. He said, 'Do you not like mushrooms?' I said, 'No'. He said, 'Why did you not say so? Fool! I hate waste.' He then told me that I was to go to the English Presbytery College in

Toulon that same day. 'Be grateful for the opportunity it gives you, and which you, a Gilbey, do not deserve.'

Another dreadful memory came to me, as I sat looking at Pete across the table. I thought for a moment that someone, maybe my father, was showing it to me. It was of the great serrated knife that the maid at Les Arcades used to slice up bread, being drawn slowly over the bulging flesh of Mr Bevington-Ward's throat, which in memory at least was strikingly similar to Pete's.

I had almost carried that out as my first murder. But I did not then have the technique, and maybe not the gumption. I remember thinking of my mother, and what would become of her. So I had smiled and said, 'Thank you, sir.' I left the room. Never to see Bevington-Ward again; never again to see my mother, who had gone to the village to fetch cleaning and balls of purple wool for the master's Christmas sweater, an annual present from his wife, assisted by Mademoiselle Prevert. A taxi (I used the house phone quietly and put it on the Bevington-Ward account) came for me before my mother returned.

As I thought of that taxi to the local French station I heard another car draw up outside. Pete was calm. He must have expected the visitors. He left the breakfast table. I stayed where I was for a few minutes. Then I moved to the window to look out. The car, a big Mercedes like Pete's, had a uniformed chauffeur in the front, and a bearded man next to him. The bearded man looked up at me. His eyes were intense and threatening. Pete had gone to sit in the back, next to a smaller man, who wore a bright, white shirt that caught the lights from the farmhouse and a green spotted tie. He was not relaxed like Pete though, or the men in the front. He was agitated, his hands waving in the air.

I sat down. Pete returned and instructed his henchmen. Again, he was calm and collected. Then, he told me that I had been right. 'Intelligence from good and reliable friends' was that 'my party' were on their way to Holyhead. There was a ten o'clock ferry to Dublin. There was already a 'welcome' for them at the terminal, if they could not be intercepted before then.

The meeting in the car, his greasy breakfast and the apparent progress of his plans seemed to mellow Pete. He said that he was working on the assumption that Eireann and her men knew that they were being followed. If necessary, if it got 'messy', the pursuit could be taken, Pete said, all the way to Ireland. That had been his basic plan 'and my friends agree.'

But Pete also said that, actually, he didn't want to take it that far; also he admitted distress again at having been taken in by Colin. 'I wish I could have that explained. I really do wish that, William. I liked Colin. He seemed to be my kind of man, devious and bent, but knowing his mind, the sort you and I could trust. It has upset me. I don't mind telling you that, William.

'But, despite that,' Pete continued, 'do you know I've been thinking about it, I wouldn't rule out some sort of sharing agreement with the Irish, including Colin. Maybe you could help out with that. Miss Eireann Canning seems to have taken a fancy to you, William. Of course, I can't bank on it: but if they have got the clues to what we're all after, a house, an address, a vault number, at the end of the day there'll be enough to go round. I'm not a greedy man am I?'

Charlie laughed.

'And, you know William, maybe they will have information to help on other things, even the Churchill story. Maybe that'll turn out to be true, who knows? Who the fuck cares, though?'

Charlie laughed again.

I dozed when we all got back in the car, although I was jolted awake a few times by the busier, slowing traffic, and then by light. It was a cloudy, rainy morning. Eventually I saw a sign for the Menai bridge. We were crossing into Anglesey, its Welsh name on the signposts 'Ynys Mon'.

'This, they say, is the sacred heart of Wales,' said Pete. 'All the Celts, the Welsh, the Irish, they are all romantics aren't they?' He made more phone calls. 'No sign of them. No sign. They were lost after the bridge apparently. Incompetent bastards, they couldn't run a piss-up in a brewery, now it comes to it. Yet, I've been impressed with their work before. I'll have to forgive them this time, I suppose. It may all end well. Let's hope so.'

We stopped in a lay-by. The sun was coming up. Pete leaned back.

'The Irish are said to be in a Toyota people-carrier. Maybe they've decided to lie low, for days, or maybe even longer. But, surely, your lady Eireann wants to get back to Ireland, William. After all these years of searching, who'd wait?'

I had another idea. I said to Pete that there was a

particular point in the story of the meeting between Churchill and Eamon de Valera, that they had met on a hill *'a promontory',* outside Holyhead and that they had stood by a plinth, bearing a sundial. Maybe Eireann, believing the story, maybe or maybe not, or just taking it as a clue, expected to find something there or perhaps she just wanted to connect with the past.

'Mr William Gilbey, you are a genius. You deserve a round of applause.'

Pete made more calls. He demanded local knowledge. Soon an answer came. We turned off a main road that led to the port of Holyhead. We drove into the countryside that surrounded it. The air was misty, and the roads empty. Pete ordered reinforcements.

At seven-thirty, we passed a Toyota, just short of the summit of a hill. It was parked next to a monument, a mushroom shaped stone plinth topped by a metal dial. Alongside it was a shelter with seating for walkers. There was a lay-by, with room for three or four cars. The scene must have been the one my father had described to me, yet there was little view to be had. Trees obstructed it. The whole panorama seemed smaller. The views here did not match the sweep of my father's story. Maybe he had exaggerated for effect. But, at least, the car matched the description Pete had been given.

The road bent round. We stopped. 'Well, they've seen us now.' Pete thought for a moment. Then Pete looked at me. 'Now, William, you have a chance to shine and to thank me for all I have done for you, and all that I have told you, and to earn, let's say two hundred thousand pounds, but given that you owe me about thirty thousand, let's call it one hundred and seventy thousand cash clear for you, in your hands tomorrow, in London. Then your troubles will be at an end and your future nice and comfy. I guarantee you that.' I nodded.

Pete gave his instructions carefully. 'So, William, just walk towards the Toyota, slowly, hands clear. Then, please, arrange an introduction for me with Miss Eireann Canning. Tell her this. No shooters, no fireworks, just a parley about our mutual interest. Tell her that it's been arranged for some roadwork signs to be put up on each side of the hill as diversions. So we won't be interrupted for an hour or so, until the local council gets a call from some nobby busybody and has to send out a van to sort it. We've got plenty of time to do what we have to do, *comprende*?'

I was set to go. But Pete, my bossman, to whom I apparently owed such thanks and loyalty, tugged my arm and held me back for a moment. He said slowly: 'If she won't do that now, tell her we will withdraw, and I can arrange that all involved will meet another time. Tell her that this is too sacred a place, in the shadow of our great leader Winny and her Irish leader Val–aer-reeyar for a pointless shoot-out. We'll live to fight another day. Understand?'

I did as I was told.

As I approached the Toyota, Eireann Canning came out of the car. I saw skinhead Colin and another man come out after her.

Eireann beckoned me towards the plinth. Colin and the other man crawled over the ground behind the car, out of my sight. I assumed that they were armed. 'Well, William, I can understand why you came here.' Eireann pointed to writing at the upper edge of the stone block, a sundial and faded panorama, that stood on the plinth. Some of the engraving on it was faded. But I could still read the top lines:

*'IN MEMORIAM: 'THE COLONEL'*
*A C WARD MCMXIX'*

'That must have been your guardian's grandfather. We know all about the cheating Wards, the Bevington-Wards as they became don't we? You know that the family came from Ireland to Flint in North Wales, across the Menai straits from here?'

'I hadn't thought much about all that, Eireann. It didn't seem important.'

Eireann said: 'I guess that the colonel commemorated here in 1919 must have survived the 1914 to 1918 war, just by a few months maybe. Another victim of a war started by the high and mighty. Yes, in his way, Colonel Ward was a victim. He may have died of the influenza, the plague after the war that killed so many Englishmen and Irishmen. This Colonel would not have been of my class, but I can still mourn him.'

I said: 'That shows, and I know, that you are at heart a good woman, Eireann.'

I said that, because that is what I felt.

I glanced back at Pete's car. What I really wanted was for everybody else – I sensed that there were more watchers, not just Pete's people and Eireann's, including Colin, but others, all of them please, I begged silently, please, to go and to leave us with our history. Maybe we could work something out. Maybe all could be explained once and for all: the hanging of my father, the suicide of my mother, the murder of Roy Harvey. If there is a God, as my mother believed, he must surely have a plan for all this.

Yet, much as I wished otherwise, again I knew the logic of our situation. There was only one path to be followed. I was an underling. I needed money, if I truly had no money of my own. I must play my part. I had no choice. Events had forced this on me. I had to give Pete's message to Eireann, quite straight. There had already been too much delay.

Thus, for the next critical moments, I became the voice of Pete the bossman. I became a spokesman for gangsters. I was no longer William Harrison Gilbey, the man that Eireann Canning seemed to want to help, the man who had started an innocent search, just a week before, to find out the truth about his father.

I said loudly what I had been asked to say. I asked Eireann if she would talk to Pete to see if an agreement could be reached. I said that there would be no fighting and no killing but a parley of truce, on the honour of all.

Eireann replied loudly, carrying to the people beyond me: 'William, do you think that a patriot like me, indeed a group of people like us, would do business with the thugs that keep you company? Do you really think that?'

I said quietly that, until a few hours earlier, I had had no idea what was at stake.

Eireann also replied in a quieter tone. 'What is at stake, William, is the honour of Ireland. I won't negotiate with your Pete, the one you call bossman. Everything I do is for the honour of Ireland. Tell him that.'

I asked Eireann why Roy Harvey had died.

'Yes, I know that Roy Harvey is dead. But I shed no public tears. Because he was one of those that had leeched off the Irish people, one who had lived a life of comfort, ease and riches, ending up in a home where they slavered over him. As long as my country is not united and truly free we have the right in the name of our people to let such trash die.' Eireann paused. Her voice mellowed 'But the truth is that, whatever he knew, he wouldn't say. No drugs would have dragged it out of him.'

I did not speak. Eireann turned and leant forward, her arms stretched over the plinth. After what seemed like several minutes (but was probably only one or two) she turned to me. She said that we should 'all go our separate ways, without violence'. She told me to go back to my car and to tell 'my friends' that. Eireann told me to say that we had reached an impasse, and that there was no purpose in a fight today: 'I offer a truce, on our honour.'

I went back to the car. I told Pete what Eireann had said. He nodded. He sent a text on his phone. A moment later, a bleep from the phone showed that the text had been received, and answered.

Pete turned to me. His words were quiet, and unemotional. 'Ok, William. Well, on her honour, on my honour, if that is how it's got to be. Honour is a great virtue. She's right, I suppose.'

Pete, the bossman, tapped Charlie on the shoulder and said: 'Turn round. As we drive past, I'll give her the thumbs-up, a good English sign of peace, *comprende?* She will understand that. *Comprende* Charlie, *comprende?*'

Pete then turned to me and spoke, still quietly: 'I'm glad that she has seen sense. Well done, William. No need to continue this. We've made the contact. We can continue later. There are other routes to the Irish gelt.'

Charlie did as directed. Pete opened the car window on his side as we passed the Toyota. Eireann now stood rigid between the car and the plinth. Pete called out: 'OK, OK, stand down, well done my Irish lady, Eireann.'

Our car went forward slowly. Then I heard a shot behind us, fired from the bushes. Pete's text had been a signal. Our car stopped. Pete smiled and coughed. Then he looked at me, and smiled again. Checking first in the rear-view mirror, he slowly opened the car door from the inside. He got out. He waved to me.

I followed him, shaking.

From within the undergrowth a uniformed man and two men in suits, in fact the men who had been in the Mercedes at the farmhouse, joined us. Coming close to them, I was certain that the bearded man was the man who had followed me, outside the probation office, in Dublin, and in London. A more incompetent agent could not be imagined.

The small man pointed to Eireann: 'Well, this is the end of the yellow brick road for her.'

A gag was quickly put over Eireann's mouth by the man in uniform. The small man then looked down at a body, which was of Eireann's friend the professor, I assumed. I looked at the calm, frozen face, no hint on it of the agony nor the dignity of death but a plain and ordinary face, one that I had seen before.

I remembered where: The Duke of Connaught. Was it Cyril or Ray or Larry, friends – so she had said – of my Gillian, or, as she was really called, Debra?

No, it was the surly Irish landlord Tony, the man who was 'good with our slate'. Another double-crosser, another fraud.

Skinhead Colin was nowhere to be seen. He must have made his escape. If he gets away, I thought, Colin could one day be a bossman. He is clever and treacherous.

The small man said to Pete: 'We see here the casualties of a war, a war of apparently never-ending troubles. I wish I understood the Irish.' Pete laughed. 'One day, Peter, I will go to that Emerald Isle, and I will make them see sense.'

'I'll come with you, Mr Robbins,' said Pete, laughing even louder, a triumphant laugh.

The bearded man then left the group to look at the sundial on its plinth. The small man, Robbins, handed over a briefcase to Pete, while calling to his colleague: 'Nicholson, no time to be a tourist! We must go.'

Nicholson said something and then came over and stared at me. I saw hatred in his eyes. His fists were clenched white, as mine clench when I am troubled or angry. Robbins said to him: 'Nicholson, you can leave him. Gilbey will be dealt with.' Then all three, Robbins, Nicholson and their murdering, trigger-happy military escort, got into their big car. They drove off, taking Eireann with them.

I would like to record that Eireann called after me,

or even looked at me. But she did not. I guess that she could not.

The noise of the vehicle receded. Pete waved after them, with a pointless, cheerful wave that reminded me of happy children in the junior school I had attended for a few years in Burnley. Memories of such triviality and happiness come at strange moments, it seems.

Pete opened the briefcase. It was stuffed with money.

It was at that point that I took out my revolver. I walked up to Pete.

I had made my decision in the car half an hour earlier. This so-called bossman, this arrogant Pete, had broken the trust that the Uncles must always have between each other. He had told me lies about my father and my mother. He had insulted my father's memory. He had told me that my jewellery was 'paste', when I knew differently. The jewellery that Eireann Canning wore was paste, not the jewellery that my father had given to my mother.

This Pete was also a bogus bossman, who had made me sign forged bank documents. I had never been allowed to meet Mr Imoglu. He might not even be real, but just an invention, like Pete's spreadsheets and graphs.

Pete was clearly an officer of the state, like Mr Piercey or Mr Ross. Or, at the least, he was in the pay of the state. And Robbins and his colleague Nicholson, the bearded man, they also were the state, the sort of people that my father hated, and who he had tried through his stories, and his death, to teach me to hate and to destroy.

This pretend bossman, this Pete with his big Churchillian cigars, his huge appetite, his temper, was as much one of my father's enemies as any politician or policeman. He was not fit for his job. I must protect the other Uncles. I must let Colin, or if not him then Swiss Joe, or even Artie, have a clean inheritance.

As Pete turned towards me, he saw the revolver. His face took on a look of surprise and irritation. He would never have imagined that anything could happen to him. He believed that his life was charmed.

I walked straight at Pete, the bogus bossman. I looked directly into his eyes. With my left hand, I lifted up the lapel of his black cashmere coat. I held the revolver with my right hand. My hands were shaking.

I shot Pete at close range. Then, grasping him, and turning him round as he fell, I shot again into the top of his spine. I then hit Pete on his head repeatedly with my revolver. I broke deep into his skull. I did this over and over again, until I thought that I could see his brain.

It was my easiest murder ever.

As that sweaty, over-fed, obese body collapsed dead, squirting blood, I said loudly:

*'Violence begets violence; evil begets evil; and good begets good.'*

# PART EIGHT

# 8

## 8.1

*the mémoire, posted to important persons, concluded.*

I went free from the confrontation outside Holyhead. There was no more shooting. Pete's henchmen seemed, for those moments at least, in awe of me. It was a natural gang reaction. 'Our bossman is dead, long live the new bossman!' Of course it helped that I had shown that I would kill in cold blood. Perhaps the henchmen had not thought that of me before.

But I had no wish to pretend to be the new bossman for anything other than a few hours. I told the others so. After deleting the directory of contact numbers, I threw down my 'special' mobile phone in front of all of them, as a sure sign of my withdrawal from their gang, for ever.

I told Charlie to take me immediately to the Holyhead to Dublin ferry terminal.

As I left, the clean-up ordered by Pete continued.

On arrival in Dublin a taxi took me to Moore Place. An old lady answered the door to number three. She was not wearing make-up, but I saw straightaway that she was the woman who had been Eireann's secretary at The De Valera Foundation on my earlier visit.

'Hello, Bridie,' I said. She looked at me sadly. She asked for news of Eireann.

I asked to come in. While she went to her kitchen to make tea I found a thin, dirty and unfashionable cream coloured scarf among the coats hanging in the hallway. I moved up behind Bridie. Using the piano wire I had brought, and her scarf, I killed her. Slowly and quietly.

It is extraordinary how one can become numb to violence. The tragedy processes. One act of violence follows another.

I left Bridie's body hanging over a sink. I made no effort to cover the crime.

After a pedestrian lunch at a Fearney's of smoked salmon followed by Atlantic sea trout 'on a bed of Irish fennel', I took a fast ferry back to Holyhead. I then went by taxi and evening train to Chester. It was strange arriving in the famous cathedral city, which I had only previously experienced through my father's brief account. But Chester produced no immediate inspiration. It seemed anonymous and dull in the late evening. My spirits were low, a reaction to the earlier excitements I suppose.

I checked in at the Grosvenor Hotel, as recommended by the taxi driver from Chester station. Might the Grosvenor have been the fine hotel where my father had stayed on his way back from Holyhead, years before?

I ordered wine and food. Both were excellent. I sat at the desk in my room working on this mémoire. It was a big task. So many names to remember, and to spell. So many events to recreate.

I must have dozed off. When I woke I saw two figures framed against the bedroom wall, as if in a vision. They were two men walking across a hill. One was waving a cigar; the other, tall and serious, carried a thin case. I need not tell you who I thought they were. They leaned for a moment against a sundial.

Then the mists surrounding the vision cleared. In front of me stood my father. He was exactly as I remembered him when I was eight. He was wearing a collarless shirt, with a stained front, and wide trousers with baggy turn-ups. There was a smell in the room of cigarette smoke and sweat.

'Do not believe them, William,' he said in a confident voice, with a Lancashire accent that I had almost forgotten. 'Look at my neck.'

I could see red marks on the bottom of his neck, in a circle; and whiter marks higher up.

'Do not believe them, William. They took me from my cell. They gave me a last smoke. A parson prayed over me. Then I was killed by hanging. I shat myself as the rope burned through me.

'William,' my father continued, 'I knew too much. I had said too much. The powers that be wanted me out of the way. The truth is still to be revealed, even if it cannot be told by you. Forgive me, son, if you have been deceived by me, or if your life has not been as it should have been. I cannot now help you directly. That is forbidden.'

I tried to speak.

'Now, don't say anything, son. You still have a mission to complete. You will understand, after I have told you a story.'

I felt a light hand, a gentle and loving hand, over my face. It did not smell any more of my father. Maybe, in the afterlife, there are only the scents of goodness, the smells I still link with the time of my childhood, the brief time of demi-paradise in Les Arcades.

'I want to complete that story, the one your grandmother, my mother, told me, the one you started to tell Mr Ross. But he was too arrogant and impatient to listen and you never heard the full version.

'Your grandma Charlotte died young. Sadly, you never met her. I hope, William, that you may now see the story in a different light and that, in its fuller form, it may reveal to you something new.'

I could only listen, like Roy Harvey could only listen when I first questioned him, my eyes closed to help my concentration, my fists occasionally clenching at my side, as my father told me his story.

When he had finished, and I had snapped awake again, I found, by some miracle, that the second part of the story had been written down as part of my mémoire, exactly as you have it here.

'This is the story that I must complete, William. I told you, and you told Mr Ross, how at the big house, the housekeeper and his wicked wife had made an innocent girl into a devil for their own pleasure. A more innocent and honest victim had never been seen. But, do you know, no-one ever dared protest or make amends to her, she who was made mute by her pain and shame, she who never smiled again, or who enjoyed proper food or drink? Instead, she was confined to a room converted from a shed, which lay down a hill next to the gardeners' outhouses. Every day, scraps of food and water would be taken to her.

'Once a week, the poor girl would be taken to a nearby village, they said to take cleaning or shoes to be mended, and to buy lace and silks and other fine objects. But, really, they wanted to show the girl off, first to the shopkeepers; but then for other men, while the housekeeper's husband got drunk at a pub. Local children would also be encouraged by their parents to come and laugh at the mute girl, especially if it was raining. They would taunt her with the slugs and the snails that appeared with the heavy rain they have in Flintshire.

'Once a month, at a certain time of the month, the girl was brought up to the house and made to play the harp for the housekeeper's husband, and to do other things for him, it was said. New servants were taken into the girl's simple shed and shown her breasts, and the Devil's mark on the girl's back, the 666, as a warning.

'My mother – your grandmother Charlotte, William – she kept quiet about all this, to her lifelong regret, she said, because other jobs couldn't be had at her time of life, after she became a widow. She told me of her own guilt about this. She wept in front of me, although at least she knew that she had, at the outset of the troubles, saved the girl's life. Yet, might it have been better had that poor girl died under the first flogging?

'The master and the mistress of the house, he now with a knighthood and celebrated in the press, and she known as Her Ladyship, carried on living as though nothing had happened. They never spoke about the girl, or to her. Their house was so big, and the shed so far away out of the line of sight of their bedrooms, that they needn't give her any thought. They spent their time writing to the former President Theodore Roosevelt, The Colonel as he was known after he left office. They even put up monuments to him. They implored him to visit again, so that they would get the reflected glory that they thought they deserved. You have seen one of the monuments, William. But Mr Roosevelt never replied, even when he came to England for the funeral of King Edward in 1910. So, the master and mistress became embittered and lonely. They changed the name of the house back to Flint Manor. They spoke only to the evil housekeeper or his wife. They conspired with them. They treated the few other staff with contempt. No-one visited the house.

'When the innocent girl died, she was only sixteen, your grandmother said, she was buried in the grounds next to the darkest and dankest of the house's storehouse and cellars. An old drunk from the village who dug graves was at the internment, together with your grandma, who put on the resting place a small wreath of daisies and clovers.

'William that was the end of the story I originally told you. But now I can complete it.

'Something miraculous happened. The curate who had put the girl in the house had long moved on to a better paid living. One day, he became a bishop. He remembered the girl, and asked after her. At first, no-one would tell him the truth. Your grandma heard of this. It opened her heart. She wrote to Bishop James. He was so filled with remorse and anger when he heard of what had happened that he visited the graveside. He spent some private time there. He ordered a reburial. When the coffin was placed in the ground, he lowered with it an iron box containing jewels and all his worldly wealth, amounting to tens of thousands of pounds, worth hundreds of thousands of pounds in our day, William. Indeed, maybe more. Stones were then placed over the coffin to try to prevent thieves getting to it. The Bishop also solemnised the place. He preached that anyone who violated it would be cursed, and would never leave Purgatory.

'Bishop James then left to spend the rest of his life in a monastery. The world was too evil a place for him, as it is for most godly people.

'Of course, as soon as Bishop James left, the Master and Mistress, and the housekeeper and his wife, who had hidden inside the house, scrambled to unearth the treasure, like four desperate wolves. There was no class distinction between them. The two men used shovels and picks, as though they were Irish navvies. The women pushed and swore at them, if they relented for a moment. But, as they neared the treasure, the heavens roared in the greatest thunderstorm Flintshire has ever seen. Bolts of lightning struck the house. Great hailstones, like shrapnel, tore into the garments of the women and blinded the men. But all of them carried on scrambling and digging. They didn't even notice that a fire had started in one of the dining rooms. They ignored the cries of fire. They were obsessed, and blinded, by greed.

'The fire roared through the house. But still they ignored it. Then, with one great lightning bolt, all four of them were struck dead. Your grandma saw them falling into the pit of the Hell they had created. Their bodies lay on top of the great stones still protecting the privacy and sainthood of the girl with the so-called devil's mark, 666. Her resting place and her worldly wealth was preserved. The house and all it represented lay in ruins. No-one has ever found the treasure. No-one will find it now.'

## 8.2

As I re-read in the morning the astonishing and moving ending of the Welsh 'devil girl' story, dictated to me and written as if in my own hand by my father, I remembered that the envelope I had picked up in Kensington, addressed to me and left next to my computer, was unopened in my bag. This is the letter that it contained:

*'My dear William, Mr Gilbey,*

*I have composed and printed this letter to you on the computer that Colin set up for you. I have written this hurriedly, with no time for correction, in the hour while you have been out meeting a friend. From the look in your eye and the smart clothes you put on (what a contrast you are to the dressed-down in London!) I could tell that it was a special meeting for you.*

*I am sorry, first of all, that I could not have become that friend myself. I have been deeply attracted to you, by your gentleness, your honesty and your search for your father. You are a gentleman of a kind now rarely encountered in any of our islands. I was touched by your troubles and, although my mind was far away when you told me – I am so sorry – by the sadness of your story of your mother's death. A deeper relationship was not meant to be, however, if only because you may well already have discovered that what we had begun was founded on a series of lies. They were lies that I carried through, for the sake of a greater good.*

*My name is not Eireann Canning. It is Justine Costello. I am not Director of The 'de Valera Foundation', as there is no such thing, but I deeply admire 'The Long Fellow', Mr de Valera, one of Ireland's greatest patriots. I have been a part of the true Irish nationalist movement since I was a girl. My mother was English, born in Birkenhead, and called Honour. She despised the Americanisation of Britain. She would have been even more horrified at the way Ireland has become equally 'globalised', and how it has lost its soul – had she not died young.*

*I, and others of our group including my mentor Bridie who you met in Dublin, became interested in you a few years ago because of your father's links – which I think now were unknown to you – to a gang that stole and extorted money and objects rightly belonging to Republic families, over a period of many years, but especially during the second war. Colin says that he found this out through the man you know as 'Swiss Joe'.*

*You do not need to know the full history of this. Only that we hoped that, after your release, you would* lead us to one or more of the leaders, the people who know where the ill-gotten loot is that belongs to the Irish people. Others believed the same thing, and that has led us into such trouble and violence. I do not eschew violence in the defence of liberty and as a patriot. But I regret the necessity of it, as every human being should.

William, you led us to Roy Harvey, who we think was a key person in those crimes. Sadly, as you will now know, he died before he could tell us anything. I do not think I, or you, are, in truth, to blame for his death, any more than those who kept him on extreme medication are to blame. I will pray to the Almighty God for forgiveness if it should be thought otherwise, especially if you, William, would ever think such a thing of me. Mr Harvey simply could not take the trip we imposed upon him. I did my best. But he died in my arms.

I suggest that, when you get this note in an hour's time, you either call an ambulance and the police, or you let those who helped us to remove him from his care home handle the matter. I am sure that, ultimately, it will be decided that Mr Harvey died of natural causes; and that you will not be held to account. If I hear otherwise, then you have my word that, on my mother's name of Honour, I shall make the position known to the authorities. I would move Heaven and Earth to have you absolved. I know that you have a criminal past, William. But I also know that you are a good and reformed man.

We discussed your love of the work and ideas of Ezra Pound. One of my associates sent me this statement of Pound's, which sums up our all too common *predicament, does it not: 'the real trouble with a war is that it gives no-one a chance to kill the right people.' So it may ever be with Ireland.*

*My dear William, you came to me with a story. We should all listen to our parents' stories.*
*I urge you to continue to research your father's and to promote it, as I will.*

*I do not think your father lied to you. I believe with all my passion and all my faith, and maybe against all reason, that Winston Churchill met Eamon de Valera on that hilltop in Wales in July 1940, and that it is one of the great untold stories of the twentieth century. Our only regret should be that their meeting came to nothing and that the issues they were both boldly prepared to face, even the issue of war between the Axis and the Allies itself, were not then resolved. What a better world that you and I might then have known.*

*One day, William, I am sure that we will meet again. We will beg forgiveness together. Interceded by Our Saints and by Our Holy Mother Mary, we will wait on the judgement of Our Lord.*
*To then, and to a better world.*

*Your true and ever friend, JUSTINE COSTELLO*

Yes, I thought, the guess that I had suppressed, the experienced criminal's instinct, the smell for the truth, was right. Those marks, made by an electric iron on Roy Harvey's body, had been burnt there after he had died. I knew it. After all, anyone but an arrogant and lazy bossman would have remembered to unplug the iron! My 'Eireann', my 'Justine', was not guilty of the desecration of Roy Harvey. The pleasure in that sort of torture was the work of a criminal like me, a bossman, maybe sadistic because of the role I and other Uncles had required of him, but vindictive and inhuman still.

I dwelt also on my father's story. I have already speculated in this mémoire about the nature of my guardians, trying to identify those who were looking after me, as we are all looked after in some way. Now I also wondered whether there was a bishop in my story, a man or woman who would rescue me, maybe even sacrifice their livelihood for me. Was there someone who would smite my enemies? Or is that just for fairy or religious tales?

I had thrown away my mobile phone, so I had no way of contacting Eireann/Justine, to ask her advice, even if she was free to speak. Nor could I have saved her from whatever evil was planned. There was now no-one I could have trusted. I was surrounded by corruption and fraud. I resolved that my only remedy, and my tribute to Justine and to the apparently innocent Bridie, lay in acts of revenge that must surely bring all our stories to attention, in Britain and in Ireland, so that others can form a judgement. I have been left with no option. Murder is my profession, after all.

Having this certainty of purpose is elating, and inspiring.

I have had ten copies of this handwritten mémoire (and the letter from Justine) photocopied for posting to newspaper editors and other important people. A helpful concierge at the Grosvenor, George, opened up the Business Centre there especially for me early this morning, for two fifty pound notes. He provided the envelopes, weighed a sample, and sold me the correct stamps.

'NOT FOR PAY: BUT FOR TRUTH'

*William Harrison Gilbey, to be posted at Euston station, June 22 2014*

## 8.3

*These additional pages are attached to two copies of the mémoire to be posted to the Cabinet Office and to Mrs Llewellyn of the Probation Office.*

Yesterday, Sunday morning, after I left the hotel, I planned to catch a slow series of trains from Chester to London, where I am now completing these pages. My departure was delayed. Half-way from the Grosvenor Hotel to Chester station I realised that I had taken only the copies of my mémoire from the Business Centre of the hotel. I had left the original, some two hundred and fifty pages in all, with George, the concierge. I therefore had to get the taxi to turn back to the Grosvenor Hotel. I needed to keep my own mémoire!

My return was what Pete the bossman would have called '*ser..en..dip-ity*'. I walked into the reception to find Mr Harry Ross in earnest conversation with George. They were looking through my material.

'I won't pretend that this is a coincidence,' Mr Ross said. 'You must have been up early.'

I nodded. Obviously he had followed me to Chester (although I discovered later that he had not been to Dublin). But Mr Ross was a lazy man who slept late.

Anyway, it was a good thing that I had caught him with the original of my story. I had already prepared a copy for the Cabinet Office, where Mr Ross's card showed he worked. His was one of two I was saving to be posted later. But I didn't want Mr Ross, or anyone else at that point, to have an earlier sight of it. That wasn't in my plan.

It was critical that on this day of all days that I should retain control. I wanted my final plans followed, not interrupted either by officers of the state, incompetent hotel staff, or by old bitches who bang on walls. I had been in an elevated mood when I reflected on my father's story. I had felt blessed and privileged. I was not going to allow an incompetent man like Mr Ross to distract me.

Mr Ross then said that he had heard from Mr Piercey that I had gone north, and that he had decided to follow me so that we could 'share any leads'. He said, 'We are both investigating the same story aren't we?' and 'Clearly, Mr Gilbey, there is a Chester and a Flintshire angle.' I nodded at this nonsense. I could not believe that he thought that I believed him. I had not told Mr Piercey anything. But what could I say? I let Mr Ross believe that I accepted his version of events.

The concierge, George, was apologetic about his error in retaining my original. I forgave him. I gave him another £50 note. Out of relief, I said.

Mr Ross asked me if I was still planning to return to London. I said yes. He then asked if he could accompany me. 'Why not?' I said. 'I am travelling first class, though.' Mr Ross smiled 'Well, normally the government travels as cheaply as possible. But for you, I mean to have the pleasure of accompanying you, I will make an exception.'

So Mr Harry Ross and I travelled together. We made polite conversation. I talked about France. I told him about my plans to be a chef or a concert pianist. I told Mr Ross about my time with Guiseppe Carnarolo, although I did not tell him the ending. I did not want to alarm him.

I told Mr Ross about my first concert, which is otherwise not in this mémoire. It was at a piano festival organised by Mademoiselle Prevert at the Mairie of St Laurent du Var. I was supposed to be the star attraction, playing her favourite piece, Beethoven's 'Moonlight' sonata. But I was distracted by the murmurings and shuffling of the audience, which consisted mainly of parents of other pupils of the local music teachers. None of them could concentrate on music, as I have always concentrated. So, midway through the piece, the demented noises of coughing and whispering defeated me. I slammed down the piano lid. Hard. Two of the strings broke. When I looked down, only Nicholas Prevert was looking at me, and laughing. Mademoiselle, Mr and Mrs Bevington-Ward and my mother all looked away. That was the end of that career. Since then I have found it impossible to play properly in front of an audience. My music is inner music.

Mr Ross was sympathetic. He talked about his parents and the school and university he had attended. He asked me a few sly questions about my plans. But I did not respond. Occasionally we snoozed. We both drank coffee and ate sandwiches. We leafed through one of the big complementary newspapers. I wondered whether to tell Mr Ross a proper story, but he had not been receptive on our first meeting. Then I teased Mr Ross. As we were stopped at Milton Keynes, I pushed across the table my mémoire. I suggested that he might read it. This he began, 'with pleasure', he said. He could not contain his enthusiasm. He became animated, for the first time in the journey. He was certainly a fast reader. I noticed across the table that Mr Ross was coming to the point where he made an appearance. I interrupted him, to his obvious annoyance, although he remained polite. I asked whether he would like me to go to the buffet car and get some more coffee. He said, politely, just as I expected, that instead he would go. When he did this, I stood up and went off in the opposite direction, taking my bags with me.

I knew that Mr Ross would follow me. The train was not crowded, so my plan worked well. I simply left the bags in a rack and across some seats further up the train. I then found an empty toilet. It was fitted for the disabled so it was not as small a space as is found on an aircraft. I knew what to do. I had the necessary materials with me, including piano wire from the badly maintained piano in Twickenham, in my holdall.

I observed Mr Ross, whistling and looking very cheerful. I think that was in his nature. He was an agent of the state but not otherwise a bad man. Mr Ross passed the toilet compartment. He found the bags and then went to sit down. But I managed to attract him, and call him over, indicating that I had a problem and needed help. Obviously he could not ignore me. I need not record what I did. You will find out soon enough.

Suffice it to say that Mr Ross did not get off the train when it reached Euston.

On arrival there I posted most of the copies of the mémoire, knowing that there was no collection until today, Monday.

Mid-afternoon I took a taxi to Twickenham. I went into my house and played the piano. I chose the third movement of the fourth Beethoven concerto, humming to myself the orchestral parts. At first there was no reaction from next door. Then I heard a door banging shut. The woman had probably been to church or had been to a whist drive, or wherever *old bitches gone in the teeth*', as Ezra Pound called them, amuse themselves in London on Sunday afternoons. I knocked on the bitch's door quietly. She seemed reluctant to open, but then curiosity got the better of her. She opened the door slightly. I pushed in and performed the same service for her as I had for Bridie Costello in Dublin. I did not cover anything up. So I could not risk returning to either Kensington or Twickenham. Instead I stayed at the hotel at Charing Cross station. I ate a last dinner, of twelve Breton oysters with a bottle of Laurent Perrier champagne and two glasses of armagnac, at Sheekeys near Leicester Square, one of the restaurants on my earlier list. I close here as I leave the hotel to post the last two copies. I have one last act to commit. As I have already written through this mémoire I will face the people's verdict.

*W H GILBEY, Charing Cross Hotel, London, June 23 2014*

# PART NINE

# 9

## 9.1

*Monday June 24 2014, 10am:*
*MI5 HQ, Vauxhall, London.*

'This is a distressing occasion, Wilfred.'

'I agree that the premature death of any young man, especially a colleague, is a cause of distress, Sir Rory.' Wilfred Robbins wrapped his right arm around his left shoulder. He adjusted his glasses. 'But, at least, provided we are consistent, the death should cause us no undue embarrassment. The discovery was handled efficiently.'

'The circumstances were extraordinary, weren't they? Why did the train company not find anything before we did?'

'It appears that the train was taken out of service at Euston station on arrival at about four o'clock yesterday afternoon. Our operator immediately noted the static nature of the signal sent by Ross's special telephone. I was consulted. I had just returned from my own trip north. I was in the office to write things up. We were able to get to the locked toilet compartment just before the train cleaners. Ross had been garrotted, using what appeared to be piano wire. He had been bound and gagged first. The technique is well known to us.'

Sir Rory shuddered.

Wilfred Robbins continued: 'It was cold blooded murder. But I made the position clear to the police. They will not cause us any difficulty. As far as the family is concerned, Ross has been killed on active service. They need know no more.'

'I understand. Well done for all of that, Wilfred. Sir Brian and Mr Cameron will be grateful. But, you say that Gilbey had murdered in this way before?'

'He claims to have murdered a man in an aircraft toilet. It is in his mémoir, which I read overnight. Some of the stuff is pretty fanciful, in my view. However, he certainly knows how to murder, swiftly and efficiently.'

'Why was Ross travelling with Gilbey?'

'I sent him up on Saturday evening to intercept Gilbey in Chester. Gilbey had been followed by us and our Irish friends throughout. I wanted Ross to confront Gilbey himself to see whether he had found anything useful that we would not get from Miss Costello.'

'Did he?'

'Apparently not. Or, if he did, he did not communicate it to us. His only messages before Gilbey trapped him were to a friend in the office.'

Sir Rory raised an eyebrow.

'They were of no substance, Sir Rory.'

'Yet you were confident earlier, Wilfred – indeed it has been the whole basis of our involvement – that Gilbey had inherited a store of knowledge from his father.'

'We seem to have been wrong about that, as indeed were others.'

'In fact, it may be that Gilbey knows even less than we do?'

'That is possible, Sir Rory. His mémoire, as he calls it, is full of tales and fantasies. But nothing concrete, on my first reading anyway. I have arranged for other colleagues to read it more carefully, word by word. There may yet be clues.'

Sir Rory raised his eyebrows. Wilfred Robbins adjusted his glasses again.

'Where is Gilbey now?'

'He is at the Charing Cross Hotel. He is being watched, of course. But my instructions are not to intervene, yet. He may lead us to other people, or material. Gilbey has already finished off one old enemy of ours, in Dublin. If we leave him one more day he may dispose of others.'

'He planned a wide distribution of the mémoire?'

'Yes. But all the copies he posted were intercepted immediately. It is essential that we have any remaining copies and the original, and any other material. The places he has been staying in, as well as the train he was on, are being searched by our people.'

'Oh well, good.' Sir Rory poured more darjeeling. He spoke quietly 'You know, Wilfred, that I could never be as cold as you about personnel matters. I am sorry to say that, but it is true. Perhaps you should have known that the obsessive William Gilbey, this spinner of tales, would turn violent when he encountered Ross. I do not feel responsible myself, but it is me that has to carry the can. All that training wasted, our being economical with the truth and so on.'

Robbins said nothing.

Sir Rory continued: 'You say that we have a transfer request from Morgan Janvir. Ross's death has upset him?'

'I called to tell him of the incident early this morning. Janvir is, yes, most upset. I could use the word unhinged.'

'It would be tiresome to lose the services of two trained staff, especially Janvir, who is highly talented. Where is he?'

'He came in an hour ago. I have given him gardening leave. So now he should be on his way home. He seemed content with that, as he has other problems to deal with. He told me last week that his father had been admitted to a care home, Foxdale Lodge in Esher.'

'I know it well. Indeed, our personnel people would have recommended it to him.'

'As you also know, Sir Rory, the father was a political refugee from Iran. But I think he and Morgan hardly speak.'

'That is sad. But of course we rely nowadays so much on the depth of information we hold on everyone, including all our staff. We cannot rely on duty and deference. The Iranian connection gives us that hold over the Janvirs. Such holds are useful.'

'Surely.'

'And the agent we called Colin?'

'He carried off his triple role. We need more men like him.'

'And Miss Ingham, Gilbey's prison confidante?'

'She has been assigned to another case.'

'An extraordinary woman. So, once again and despite certain – how shall I describe them, Wilfred, *hiccups* – we have acted efficiently and have defended the good name of the state. The necessary national myths have been preserved. Even if we have not finally solved the puzzle of the missing documents, nor all of the missing art and money. As you say, more information may come from Gilbey.'

Sir Rory paused. Wilfred Robbins adjusted his glasses, in his characteristic way.

'We shall just have to carry on, anyway. Let us hope that your confidence in Gilbey is rewarded. By the way, do not forget, Wilfred, to brief Douglas Smythe, our excellent public relations man, so that he can find lines to explain the various incidents. He will put a breach into any leaks.'

'Of course, Sir Rory. Smythe is very inventive isn't he?'

Very much so, yes. As usual in his profession he will lie as much as he needs to. That is how he made his fortune in the commercial world. It occurs to me, incidentally, that there may be some way that he can turn the discovery of the Sagamore connection to our advantage, should there be any local publicity about the events there. One Ministry or another may be able to claim some credit for rediscovering the local history during civil defence manoeuvres. That sort of thing.'

Wilfred Robbins put down his teacup, shakily. 'Incidentally, although Nicholson could not translate the Latin part of the inscriptions, he saw straightaway that the plinth at Holyhead commemorates not a member of the Ward family, as is now assumed locally, but the American President Theodore Roosevelt, known as The Colonel, who died in 1919. He had visited Flint Manor as a young man while on a tour of England and Wales. For a time the Wards had even changed the name of their house to that of his house Sagamore in Virginia, to play on the connection, and to curry favour.'

Sir Rory smiled.

Robbins continued. 'William Gilbey's grandfather was a chauffeur in service at that time. He and Gilbey's father seemed to have continued to use the Sagamore name – mainly in mockery, I suspect. Anyway, Nicholson is a keen amateur historian, as well as having a policeman's photograohic memory. He remembered a reference to a memorial at Holyhead in one of the American biographies. It is doubtful whether any of the Roosevelts ever visited the site and, sadly, Flint Manor, or Sagamore, was destroyed in the war, and built over. There are now tower blocks where it used to stand. So, although I have made arrangements for the area to be checked, I doubt if there is any possibility of our finding anything more, even if it was used for storage of a large part of the Irish stuff.'

Sir Rory said, 'That is a great pity. The name had long intrigued us. I had hoped that we might find there both a treasure trove, and the final documents we have been seeking so long. You thought that Gilbey could lead us to what he called 'saggermore'. Well, he has, but not in a very productive way. That is really a pity, for you, especially for you, Wilfred, after so many years.'

Wilfred Robbins nodded. He regretted, and also feared, Sir Rory's disappointment.

'So, what is next for you, Wilfred?'

'I will go now to meet Gilbey's probation officer, Piercey. At the same time Nicholson will see Piercey's boss, a Mrs Llewellyn. Gilbey's papers confirm various things we knew. It will help us ensure that there is no further involvement from the probation service, nor any other meddlers. It is time we ran things our way, complete and uninterrupted.'

Sir Rory nodded.

'Later, Sir Rory, I will travel to our location near Birmingham to assist in the interview of Miss Costello, before her rendition.'

Sir Rory smiled. Wilfred Robbins's fingerprints were on this case, and its aftermath, not those of Sir Rory Armitage.

## 9.2

*Hendon*

An hour later Sir Rory's car drew up outside a small terraced house.

A policewoman answered the door. She showed Sir Rory into a tiny room, apparently the main living room. A woman remained seated, sobbing. The man of the house, in open-necked shirt and stained trousers, stood up. 'Please sit down, Mr Ross.' Sir Rory sat down as well. 'Mr and Mrs Ross, this is a very sad duty.'

Mrs Ross dabbed her eyes with a little embroidered handkerchief. Mr Ross asked Sir Rory if he would like some tea. Sir Rory said that he was sure that the policewoman would make some for all of them. He said that he preferred his tea without milk. The officer went into the kitchen.

'I want you to know how brave your son Harry was. We had to send him on a mission, a very secret mission, in the Middle East. And I want you to know how valuable his work was. He was one of the officers I personally held in the highest esteem. Later today we will announce the sad deaths of several of our military, young men and women. Harry will be listed among them. No further information will be given. Of course we rely on you to honour Harry's memory and to safeguard his true role. He told me often how proud you were of his work.'

'We knew nothing,' said Mr Ross.

'Only, that it was very secret,' added Mrs Ross.

'And so it must remain,' said Sir Rory, wiping his eye with a large white handkerchief.

After tea and further tears Sir Rory was able to tell the Rosses the pension and other special arrangements that had been made.

Tom and June Ross thanked Sir Rory. They had never expected to meet anyone so grand, or so generous. It just showed how valued, and how important, their only son's work was.

Rory Armitage returned to Vauxhall, to look at a Monet just delivered. His job was completed. How he wished that he could rely on others in his command to do their jobs as well, or at least as authoritatively, as he did his.

At the same time as Sir Rory was in Hendon, Wilfred Robbins was drinking milky coffee in a nasty cafe near Twickenham station. Lloyd Piercey was late. Then a hand lightly touched Wilfred's shoulder. 'Sorry, court business, had to leave my car at the office, parking hopeless at court. But no taxis. You must be Wilfred.'

'Indeed, I am Wilfred Robbins. Let us go somewhere quieter.' Robbins's left arm rose and scratched the back of his right shoulder in a monkey-like movement that amused Lloyd Piercey.

'Stranger and stranger,' Lloyd Piercey thought. 'Life is becoming stranger and stranger.' He had wanted to get a coffee to take away, but Robbins was out of the door before he could do so.

'I suggest, Wilfred, that we go to Gilbey's place near here. I have not been able to contact him today, so I should check up on him anyway. If he is there, or if he turns up, we could find somewhere else.'

'Yes, that is where I expected we might go. I am confident that Gilbey will not be there.'

Lloyd Piercey was curious about Robbins's confidence, but said nothing. As he opened the door to the terraced house Piercey said, 'Shall I try to find some coffee for you, Wilfred?'

'No,' said Robbins. 'I do not have much time, Mr Piercey. Frankly, I never have much time. I do not intend to waste it on you. Please sit down. I will remain standing. Please listen carefully. Please take full note of what I say to you.'

Lloyd Piercey sat down. 'What is all this about?'

'Just listen. Mr Piercey, the critical thing you need to know is this. I am an officer of that part of the essential security of the state which, in the normal course, you need to know nothing about. Don't smile Mr Piercey. Just believe that everything we do is in the interests of our country. That includes your interests.'

Piercey continued to smile.

'You may chose to believe me, or not to believe me on that point, Mr Piercey. But that is of no consequence to me. All you have to do is to listen to me. Then, you must agree to remain silent.'

'Are you threatening me?' Lloyd Piercey's mood, after a good morning in court, was changing. This could not be a wind-up, surely? He fingered his mobile phone.

'Listen, Mr Piercey. I am telling you today that you are being relieved of the case of William Gilbey. To you, he is now a man of no importance. As of today, he does not exist for you. All the files on Mr Gilbey are at this moment being removed from your office by your colleague Mrs Llewellyn, under the supervision of my colleague Mr Nicholson. They will be sent to join the copious files that we already hold on Gilbey. All traces of electronic and mobile communication between you and Gilbey are also being removed. William Harrison Gilbey will now be as much a non-person to you as his father Herbert.'

'This is outrageous, ridiculous, nonsense.' Lloyd Piercey could hardly find words. This was a bad dream. 'I want to speak with Mrs Llewellyn.' Piercey pressed a speed dial number on his phone. He got an engaged signal.

'Engaged? Mrs Llewellyn? Yes. It will remain engaged as long as I am here. You will then be able to speak with her, to find out what she has agreed with my colleague.'

Lloyd Piercey stood up. Robbins waved his hand in the air as if to say 'don't be tiresome'.

'Don't try and leave, Mr Piercey. I have people outside.'

Lloyd Piercey opened the front door. Indeed, there was a man, a smiling but well-built man, standing in the pathway. Piercey shut the door and turned back.

'Calm down, Mr Piercey. Things could be worse for you.'

Robbins helped Piercey back onto the sofa. 'Because I can offer you something very important. All we want is your silence, nothing else. In return I will give you *our* silence about your private life, and also silence about Mrs Llewellyn.' Robbins smiled. 'Listen carefully, Mr Piercey. We know every detail about your relationship with Mrs Llewellyn. That is our starting point. It must be yours too.'

Lloyd Piercey's stomach sank. But, as far as he knew, he neither moved nor made a noise. He just listened, as if to a voice in a nightmare.

'I repeat, Mr Piercey, that we know every detail. Most people would find what you have done, and are still planning, despicable. But I am not a moral censor. I am just a practical man who serves his country. So, if you chose not to forget Mr William Gilbey, and everything that he told you, I promise you that this will happen: every detail of your behaviour, every detail of Mrs Llewellyn's behaviour, the locations of your sex acts, here in this house for example, using people in your care like poor Mr Gilbey as a cover, will be made known in as damaging a way as possible. I also read in a report last night that Gilbey claims you have been dealing in drugs, which presumably Mrs Llewelyn also knew about.'

Lloyd Piercey shook his head. 'No, no: drugs never!'

'Well, maybe not, but does the truth matter in every detail, when a villainous, lying reputation is exposed? We have definitive evidence about the intercourse, the fetishes, the oral sex in Mrs Llewellyn's office and yours, in cars, in car parks, in the toilets of a public house. We have all the details of your ideas of moving first to the flat upstairs here, and then eloping to France, abandoning your families, including young children. Your recent trysts have been photographed. Your text messages are all on file. If we have to, we can release them, slowly for maximum impact, to the press, on the internet, to your wider family and friends. When we do that, there is no turning back. Believe me. You and Mrs Llewellyn will lose everything. Most of all you will lose all your respect. We will see to that. It will not be a matter of simple divorce. We will make it a scandal. You may as well spend the rest of your lives in the hostels to which you send your clients.' There was a long, long silence. Lloyd Piercey's stomach sank further. He could no longer feel anything. This was not a nightmare. It was real.

'In our service, which in my view is the highest service of the state, Mr Lloyd Piercey, we have long memories. We deal with matters that cross generations. I will personally see to it that, if you do not co-operate and remain silent – that is all, I repeat, all that I am asking, just that you remain silent – then yours and Mrs Llewellyn's lives, yours and her families' lives, will be destroyed.

'For ever, Mr Piercey.'

## 9.3

*Hammersmith, London*

At eleven-thirty, exactly, William Gilbey entered the Inner London Probation Office through the car park. He remembered the security code used by Mr Piercey on their first meeting ten days earlier. Mr Piercey's car was parked in the same place. The same code opened the door to the staircase that led up to Mr Piercey's office. To William Gilbey, that was typical of so-called 'security'.

Gilbey paused at the top of the stairwell. He heard a door opening, and voices. They came from beyond where he remembered Mr Piercey's office to be. A deep voice said: 'Thank you, Mrs Llewellyn. We have understood each other. I'll just use the toilet, if I may. Then I will take the files and disks.' A woman's voice said: 'It's at the end of the corridor.' There was then the sound of someone walking, fortunately in the opposite direction to the stairwell.

Gilbey moved out. This was, perhaps, the final murder. He must not hesitate. But he had heard that deep voice before, at the shoot-out at Holyhead. Was it the small man called Robbins? No, it was the tall man, the man with hate in his eyes, the bearded man. Of course it was him, the bearded man who was Gilbey's main follower. He was the principal spy, the eager agent of the overwhelming state

Gilbey opened the door to Mr Piercey's office. It was dark. Mr Piercey was not there. Gilbey had an obvious new target. He must go to the toilet. He must kill the bearded man. He had killed twice before in toilets.

But, as Gilbey shut Mr Piercey's door, a woman came out of the next room. She bumped into him. Her eyes confronted him. This was certainly Mrs Llewellyn, Mr Piercey's boss. Gilbey had just posted a copy of his mémoire to her. He had wanted it to arrive after he had killed Piercey. Then she might have understood the need for murder.

Gilbey put his hand over Mrs Llewellyn's face. He pushed her back into her office with all his strength, right back until she lay against her desk. Gilbey hit the door behind him with his foot. It banged shut.

Gilbey picked up, from the desk, a jar of sharp pencils. He stabbed three of them into Mrs Llewellyn's hands.

Above the screaming, the sound of choral music came into William Gilbey's head, music that his mother had loved, music that even his father, one dark night coming home from a pub in Burnley, had sung along to, to drunken words of his own invention, before William's mother had noticed. She had then stood and had angrily turned off their Dansette record player, the one that they had left behind when they had gone to France.

William had been standing on the stairs when his mother did this. Seven years old, William had watched as his parents' argument had become violent, demonic and cursed.

The music was Haydn's, from his oratorio 'The Creation'. It was a chorus, 'The Heavens are Telling the Glory of God!'

Gilbey held Mrs Llewellyn with his left hand around her throat, pushing his fingers into it as hard as he could. He lifted up her skirt, stabbing her again and again in the midriff with the sharp pencils. All the time he was hearing the choral music. Gilbey started singing it out aloud. *'The Heavens are telling...'*

Gilbey then shouted rather than sang:

*'My God is Your God. My Glory is Your Glory. My Glory is the Glory of Our Fathers and of Our Mothers. Praise to the Virgin Mary, praise to Jesus, praise to God, praise to Ol' Ezra. His gods were violent gods, his true gods, praise to Baal… praise….!'*

Then Gilbey suddenly pulled back, as if a voice there in the room or from within, from his head – Gilbey himself knew that it was his father's voice – told him to do so. Gilbey heard the words: *'You have done enough, son. Someone else is taking over the story.'*

Elizabeth Llewellyn, saved from the certainty of death or rape, choked. She wept. She screamed.

Then there were people in the corridor, and two new people in the room. One picked up Gilbey's holdall.

William Gilbey felt a tremendous single hammer blow to his head. He was picked up and turned around. He felt himself flying through the air, through a window, open as always, as Mr Piercey had said. Gilbey was thrown out of Mrs Llewellyn's office. He landed face down on Lloyd Piercey's Audi.

The recidivist William Harrison Gilbey, fifty eight years old, of no fixed abode, in the care of the Inner London Probation Service, was killed instantly. He had willingly surrendered himself to death.

With the eyewitness support of Mrs Llewellyn, and following their earlier talk and a second talk in hospital, John Nicholson could assure Wilfred Robbins that an accidental death verdict on Gilbey would be certain at the inquest. All his papers and posted material had been intercepted.

Robin, Elizabeth Llewellyn's husband, rang Lloyd Piercey at Elizabeth's request, on return from visiting her in hospital. Charlene, Lloyd's wife, answered the phone. Robin asked Charlene to pass on a message to Lloyd, Elizabeth's colleague, whom Robin had never met, that Elizabeth was 'doing well' after 'that madman's attack'. But, Robin said, Elizabeth would not be in work for a while. Sadly, Elizabeth had miscarried.

When told this, Lloyd Piercey had broken down in front of Charlene. He had shed tears, the first time he had done this in her presence. *He is a good and noble man, as good a man as ever has lived,* thought Charlene. *And the filth he has to deal with!*

Despite his crimes, and his pain, during that period after death when the soul passes through Purgatory, William Gilbey was happy. The Roman Catholic faith of his mother Marjorie was vindicated. Her suicide had been forced on her, so God had forgiven her. William heard her singing, and the distinctive piano playing of the collaborator Alfred Cortot. He heard the chatter of Uncle and Aunty Bevington-Ward, and their deep, deep regrets for the harm they had done to the Gilbeys. William heard The Milky One and Artie giving him their best of luck from their hide-away in Paris, as did a red-faced Guiseppe Carnarolo, long dead, also in Paris, lying in the same cemetery as Oscar Wilde. 'I was jealous of that Maitre d', you know, William. I wronged you. I was heartbroken when they convicted you.' A lady called Bridie said that she bore no grudge. Governor Spratt cheered William on.

William Gilbey sensed that his mémoire, with his father's most important stories, was being read, with great intensity, by several people. His life task was thus, perhaps, accomplished. Gilbey saw and loved again Gillian/Debra, now relieved of pain. She was laughing at Roy Harvey's jokes. Gilbey felt the presence of Eireann, now Justine. She would soon join William and Ezra Pound. 'Good ole' Ezra here!' an American voice shouted: 'Come and join my party William Gilbey! Meet Mussolini and my other friends!'

And above all of them – above even the combined choirs of Heaven and Hell, alternately singing *'The Heavens are Telling the Glory of God!'* and *'Baal we cry to thee',* another favourite of mother's, from Mendelssohn's 'Elijah' oratorio, William heard the voice of his father, Herbert, 'Bert', Gilbey, telling stories to all who would listen.

The immortal Bert Gilbey who, according to the story believed by William, was the last man to be executed in England, by hanging, on the 18<sup>th</sup> of July 1964, fifty years ago, and whose earthly body, William believed, rested in the precincts of Pentonville Prison in London.

Herbert Gilbey, forever 'Mr Churchill's driver'.

# PART TEN

PART TEN

# 10

## 10.1

*Three weeks later. Holyhead Heights, Anglesey.*

It was a rainy July morning. Morgan Janvir stood looking at the sundial on the headland for several minutes, his head uncovered and without an umbrella, no doubt to the bemusement of the day-trippers parked nearby. Day-trippers, he assumed, or was he being watched?

It was Wilfred Robbins's notes in the file on the Gilbey case that had brought Morgan to Holyhead.

For probably the first time in her working life Amy Moynihan, Wilfred Robbins's secretary, had misunderstood her duties. On that terrible morning when she had learned of the death of Harry Ross, Amy had thought that Robbins had intended her to attach to the main A Group files the new Gilbey material he had left on her boss's desk, as was his standing instruction for loose papers.

Mr Robbins had gone to meet Sir Rory Armitage. Amy was distraught. But she composed herself and immersed herself in her work. She had to carry out instructions. She had to carry on. She told herself that it would be what Harry would have wanted. But she dreaded the work day coming to an end, and how she would occupy her thoughts, if not of Harry.

Amy knew that the main Gilbey files were where Harry had left them, in the safe he shared with Mr Janvir, and it was thus to the cold Mr Janvir that Amy had delivered the new documents and notes. In her distress she had not registered Mr Robbins telling her of Mr Janvir's gardening leave. But, when Mr Robbins came back after his meetings with Sir Rory and Mr Piercey he had angrily demanded to know, where the loose papers were and why, when Amy told him, had she taken them to Mr Janvir; and why was Mr Janvir still in the building anyway?

Amy spoke to him, and Mr Janvir had left immediately. But he had had two clear hours to look over the main files and to speed-read the recent additions, including William Gilbey's scrawled mémoire. Morgan had looked in vain there for anything other than a passing reference to Harry. But what he had absorbed of Gilbey's stuff had a strange conviction, even if it was the work of a fantasist and confessed killer. Violent criminals could still reach out to the truth, perhaps; and a son's loyalty to his father could overcome all obstacles, even the separation of death. Most importantly, among the loose papers Morgan had found –'for future action' – a note by John Nicholson, about Latin words and numbers at the base of the Holyhead plinth. Nicholson, with his photographic memory but lack of Latin, had mentioned them to Robbins, as they had driven away from the scene. Robbins had been keen to get away.

Now, at the plinth, Morgan, a classicist, saw them properly:

## 10.2

It had not been an immediate decision by Morgan to come to Holyhead. Over the three weeks since he had been sent on gardening leave he had repeatedly put off the trip. He had no official business there. But he was still a civil service 'high-flyer', a career his father had chosen for him after he had refused to go into the Janvir building business, and which Morgan thought that he should still care about. He knew that really he should back off. Yet what had happened nagged at him.

Morgan rifled through the boxed-up sets of his father's books. He found books about Churchill and the Second World War. He knew much of the history, but he read and re-read. From the internet he purchased books about de Valera, and about the critical days of 1940 when, according to Herbert Gilbey's story, Churchill and de Valera had met. He found nothing to prove or to disprove such a story. Morgan also bought two books on the psychology of serial killers, to see if they would tell him anything about William Gilbey, this strange partly French-educated serial killer. Really, they did not.

When not reading, Morgan paced up and down his flat. He cleaned compulsively. He went to see his father twice and drank mint tea with him at Foxdale Lodge. They made tedious small talk.

A decision had effectively been forced on Morgan when he was told in a phone call from his personnel manager that his 'gardening leave' would end that week. He was told that he would be leaving MI5, on a temporary secondment to the Cabinet Office, shadowing the Treasury. This still demanded a high security clearance. It was close to the political centre of power. It was a good job.

So, Morgan's decision was made for him. But his doubts lingered.

With no-one to consult – Morgan had dropped most of his Oxford friends when he had joined MI5 – he convinced himself that no harm could come from using his last few days of leave to take a short trip to the scene of the confrontation described by Gilbey, which seemed to be at the centre of so many events. And maybe some good – well, at least, a break from London and from his father would result.

Within an hour of the personnel manager's phone call Morgan Janvir had taken a taxi to Euston station. There, he had boarded a first class compartment in a train going north-west. He told himself that he had a few days to satisfy his curiosity; then to come back and to forget, if necessary, the whole thing.

The better hotels in north Wales had been full. Eventually Morgan, hiring a car, found somewhere.

But Morgan had tastes which were not going to be satisfied in this part of the world. Even the Chablis was lukewarm. After a poor dinner Morgan almost went back to Hampstead there and then. But, Morgan thought of his father, and of Harry Ross.

Morgan had tried hard to get the cold sacrifice of that

handsome young man – with all his life to look forward to – out of his mind. Morgan had warned Harry, almost pleaded with him, hadn't he? He could not have done more, surely? So, in truth, he should feel no guilt.

Yet, he did feel guilt, and he could not let go. The abandonment of Harry Ross by his superiors was a criminal act.

What would Morgan's father in his earlier years, battling the powerful in Iran, have done?

## 10.3

Morgan spent most of his second day in Wales in the local library. The archives of the Anglesey Chronicle, a thin newspaper in wartime, had been transferred to film. It did not take too long to find what he had hoped for, but had also feared.

On the lower front page of the edition of the 12th of March 1942 was a paragraph headed '*Restoration of monument*'. It read that, following special permission of the Ministry of Works, the damage done to the sundial and panorama overlooking Holyhead had been repaired. Volunteers had carried out the work over several weeks, during the mild winter, and the whole project had been financed in full by the Ward family of Flint Manor, now resident in London, Sir Alec Ward having paid for the original. The Mayor of Holyhead had been present at the unveiling ceremony, as was Lieutenant Andrew Bevington-Ward. The Mayor had said that it was good for the Welsh spirit that even in these terrible times we looked after our past.

The report stated that, at the request of the Ministry of Works, a time capsule, including a sealed envelope containing 'papers signed by Mr Churchill himself', had been prepared. It also included a verse of praise in Welsh by Reverend Christmas Jones, and a letter from the American Embassy, with photographs of the two Roosevelt presidents, Theodore and Franklin. The newspaper reminded its readers that the Holyhead sundial had originally been erected in honour of Theodore Roosevelt. He had visited Flint Manor and was such a friend of the Ward family that, for a while, they had renamed their house Sagamore, after Roosevelt's family home, Sagamore Hill. The name had since been changed back, however, at the request of local people. The strongbox also contained nature drawings by evacuee children.

All these items were buried in a strongbox adjacent to the sundial. This was not to be opened for at least a hundred years.

So the words on the monument, in Latin presumably as an act of diplomacy, to avoid choosing between English and Welsh in 1942 when Welsh speaking and nationalism were more prominent than in 1919, were appropriate.

Morgan Janvir had translated them as:

*'Restored, with patriotic confidence in our future, March 1942.'*

Morgan wondered if anyone now remembered that the time capsule was there. It was most likely forgotten.

Then Morgan saw the truth, as if in a flash of light.

The date was critical. March 1942. Three months after the Japanese attack on Pearl Harbour, when the United States had entered the war. Churchill had rejoiced at the news and at Hitler's subsequent declaration of war against America. Churchill and his advisors knew that, with the capacity and resources of the Americans, the war would eventually be won. So, maybe the Prime Minister had taken as an extraordinary opportunity the invitation, just a few months later, to contribute to a time capsule associated with a Roosevelt. It was his chance to be rid of, and to pass to the verdict of history, in one sealed envelope, the only full record of the last, unwilling effort at appeasement.

The strongbox buried near the plinth at Holyhead must surely contain an account, and possibly the final text, of the fabled agreement signed with the neutrals' leader Eamon de Valera.

Various drafts, each headed 'Heads of Agreement for a European Peace' were in the files that Morgan Janvir and Harry Ross had seen. Wilfred Robbins had correctly stated that those papers were incomplete. But in general the peace terms followed the outline that was known to historians and referenced in several of the specialist books that Morgan had consulted. With Britain out of the war, they included the recognition of the German sphere of 'influence and control' in western and central Europe, and of Germany's claim to 'living room' in the east. German colonies in Africa ceded in the Treaty of Versailles were to be handed back. Favourable tariff terms for Axis goods, and the transfer of weapon technology were to be agreed as were the installation of a British monarch (presumably the Duke of Windsor) and a government 'sympathetic' to 'the new Europe'. British 'volunteer forces' were to be allowed to support the Germans, if required. And, most important to Morgan's eyes, the whole of the island of Ireland was to be united and administered from Dublin. The Germans had also apparently demanded the repatriation of German citizens, mainly Jews, who had immigrated to Britain, including Northern Ireland, since the Nazis had come to power.

Britain itself would not have been occupied, nor its armed forces and those of its allies disbanded. Most of its Empire, which Hitler claimed to admire, would have remained intact.

These terms would, no doubt, have been subject to intense negotiation, and the more offensive, especially those affecting sovereignty and the refugees, refused. But basically these were the terms Morgan knew that a few modern historians believed that Britain should have used as a basis for negotiation. Instead we had continued a war for five more years, which, at its end, had left Communism in control of half of Europe; and which, by bankrupting Britain, had ultimately destroyed our empire.

However in the incomplete documents in the Gilbey file there were references to a codicil to the settlement that Morgan was sure was truly unknown, and truly explosive. It referred to Ireland alone. It was explicit in only one draft, itself heavily crossed through and amended. But it seemed to say, as Morgan recalled, that Ireland would insist not only on re-unification of its island, but millions of pounds of 'reparations' from the British. At Holyhead, it appeared that de Valera had confirmed his demand that, when Britain withdrew from the war she should repair Ireland, in the words of the paragraph, 'from the damage of centuries of British occupation'.

That admission, and that national humiliation, was to be the price of de Valeras leading a negotiated peace, with better terms achieved for the British than they might get without the help of neutrals. Alternatively, it could have been the additional price for Ireland entering the war on Britain's side later, should the war not be ended by negotiation, and the tide turn in Britain's favour. That was 'their moral duty', Churchill had said to General Brooke, according to Herbert Gilbey's account. Perhaps Churchill was being ironic.

Every circumstance now pointed to the heads of agreement, including the Irish demands, being initialled by the two leaders, then Churchill, back in London, playing for time, drafting and redrafting, and ultimately reneging, holding the line against Halifax and the peace party in his Cabinet. Morgan could see him using the reparations issue as the clinching argument 'to fight on'.

*'Thank God for Churchill,'* thought Morgan.

So the draft agreement of Holyhead had led nowhere, neither to Ireland's entry into the war, nor to its reunification; and certainly not to reparations. But the possibility that such humiliating terms existed must have poisoned relations between the leaders of both Britain and Ireland for generations, if they had been informed. Wilfred Robbins had said that at least some of the British Prime Ministers had been told.

But now? The peace process for Northern Ireland had been concluded. What reason was there to hide matters?

Morgan decided that the issue was, for him, beyond reasonable doubt.

*Herbert Gilbey's story told to his son William about the encounter between Churchill and de Valera was true.*

Its proof lay in a box, not buried beyond reach beneath the tower blocks of flats that had replaced Sagamore or 'Flint Manor', as had been assumed, but buried two feet below the earth, adjacent to a sundial on Holyhead Heights.

Added to that, and more to the taste of the thugs and criminals that had pursued William Gilbey, as described in his 'mémoire', there was the missing art that the bossman Pete and others had talked about. Morgan realised, with a second blinding revelation, that some of it (he knew not what proportion) was already hanging on the highly decorated walls of The Second Floor of the Security Service building, admired and pointed out to all-comers by Sir Rory Armitage, Second Permanent Secretary, and changed regularly. The bulk of the art was, however, still missing. Hence Harry Ross's fateful mission.

The apparent hunt for truth was, as ever, also a hunt for money and possessions.

Morgan Janvir's confusion of mind was over. Here was a chance to assert the values that his father had tried to teach him.

Morgan now had the opportunity, through an upbringing and an education denied to the self-taught and isolated serial murderer William Gilbey, to reveal the truth. That would be uncomfortable for the establishment, the 'nobs' of the Gilbey story, and maybe it could lead to criminal charges. But there were matters that the British and Irish people had the right to know. Morgan himself had the right to a conscience, and to act on it.

Morgan went for a long walk, and ate calmly. He slept soundly. After breakfast he went to a telephone box. He called an Oxford friend who worked for The Guardian. He had not spoken to him for three years. But Morgan, speaking calmly, gave enough information to justify Tony agreeing to take a taxi to Euston immediately, and to meet Morgan at noon at Chester station.

Morgan checked the route to Chester on an AA map in his hire car. He reckoned that he had time for a second visit to the sundial. It was a sunnier and warmer day. There were new road works on the road up the hill, which was otherwise quiet. There were no cars in the car park.

Morgan felt good. He stood and looked across the landscape. He tried to feel inspired by it, as perhaps others, over seventy years earlier, had been inspired, for good or for bad.

After a few moments of silent prayer, not to the angry, violent Gods of William Gilbey's mémoire, and his favoured poet Ezra Pound, but to the Gods of peace, Morgan used his mobile to ring his father at the care home, Foxdale Lodge, in Esher.

It took a while but eventually Mr Alexander, one of the staff, put Morgan's father on the line.

'Father, Father? How are you?'

Mr Janvir mumbled something.

'Father, Father, why are you so surprised that I, Morgan your only son, should call you in this way? Father, sit comfortably and relax. I want to tell you a story that has been passed down from father to son, and will soon be well known. You are going to hear it from me first. It is called 'Mr Churchill's driver'.'

But before Morgan could start his story the line went dead.

From beyond the summit, where two large cars were parked, emerged, among others, Wilfred Robbins and John Nicholson.